SHE WASN'T READY
TO TALK ABOUT IT

Impatient with the entire situation, she gestured with her hand. "Oh, I don't know. Things seem so complicated now."

He remained silent for a few moments. Finally he said, "We're back to that now, are we? You're remembering that you didn't want to get involved."

"I thought you felt that way, too," she said resentfully. Why was he making it sound as though this were all her fault? "After all, you said you weren't interested in a relationship right now—"

"No, you said that, not me."

"You said it, too!"

"Well, I felt that way before I met you."

And my new equipment, she thought, and was surprised and ashamed of herself. Where had *that* thought come from? Why was she so suspicious? Because she wasn't sure of her own motives—or his?

ABOUT THE AUTHOR

Playing with Fire is Risa Kirk's fifth
Superromance. A native Californian with a love
for animals, Risa is known for her lighthearted
stories and witty characters. Fans won't be
disappointed by her latest effort. And they can
look forward to her next Super—a comedy-
adventure, complete with glitzy backdrops and
ultra-glamorous protagonists!

Books by Risa Kirk

HARLEQUIN SUPERROMANCE
200–BEYOND COMPARE
238–TEMPTING FATE
273–DREAMS TO MEND
300–WIHOUT A DOUBT

Don't miss any of our special offers. Write to us at the
following address for information on our newest releases.

Harlequin Reader Service
901 Fuhrmann Blvd., P.O. Box 1397, Buffalo, NY 14240
Canadian address: P.O. Box 603,
Fort Erie, Ont. L2A 5X3

Risa Kirk

PLAYING WITH FIRE

Harlequin Books

TORONTO • NEW YORK • LONDON
AMSTERDAM • PARIS • SYDNEY • HAMBURG
STOCKHOLM • ATHENS • TOKYO • MILAN

Forty Years of Romance

Published June 1989

First printing April 1989

ISBN 0-373-70361-9

CHAPTER ONE

"IT'S NOT ME," Mary Nell Barrigan said, tugging at the pewter-colored, strapless cocktail dress her sister, Stacy, had just zipped her into. "It's awful. It just won't do."

Exhausted from running back and forth trying to find Mary Nell something to wear, Stacy threw herself into the dressing room's only chair and blew a breath upward. She was twenty-three, seven years younger than Mary Nell, a nursing student in Seattle who had driven home to Tacoma the previous night for semester break. Looking as though she wished she'd stayed at the dormitory studying, she said, "Give it a minute. Maybe it will grow on you."

Mary Nell looked back at the mirror. Unlike Stacy, who was sturdy and blond and blue eyed, she was petite and small boned, with emerald-green eyes and a deceptively fragile air enhanced by a cloud of unmanageable fiery red hair. No one looking at her would have guessed that she owned Barrigan Design, a mechanical engineering firm; she looked like a delicate Southern belle.

"It's not going to grow on me. I hate it," she said flatly. "You've got to find me something else."

Stacy rolled her eyes. "There *isn't* anything else! You've tried on everything in the store!"

"There must be something! I have to have a new dress for that fund-raiser this weekend! Come on, Stace—you know I'm desperate, and you promised to help."

Glancing pointedly around the cluttered dressing room, with discarded dresses draped over every surface, Stacy said, "If I'd known this was going to turn into such a marathon, I'd have brought lunch. You *do* remember lunch, don't you? That's a meal we should have had yesterday."

"We'll eat as soon as I find something to wear," Mary Nell said stubbornly. "Ask someone to help you."

"There isn't anyone," Stacy retorted. "You've driven them out. Everyone quit." She narrowed her eyes. "They all went to lunch."

"Very funny," Mary Nell said, beginning to struggle out of the dress. The zipper was at the back, and she couldn't reach it. Impatiently, she looked over her shoulder. "Would you *mind*?"

Sighing heavily, Stacy got up and gave the zipper a pull. "If you don't buy this one, what are you going to do?"

Wondering that herself, Mary Nell stepped out of the pewter taffeta concoction. "I don't know," she said. "Maybe I won't go. I don't know why I said I would, anyway. Robert and I were supposed to stop seeing each other months ago."

Robert was Robert Chiles, a man she'd been dating seriously until last year. She'd finally had to tell him she couldn't see him anymore. At first it had been funny, endearing—cute—that he spent most of his time assuring even waiters in restaurants that his name wasn't pronounced "chilies," as in hot peppers, but "shyles," as in "shy." But after the thousandth time, it stopped being funny and became grating, instead. And when she started asking herself if she wanted to be known as Mary Eleanor Chilies the rest of her life—it was either that or buttonholing strangers, it seemed—she knew she had to do something. The truth was, her irritation over the name was a symbol of many other things wrong with the relationship, and so she had ended it.

Well, she'd tried to end it. Robert still called her now and then, and while she knew she shouldn't, sometimes she'd accept a date. Every time she did, she vowed it would be the last, but then he'd call again and she'd give in, and the cycle would be repeated. She wanted to not see him anymore, but it was difficult to refuse. With Stacy at school so much, she was alone in the house, and even though she had the business to keep her busy, she couldn't work *all* the time. There were nights when she got lonely, and going out with Robert was better than sitting at home waiting for Mr. Right.

Grimacing at that last thought, she started searching quickly through the pile of clothes. When she pulled her own dress from the stack, Stacy brightened. "Does this mean we're leaving?" she asked eagerly. "And that we can *finally* get something to eat?"

Rolling her eyes, Mary Nell started to say yes, but then she glanced at her watch and had to apologize, instead. "I'm sorry, Stacy. I didn't realize it was so late. I have to get back to the office right away."

"What! After all this?"

"I know, I know. But I promised Lucille I'd be back by one. It's her mother's birthday, and she had plans to—"

Stacy sighed heavily. "Take her to lunch, right?"

"I'm sorry," Mary Nell said again. "I'll make it up to you."

"How, by taking me out to dinner?"

Exasperated, Mary Nell put her hands on her hips. "Is that all you think about—food?"

"No, I think about men occasionally, too." Stacy grinned. "Don't you?"

"What kind of question is that?"

"A touchy one, judging from your tone of voice," Stacy said, watching her closely.

They'd had this conversation before. Trying to hide her annoyance, Mary Nell reached in her purse for a comb. Her hair was more flyaway than ever after trying on all these clothes, and as she plied the implement furiously, she could feel Stacy's eyes on her. Defensively, she said, "It's hard starting up a new business. I don't have much time left to think about men."

"But you still need to have fun now and then."

Giving up on her hair, she put the comb away. "I'm going out with Robert this weekend, aren't I?"

"You know what I mean."

She did know what Stacy meant. But her relationships hadn't worked out well in the past, and she was starting to wonder if she deliberately chose incompatible partners or if her standards were just too high. Realizing it might be a little bit of both, she decided it didn't matter, anyway. She didn't have time to be involved now; she was committed to building up her business.

"Yes, I know what you mean," she said, her tone indicating she didn't want to pursue it. She reached for her sweater. Even though it was well into spring, the breeze that came in off Commencement Bay carried a tang, and she threw her sweater around her shoulders as she and Stacy left the store.

Seeing her expression, Stacy gave up as they hit the sidewalk. "Okay, since you obviously don't want to talk about men, tell me about Lucille. She's been working for you for...six months now? How is that working out?"

Her secretary was one subject she didn't mind talking about. With a smile, she said, "Lucille's been wonderful. I don't know what I'd do without her. She's a real help."

"She's learning the business?"

She laughed at Stacy's disbelieving expression. "Don't sound so incredulous. Mechanical engineering might not be your field, but not everyone feels that way."

"Yes, but Lucille used to be a librarian," Stacy said, and shuddered. She was a good student, but too active for the library to be her favorite place. "She still looks like one, too. I can't imagine anyone even calling her Lucy, can you?"

Picturing Lucille, with her prim pageboy, her glasses and her plain skirt-and-sweater sets, Mary Nell smiled again. "No, I have to admit, I can't."

"Does she still live with her mother?"

"She's *always* going to live with her mother," Mary Nell said, thinking that she didn't care if her secretary lived with King Kong—as long as she didn't leave Barrigan Design.

She never would have dreamed that Lucille Hendershot would work out so well in the office, but she had. It was ironic that she'd been there all the time, practically right under Mary Nell's nose. They'd known each other for years—until Lucille and her mother had moved away from the old neighborhood, after Mr. Hendershot had died. Mary Nell hadn't heard from Lucille until the morning she had answered the ad, and she still remembered how astonished she'd been when Lucille had walked into the office and told her why she'd come.

"But I thought you worked in the library," Mary Nell had said.

"I do," Lucille said. "Or, at least, I did." She looked around, as though someone might overhear. Then she leaned forward and whispered, "I quit my job."

Surprised, Mary Nell said, "You did? Why?"

Lucille hesitated again. Her hairstyle did nothing for her face, and her glasses had a habit of sliding down her long, thin nose. Mary Nell had always thought that with a little help, Lucille could have been pretty. Her hair was glossy, and behind her glasses were clear, deep turquoise eyes.

Lucille leaned forward again, forcing Mary Nell to do the same. It was an awkward position, and she felt a crick in her neck, but she had to remain that way to hear; when Lucille began speaking, her voice was barely a whisper.

"Mama doesn't know yet," Lucille said, "but I quit my job at the library because... because—" She stopped and took off her glasses with an almost defiant gesture. Once again, Mary Nell was struck by the startling blue color of the other woman's eyes. "Because I was tired of hiding out in the stacks, Mary Nell, and I wanted a little excitement in my life," she said. "That's why!"

She had tried not to laugh. Glancing around her spare little office, Mary Nell said, "I'm not sure you'll find it here, Lucille. If you want the truth, I think there's probably a lot more excitement in the library."

Lucille had glanced around, too. "I don't know why you say that. I think this is quite nice."

Nice? It wasn't *nice*, Mary Nell had thought. It was adequate... barely. It certainly wasn't the dream office she had pictured when, with Stacy's encouragement, she had quit her former job at McInerney and Glade to start her own business... but still, it *was* better than her little cubicle there. She'd been lucky to find a space near the Old City Hall, which was patterned after a Renaissance castle in Italy. The surrounding area consisted of specialty shops, restaurants and offices, and to Mary Nell it had a lot more character than Broadway Plaza, with its two gleaming high rises that signaled the growth of the hotel and financial industries in Tacoma.

Or so she told herself. Later she'd have a bigger, more important office, with more work. This smaller place had to suit her now, even if it still lacked warmth and furniture. All she'd done in the way of decorating was place a few plants around. The carpeting and drapes had come with the lease. After sinking everything she could beg, borrow or steal into the computer equipment in the back, anything else would have to wait for a while. A long while.

Six months after she'd signed the lease, Mary Nell had begun to think she'd be there forever. By the time Lucille had answered her ad, she had managed to snag several small accounts, but she needed a big contract to give her financial breathing space. With start-up expenses, plus Stacy's nursing-school bills, she was just barely squeaking by, and she longed to be given a chance to prove what she and her computer could do. She'd known for a long time that computer-aided design, or CAD, as it was called in the trade, was the mechanical engineering tool of the future, and even though she was still mastering the intricacies of the technique, she felt she was ready for any challenge. All she needed was a chance. She had quit her old job because she'd wanted more responsibility; well, now she had it. Stacy was sure she could do it—so sure, in fact, that she'd talked her sister into getting a loan to open up the office.

Grimacing at the thought of the loan, she had looked at Lucille and said, "As you can see, I'm not exactly swamped with work here. If you're looking for excitement—or more importantly, decent pay—you'd be better off applying at a more established office."

But Lucille had glanced around the spare reception area, with the simple desk, secretarial chair and two-line phone, and nodded to herself. "It looks just fine," she said. "If you ask me, all this space is . . . refreshing."

How could she refuse that? Laughing, she'd hired Lucille on the spot and knew she'd made the right decision when her new secretary showed up for work early the next morning bearing a coffee maker under one arm and two oil paintings under the other. "There are a few more things out in the car," Lucille had said. "But I'm going to need some help bringing them in."

The few things turned out to be two chairs and a coffee table and a beautiful handmade rug to place in front of the door. When everything was in place, Lucille dusted off her hands and took out the crowning glory: a brand-new copy of *Design News*.

"I've already sent for a subscription," she said with satisfaction, placing it just so on the coffee table. "Now, doesn't that look nice?"

Absurdly, Mary Nell had felt close to tears. "It looks beautiful," she said, and thought that the smartest thing she'd ever done was place that ad.

She still thought that, six months later. She couldn't imagine the office without her secretary, who had been both a godsend and a good luck charm. Lucille hadn't been at the reception desk two days before Barrigan Design was awarded a sizable contract, and then another, and then a third. Now business, while not exactly flourishing, was steady, and since it was a fledgling company, Mary Nell couldn't complain. But she was still looking for that elusive big account that would give her a little more breathing space—and she was sure she'd found it.

She had intended to tell Stacy at lunch the news that McAdam Recreation, based in Tacoma, was planning to update all its lines, and that she was trying for the account. McAdam was the biggest manufacturer of camping and recreational gear in the state, and getting the design contract would be a plum that would certainly lead to even bigger and better things. She'd already submitted a résumé that Lucille, calling on her formidable talent as a former reference librarian, had helped her to write, and she'd been delighted with the finished product. On paper, it seemed that Barrigan Design outrivaled even McInerney and Glade. She'd been filled with enthusiasm—until the envelope was in the mail. Then she was sure she'd made a terrible mistake.

It wasn't that the account wouldn't be lucrative—not that, she thought nervously. If she was awarded the contract, it would be a star feature on her résumé, opening the door to—who knew? She'd be able to write her ticket. No, she wasn't worried about that part of it.

She wasn't even concerned about the fact that the owner of the company, Anson McAdam, was reputed to be an unpredictable eccentric; she could deal with him... somehow.

Unfortunately, the problem was much simpler than that—and much more embarrassing. The plain truth was that, in this state of skiers and hikers and campers and anglers and divers and even golfers and tennis players, she was hopelessly inept. She always had been. Despite her best intentions and her fierce desire to participate in *something*, she just wasn't the sporty type.

She hated picnics, for instance, because of the dirt and the crawly things that inevitably meandered over the blanket. She disliked swimming, because no matter how hard she tried, she'd never been able to master the simplest stroke; the only thing she could do in the water was float. The last time she'd tried hiking, she'd twisted her ankle and had to be carried out, and when she'd gone skiing this past winter, she'd made a spectacle of herself snowplowing down the slopes—backward.

The list seemed endless. No matter how hard she tried, her fishing lines got tangled in branches, her golf balls wouldn't stay on tees, her tennis racket flew out of her hands, and every ball she finally batted went sailing through the trees. As popular as she'd been in school, she'd still been the last one chosen for any team—and for good reason. She'd been so proud—and relieved—when she had made the cheerleading squad in high school; it meant that she could safely encourage from the sidelines instead of humiliating herself and her teammates by making some horribly clumsy mistake on a court.

Through the years she had learned to accept her liabilities in outdoors-oriented Tacoma—had even learned to hide them, pretending allergies when someone wanted to go hiking or a bad back when she was invited to water-ski. When she thought about it, it seemed the purest folly, sheer idiocy, for her to apply for a contract to design recreational equipment, but she tried to quell her doubts by assuring herself that one didn't have to be an astronaut to design a seat on a space station or a gourmet cook to fashion a waffle iron.

No, but it helps, a little voice whispered. *Not always,* she told it firmly. Design was design; the principles remained the same. It was all a matter of lines and space and fitting all the pieces together, and the computer did that so effortlessly that sometimes she felt almost superfluous. She had the utmost confidence in her ability to handle the McAdam account—*if* she could get it. She didn't have much chance of that if she couldn't even get in the door, and after she and Stacy emerged empty-handed from the clothing store, she made a mental note to call McAdam's office when she got back to the office. It wouldn't hurt to remind him of her name again. Wasn't the squeaky wheel the one that got the grease?

"I'm sorry about lunch," she said again to Stacy. "I'll make it up to you, I promise."

Stacy sighed. "That's all right. I can see you're too preoccupied to be much company, anyway. Since I doubt

Robert's the one who put you in this state, is something going on at work? Do you want to talk about it?''

She'd planned to tell Stacy about the new contract, but now she changed her mind. Better to present it as a fait accompli, she decided, especially since her sister was aware of her pitiful sports history—or lack of it. She was already feeling shaky enough about this; she didn't need a snide comment about the absurdity of such a klutz vying for a recreational gear account. So she said, "No, there's no problem. Just a lot of things to do."

Nodding, Stacy held out her hand for the car keys. "Then I'll do the grocery shopping," she said. "Your refrigerator has exactly one half-empty can of tuna and something else I didn't want to explore too closely. Honestly, Mary Nell, don't you ever buy any food?"

She bristled. "There are all sorts of microwave things in the freezer."

"Oh, great," Stacy said, lifting an eyebrow. "Desiccated fruit? Instant vegetables?"

"Spoken like a true nursing student," she retorted, handing over the keys. Her office was only a few blocks away, and she decided to walk. That way, she could always mention to Anson McAdam when she talked to him that she was a great believer in exercise and occasionally enjoyed a walk to work. Waving to Stacy, she started off at a brisk pace.

Unfortunately, the high-heeled shoes she was wearing hadn't been designed for a brisk anything, and by the time she reached the office, she was limping and swamped with despair. If she couldn't even walk two blocks without getting blisters, how was she going to convince the head of a recreational gear company that she was qualified to design his most important lines? Groaning as she opened the door, she limped to the couch in the reception area and fell into it.

Lucille was at her desk, just hanging up the phone. She was too excited to notice her employer's sad state. "Guess who just called?" she asked, her eyes bright.

Mary Nell didn't care. She slipped off her shoes with a sigh of relief. All she could think about was a tub of Epsom salts and soaking her aching feet for about an hour. "Who?"

"Anson McAdam!"

Mary Nell closed her eyes. Why was this happening now? She'd waited on pins and needles all week, and just when she was thinking that she should forget the whole idea, McAdam called. But she had come this far, so she asked cautiously, "What did he want?"

Lucille grabbed her purse. As excited as she was, she couldn't keep her mother waiting, and it was after one. "He wants to see you Monday morning at nine. Isn't that wonderful?"

"Wonderful," she said, trying to sound enthusiastic. Her entire body hurt, and she was sure she was one giant blister. Why had she ever opted for the marathon walk to the office?

Realizing for the first time that something was amiss, Lucille gave her a curious look. "Are you all right?"

She didn't want to go into it. "I'm fine."

"I thought you'd be excited."

"Oh, I am," she said, wondering if the bathroom sink was big enough for her to soak her tender toes in.

"It's great news, don't you think?" Lucille said tentatively.

'Oh yes," Mary Nell said, waving her secretary out for her lunch date. When Lucille had gone, she sat on the couch for a few minutes, unable to move. At last, telling

herself she couldn't just lounge all day, she sighed heavily
and reached for her shoes. Carrying them in one hand, she
limped barefoot toward her own office.

"Just great," she muttered, and shut the door.

HIS HANDS IN his pockets, Cal Stewart walked along the
waterfront. Dressed in jeans and a windbreaker, he was so
deep in thought that he didn't notice several admiring
glances thrown his way from female passersby whose eyes
followed the tall, good-looking man with the dark blue
eyes and wavy black hair. He looked up once, and one of
the women was sure that a dimple would flash in that
crease in his cheek if he smiled. But he didn't. He put his
head down again, too preoccupied even to hear the sea
gulls circling above him, begging with their sharp, plain-
tive cries for scraps from the fishing boats heading into the
harbor. He was thinking about work and what he was
going to do if he and Brad didn't get the McAdam recreational gear account.

Frowning at the thought, he stopped and leaned against
the pier railing, staring at the water. He'd always loved the
water. Some of the best times he'd spent had been with his
partner, Brad Davidson—or Davy, as he'd always called
him—when they went fishing or sailing or diving. He
missed those days; God, how he missed those days.

Telling himself it was the quickening breeze and not the
thought of the way things used to be that brought tears to
his eyes, he turned away. Tacoma's increasingly modern
skyline met his eyes, and he couldn't help thinking how
much the city had changed since he and Brad had come
here to open their mechanical engineering office. The deep-
water harbor behind him handled millions of tons of
shipping every year, and the industrial plants that now
lined the bay produced everything from chemicals to rail-

road cars. This industry—and the profusion of outdoor sports—were two of the things that had brought him and Brad up from Los Angeles in the first place. Then, opening an office of their own had been the dream, and they had wanted to be where the action was. Five years ago, everything had seemed possible.

With a sad sigh, he walked on. He couldn't complain about the first three of those years. Stewart-Davidson had flourished from the start, even though—his expression became even more rueful—he and Brad had been more interested in their skis and diving gear than in their drafting boards. It had all been a game to them then; they were two young men out to conquer the world—as long as they could have fun doing it.

Embarrassed now at such a shallow outlook, he told himself he'd been young then, so young. And he couldn't deny that even with the fun times, they'd done well. Business had been steady, if unexciting, and until three years ago, it seemed the good times would just . . . go on.

Then he'd met Anna Maria O'Malley, a violinist with the Seattle Symphony. He'd gone out with girls before—dozens of them. Ski and snow bunnies abounded, and there were always girls who hung around boats. But he'd never met anyone like Anna Maria, who aroused instincts he'd thought were long buried, and suddenly, without warning, he'd started thinking about marrying again.

The idea horrified him. Already one youthful marriage had ended in a bitter divorce he knew had been mainly his fault; after that, he'd avoided commitment like the plague. When he met Anna Maria, he was thirty-two, beginning to think he was safe, immune. But she had enthralled him somehow, and once he started thinking marriage, he'd taken a hard look at both his life-style and his business and decided he didn't like the way he was dealing with either area. He and Brad had been skating since coming to Tacoma; it was time to get serious.

The problem was that he couldn't get Brad to agree. His friend had just gotten involved with a girl named Beth and was so in love he couldn't think of anything else. Cal frowned. He'd never liked Beth; he'd seen through her right away. All she could think about were her horses and her wardrobe, and in his mind, the only reason she was interested in Brad was because she thought he'd support both. As difficult as it had been, he hadn't said anything to his friend. If Brad couldn't see that Beth wanted a free ride, it wasn't his business to point it out. Besides, he was so head over heels with Anna Maria, he wasn't thinking too clearly himself. The only thing he'd tried to talk to Brad about was doing more with the business.

But Brad couldn't see that, either. He was happy designing locks and alarms and safety belts and gears; it gave him time to do other things he wanted to do, like tinkering with his inventions. He didn't want to go industrial, as Cal did—the pressure was too great.

Cal hadn't thought about the pressure; he was more interested in the challenge. That was when he realized that meeting Anna Maria had just been a catalyst. He hadn't been happy with Brad's casual approach to business for quite a while. Then he started reading about a new process, computer-aided design, or CAD, that was revolutionizing the engineering field, and it seemed the answer to everything. It was obvious that this CAD was going to be the design tool of the future, and he was eager to buy a system and explore the possibilities.

Brad wasn't. He didn't see the need to get involved in computer systems when they'd worked only with drafting tables for so long. He insisted that Stewart-Davidson had done just fine without some computer process he didn't understand and wasn't sure he wanted to. To him, the business was doing well enough without it. Unable to reach a compromise, they had agreed to table it for a while. This was the first real disagreement they'd had, and neither of them wanted it to result in a permanent breach.

Thinking about it, Cal sighed again. He'd tried to do it Brad's way, but he wanted something more demanding, and he'd been on the point of saying he wanted out of the partnership, when two things happened to drive everything else from his mind: Anna Maria accepted a position with the Philadelphia Orchestra, and Brad was involved in a car accident that crippled him for life. After that, dissolving the partnership was out of the question. Beth hadn't stayed long, of course; she couldn't face the demands of being involved with an invalid. He'd never thought of leaving, of abandoning his friend, and so he'd stayed. Getting Brad—and himself—through that nightmare time had been his responsibility, and just that had taken everything he had. There hadn't been time—or energy—for anything else.

A sea gull circled and landed right in front of him with a squawk, interrupting his reverie. The bird crouched over some scrap of something, and as it peered up at him with beady eyes, he grinned. Cheeky bird, he thought, and saluted it with two fingers before he stepped carefully around, leaving it to its find. He hadn't noticed until then that the afternoon had grown cool, and he hunched his shoulders against the rising wind. Pulling up the collar of his windbreaker, he took one last look at the now-choppy water of the bay and headed toward his car.

He'd hoped to hear from McAdam this week, but when Friday afternoon had rolled around without word, he'd decided he was too restless to stay at the office. He had to get away, to think—to plan. He still hadn't decided what he was going to do if they didn't get that contract, and as he sat in the car with the keys in his hand, he thought how much he wanted that account, how much Stewart-Davidson *needed* it, and he sighed.

Brad had spent two years in rehabilitation and therapy, and Cal had alternated between helping his friend and trying to hold down the office single-handedly. Even after all this time, they were barely scraping by. An account as big as McAdam's would pay off the last of the medical expenses and maybe clear the way for him to clear out himself. These plans had been interrupted the night Brad had been hit by that car. Insurance had helped, but neither of them had been fully covered, and he'd felt the financial responsibility was his to share. After all, Brad had been going to see a client when the accident had happened. But even if he hadn't been, Cal still would have kicked in; Davy would have done the same for him. They were friends, and he couldn't just stand by. So he'd put his own plans on hold. His friend needed him, and that was that.

Frowning again, he glanced out the car window. It had been so long since he'd been able to think about his own future that he felt guilty pondering it now. He hadn't allowed himself to plan since the accident; it seemed too disloyal. But this recreational gear contract would give them both the boost they needed. Brad would be self-sufficient again, able to handle the office by himself, and he would be free to dissolve the partnership and go out on his own, as he'd intended to do so long ago. Briefly, he closed his eyes. It was so close, he thought . . . so close.

Jerking his head, he put the key in the ignition. It was too soon to dream; he wouldn't think about it, not yet. First the contract, then he'd see. Starting the car, he drove out of the parking lot.

Brad was waiting in the outer office when he got back. No sooner had he stepped through the door when his partner crowed, "Guess what? McAdam just called!"

This was it. Feeling as though a steel hand had just clamped around his chest, Cal forced himself to say casually, "And . . . ?"

"And he wants to see you Monday morning at nine!" Brad shouted, and was so excited, he started doing wheelies with his wheelchair right in the middle of the reception area.

CHAPTER TWO

HOPING IT WAS anticipation she felt and not nerves, Mary Nell drove to her appointment at McAdam Recreation Monday morning. Her date with Robert had been a disaster, for she had so resented the time wasted at that boring fund-raiser when she could have been studying for her interview that she had asked Robert not to call her again. It wasn't fair, she said gently when he protested; they were just using each other because it was...convenient. There couldn't be anything between them, and they both had to get on with their lives. He'd been disappointed, but she'd been relieved that she'd finally had the courage to tell him goodbye. She'd spent what was left of the weekend preparing for her meeting, reading everything she could about sports and recreational gear. If she wasn't ready now, she never would be.

Her portfolio, with samples of projects she'd done at Barrigan Design, rested on the car seat beside her, and she glanced at it anxiously. By the time Lucille had returned from lunch on Friday, Mary Nell had forgotten her blisters and was hunched over the filing cabinet, going through its paltry contents with rising panic. Nothing she had done so far seemed good enough to show Anson McAdam, and she didn't know what she was going to do.

"What are you doing?" Lucille had asked in astonishment.

She had felt desperate. "I can't arrive empty-handed on Monday, but I don't want to take anything here! What am I going to do about a portfolio?"

Lucille looked down at the mess her boss had created. Files were scattered all over the floor, and she had to step gingerly over a few just to come in. "You won't put anything together that way," she said. "Would you like some help?"

Mary Nell had collapsed against the file drawer. "Would you?"

"Of course," Lucille said brusquely, and she proceeded to put together a sampling of everything Mary Nell had done since opening the office, plus some of the designs she'd done at McInerney and Glade—even a few she'd saved from school.

"I can't take those!" she'd protested, appalled.

"Of course you can," Lucille said calmly, assembling it all in a neat stack. "This is your work, and you want Mr. McAdam to know what you can do."

"Well, yes, but—"

"Then this is what you should take," Lucille said. Then she added thoughtfully, "Of course, it would be nice if you had a design for a Formula One car, or even something revolutionary in a tennis racket, but I suppose it can't be helped."

Mary Nell had to laugh, and with her amusement, some of her tension disappeared. Looking satisfied, Lucille returned to the outer office, and Mary Nell went to the closet to take out the outsize leather portfolio Stacy had given her as an office-warming present. As she ran her hand over the soft leather, she felt her confidence growing.

That blissful state had lasted until she'd started getting ready this morning. She hadn't been able to decide what to wear, and when she finally got that settled and turned to do her hair, it was more unmanageable than ever. She was still struggling with it when her sister appeared in the bathroom door.

"You're up early," Stacy said with a yawn. She was wearing a long T-shirt with a fat, very recognizable cat emblazoned on the chest, and she was holding a cup of coffee. Glancing at Mary Nell, she held the cup out. "Here, you look like you could use this more than me."

"No, thanks. I've already had some," she said, and grabbed her brush. If she didn't do something soon, she was going to be late.

Stacy glanced at the suit her sister was wearing. "Early appointment? Good suit? It must be important."

"It is," she said, and mentally crossed her fingers that she'd chosen well. She'd tried on half a dozen outfits and had finally decided on the suit because it fell somewhere between office casual and power dressing. She'd wanted to look confident and competent, but not overwhelming. Not that she could have managed that; obviously, *she* was the one feeling overwhelmed, especially because her hair wouldn't do a thing. She looked grim as she grabbed a hair clip. Maybe if she pulled it all up on top of her head into a kind of ponytail . . .

"What are you doing?" Stacy asked.

She was trying to shove the barrette into the thick wad of hair she'd bunched in one hand. "I thought—"

"Give me that," Stacy said, and tossed the clip away. Taking up the hairbrush, she gave Mary Nell's hair a quick few strokes, pulled it back from her face, secured it with a couple of combs and stepped away to examine the effect. Reaching out, she pulled a few wisps free and nodded in satisfaction. "Great. You look just like a model."

Wondering why she hadn't been able to do that, Mary Nell said darkly, "I'd rather look like a mechanical engineer—but thanks."

"Don't mention it. Are you going to have breakfast?"

The thought of food made her nauseous. Nothing could compete with the butterflies in her stomach, anyway, and she could always eat when the ordeal was over. Trying not to think how much this contract meant to her, she went into the bedroom for her things. "No, I'm not hungry. Besides, I've got to get going or I'll be late."

Stacy followed her out to the stair landing. "Where's the appointment?"

She had already started down the stairs. She hadn't told her sister about McAdam yet, and she said vaguely over her shoulder, "Oh...downtown. I'll tell you all about it tonight. We'll go out to dinner or something."

"I've heard that before," Stacy said, and raised the coffee cup. "Good luck."

Now she was about to find out if she was going to need it. As she entered the parking lot of the sprawling McAdam Recreation complex, she felt herself tense again. This was it. There was no turning back now. After parking the car in the first available space, she turned to the rearview mirror for a last check. Frightened green eyes stared back at her, and she could practically see the pulse beating in her throat.

Calm down, she ordered herself, and took a deep breath, then another. But she couldn't rid herself of the thought that this was a terrible mistake and that she was about to make a complete fool of herself. For a moment, she nearly lost courage. Then she told herself how much this account could mean to her. No more counting pennies, no more robbing Peter to pay Paul. She'd be able to pay Stacy's school expenses for the semester, not worry about

Lucille's salary and even start taking more than a poverty draw for herself. And, most important, she'd finally be able to pay off the computer.

Spurred on by this last thought, she got out of the car. *You can do this,* she told herself, and marched into battle.

Someone else was in the waiting room when she arrived. She noticed him right away—who wouldn't? Although he was sitting—*lounging*—in one of the chairs, she immediately saw that he was tall and fit—a sportsman, she thought, and felt herself shrink inside. Was he here about the contract? If he was, she was in trouble. Given a choice between her and him, even she would have picked the stranger, who, along with his supremely confident air, had wavy black hair and the deepest blue eyes she had ever seen.

Those eyes were staring at her now, and when he nodded, she returned the gesture with a brief jerk of her head. She looked quickly away from him, hoping to find the receptionist, the secretary...anyone. But the desk at the end of the room was empty, and when she could still feel him staring at her, she gave him a cool look.

"Is something wrong?"

When he smiled at her haughty tone, she flushed. But it was too late to say anything more, for he was uncoiling himself from the chair and saying in a deep voice, "Not a thing. I was just going to introduce myself." He held out a hand. "Cal Stewart."

She didn't want to know his name. Now she was sure he was here for the same reason she was, and when she realized that he was wearing slacks, a sport shirt and loafers, she immediately felt overdressed. He seemed perfectly comfortable here, while she could have modeled for an ad depicting what not to wear in this situation. Oh, why hadn't she followed her first instincts and worn a simple

skirt and blouse? she berated herself. Now Anson Mc-
Adam was going to think she was one of those female ex-
ecutives who didn't know what about lateral movements
in football or chukkers in cricket—or was that bridge?
Panicked again because despite all her study over the
weekend, she couldn't remember, she realized suddenly
that she hadn't returned the introduction or the hand-
shake.

"Mary Nell Barrigan," she said. She held out her hand
and tried to give herself more confidence by adding, "Of
Barrigan Design."

His hand was so big it practically engulfed hers. "Barrigan Design," he murmured. "I'm sorry, I don't believe
I've ever..."

He was staring at her so strangely, she just knew he was
wondering why she was here. She was beginning to wonder that herself. He seemed to fit so completely with these
surroundings that she could practically see him shooting
baskets with one hand while he swung a polo mallet, or
whatever it was called, with the other. He probably knew
all the scores of all the baseball players who ever lived, and
could recite statistics by the hour for any sport ever played.
While she . . . she swallowed. Right now, she couldn't even
remember the name of the football team everyone was so
proud of. Something to do with Indians, she thought, and
before she could panic again, she said, "We're a new firm.
We've only been open a year."

"I see. Did you work somewhere else before, then?"

Suddenly she became annoyed. Why was he asking all
these questions? Why did he want to know? All he'd told
her so far was his name, while she was so nervous she was
ready to babble her entire history. Deciding not to be so
forthcoming, she said coolly, "Yes, I did. And you?"

He shrugged, as though it should be obvious. "I'm with Stewart-Davidson. You might have heard of us."

It gave her tremendous pleasure to say, "I'm afraid not. Are you a new firm, too?"

That set him back a little, and she was pleased when she heard an edge in his voice. "Not exactly. We've been in Tacoma for five years."

"Oh, I'm sorry," she said, and smiled.

That seemed to end the conversation. He sat down again, and she turned away to find her own chair. A door opened just as she was about to sit down, and she was caught, half standing, half sitting, when a young woman who had to be the secretary appeared.

"Oh!" the girl said when she saw Mary Nell. "I'm sorry. I didn't know anyone else was here. Are you . . . ?"

Mary Nell straightened from her awkward pose. "Mary Eleanor Barrigan," she said, and flashed the cocky Mr. Stewart a glance as she added, "of Barrigan Design."

"I'll tell Mr. McAdam you're here."

The girl went off again, and Mary Nell was settling back in her chair when she realized the man was staring at her once more. She frowned at him just as he said, "I thought you said your name was Mary Nell."

She felt like an idiot. Cursing her fair skin that betrayed every little flush, she pulled herself together. Why was he affecting her this way? She felt like a tongue-tied schoolgirl. "My nickname," she said, and gave what she hoped was a sophisticated laugh and a shrug. Then she ruined the whole thing by adding, "When my sister was young, she couldn't quite pronounce Mary Eleanor, so I became Mary Nell."

"It suits you."

When she saw his amusement, she felt even worse. Why had she told him such a thing? He couldn't possibly care

about her family anecdotes, and she wondered what in the
world was wrong with her.

"Thank you," she managed in an agony of embarrassment, and wished the secretary would return.

As if in answer to her unspoken thoughts, the door
opened just then, and the girl appeared. She smiled at
them and said, "Mr. McAdam will see you both now."

Both? She had to fight her dismay. She hadn't anticipated being interviewed with this man, but with the girl
standing aside and gesturing them in, she didn't have much
of a choice. Steeling herself, she grabbed her purse and her
sketches. She had just started to follow the secretary when
she realized that Cal Stewart, coming behind her, wasn't
carrying anything. Immediately, her confidence plum-
meted again. Why hadn't *he* brought a portfolio? Was he
so confident that he didn't feel he had to prove himself?

It was too late to do anything about it now. She couldn't
pretend the portfolio wasn't hers, and she couldn't possibly hide it. The only thing she could do was put a good
face on, so she lifted her chin and followed the girl into
Anson McAdam's office. She was so startled by the sight
that greeted her that she forgot everything else.

Anson McAdam's office wasn't an ordinary office; it
looked like the recruiting stage for an athletic safari.
Camping and recreational equipment of every imaginable
type decorated the entire space, even the walls, and as her
amazed glance traveled over the tennis rackets and the
croquet mallets and the football pads and the cricket bats
and the helmets and the hunting bows and the camp stoves
and the rafts and the air tanks and the tents and heaven
knew what else, she didn't know what to say. Then she realized with a growing sense of panic that she didn't know
what half this stuff was, and she could feel herself shrink-
ing in despair again. What was she *doing* here?

"Mr. McAdam," the secretary said just then, "Miss Barrigan and Mr. Stewart are here."

With so many other things assaulting her vision, she hadn't noticed the desk before. Now a chair swung around and the man sitting there waved a pudgy hand. He was on the phone.

"Thank you, Sally," he said. "That will be all."

The secretary closed the door behind her, and Mary Nell and Cal Stewart were left with the man who had started as a golf caddie and had worked his way up to ownership of one of the top recreational equipment companies in the country. As she looked at him, she couldn't help thinking that no one would ever guess who he was or what he did; with his bald pate and protruding belly and small stature, Anson McAdam looked more like the corner grocer than a multimillionaire. As she stared, he hung up the phone.

"Sorry to keep you waiting, but His Royal Highness just called to tell me how much he liked the new polo pony I sent over for him to try," McAdam announced, and looked at them from under bushy brows. "Do either of you ride?"

Ride? She was so nervous she nearly burst out laughing. The one time Stacy had talked her into riding a horse, the beast she'd borrowed had promptly headed for the nearest tree and proceeded to rub her off. She would never forget landing hard on the ground and seeing that huge animal looming over her; she'd been terrified he was going to trample her to death with those mammoth feet. Even though Stacy, trying valiantly to control her mirth, had reminded her about falling off bikes, she'd dusted off her jeans and her ego and had started walking home without looking back. For all she knew, the horse was still standing under that tree, laughing his head off.

"My partner and I used to pack in with a couple of horses in the Cascades," Cal said. "And I still go riding on occasion."

"Good for you!" McAdam exclaimed. "I always say there's nothing so good for the inside of a man as the outside of a horse! What about you, Miss Barrigan?"

She swallowed. "I think horses are beautiful creatures."

"Wonderful! I keep a stable of Thoroughbreds and Arabians near here, and I'm there nearly every weekend. Come up and visit if you like!"

"Why, how kind," she murmured, thinking that if getting the account depended entirely upon her visiting Anson McAdam's stable, she was going to starve.

"I'll look forward to it," Cal said.

"So will I," McAdam said, and he beamed as he gestured for them to sit down.

There were two chairs in front of the desk, and as they each took one, McAdam rubbed his hands together, leaned forward and said, "We're all busy people, so I'll get right to the point. You wouldn't be here if I didn't think you could do the job I wanted, and while I had offers from bigger, more established companies, I decided to go with a smaller firm because I remember how difficult it was to get started myself. Having come up the hard way, I'm convinced that the hungrier you are, the harder you're inclined to work. Am I right?"

Thinking that he might have phrased that a little more delicately, Mary Nell seized the opportunity and unzipped the portfolio she was still holding awkwardly on her lap. "I'm certainly willing to work hard for you, Mr. McAdam," she said. "And I'm grateful for the chance to show you some of my work—"

McAdam lifted his hand. "I'm not interested in what you've done for someone else, Miss Barrigan, just what you're going to do for me."

Without missing a beat, she rezipped the case and set it at her feet. Thinking that it was going worse than she'd anticipated, she smiled and said, "Perhaps you could tell me what you have in mind, Mr. McAdam."

She was doing her best to appear calm and composed, but inside she was still nervous. It was this office; the entire space was so cluttered with recreational gear—some of which even hung from the ceiling—that she felt as though it all might come crashing down on her at any second. Uneasily, her eyes went to the model of the electric plane that was suspended over the desk. This place was so bizarre, she almost expected to hear, at any moment, the sounds of little engines and propellers revving up.

"I thought you could tell me," McAdam said.

Her thoughts had wandered. "I beg your pardon?"

Cal stirred. Crossing one long leg over the other, he leaned casually back in his chair. "I believe the man is asking you for some ideas."

Since he hadn't contributed anything to the conversation until now, she gave him a cool glance before turning her back on him. Looking at McAdam again, she said, "I'm prepared to give you what you need, Mr. McAdam. My CAD process is capable of doing just about anything."

"Cad?" McAdam repeated blankly.

She saw from the corner of her eye that Cal Stewart had abandoned his casual pose. Trying to ignore the sudden alertness she sensed in him, she smiled at McAdam again and said, "CAD, Mr. McAdam. Computer-aided design. I'm sure you've heard of the process. I have the newest 2-D equipment."

McAdam sat back. "Well, that's very interesting, but I'm afraid I'm somewhat at a loss, Miss Barrigan. You're talking about all these newfangled ideas, and I'm just an old man who makes a little camping gear. Maybe if you explained a little, it wouldn't sound so complicated."

"It's not complicated at all," Cal said before she could reply. "Computer-aided design is exactly what its name says—a computerized approach to tried-and-true design techniques."

Annoyed that he'd interrupted and that he was disparaging a process she found awe-inspiring and unique, she said sharply, "It's more than that, Mr. Stewart. In my opinion, CAD is to hand drafting what word processing is to typewriters."

Still looking mystified, McAdam asked, "How so?"

She started to explain. "Well, at the heart of the technology is the computer, of course—"

"Of course," Cal murmured.

Her chin lifted a fraction, but she wouldn't look at him as she continued, "A computer that enables us to manipulate data we simply can't do by hand."

"For instance?" McAdam asked curiously.

Sensing that he was about to interrupt again, she gave the upstart Stewart a quelling glance and then flushed when he winked at her. Pointedly, she turned away from him again. "Let's say a product has design features that have to be repeated, Mr. McAdam," she said. "CAD's ability to *replicate* means we can take part of the image and use it in several other areas of the design—"

"We can do that by hand," Cal muttered.

Now she did give him a haughty glance. "Yes, but with CAD we can transfer those parts to the screen without having to draw them all over again. I'm sure even you will admit that that saves a lot of time."

Seemingly amused by this little byplay between his two competitors, McAdam said, "Go on."

She obliged. "And CAD's ability to *translate* means that we can move images from one location on the screen to another—"

"Without having to draw them again," Cal supplied helpfully, and then gave her an innocent stare when she looked at him again.

"Yes, without having to draw them again," she said, daring him to interrupt. "But CAD can also *scale*, or change the proportions or size of one part of the image in relation to the others, and it can *rotate*, so that the design can be moved around to see it from different angles or perspectives."

Sounding impressed, McAdam said, "You can do this by computer?"

"Oh, yes," she said. "And because we *can* do all this by computer, instead of by hand, we can accomplish in moments tasks that used to take hours, or even days, with paper and pencil."

"And you can use this...this CAD process to design recreational equipment?"

"Of course," she said, mentally crossing her fingers. She wasn't about to admit that she'd never tried that particular application, so she added confidently, "CAD has proven so effective that it's starting to be utilized in other fields besides engineering. There is a program for mapping and cartography, for instance, at the University of Illinois, and one for creative arts at Purdue. Johns Hopkins is even using it for medical diagnostics, so the applications are quite wide, as you can see."

"It sounds like I'm going to be in elite company."

She smiled. "Well, it is the technology of the future."

"But how do you do it?"

To her annoyance, Cal suddenly decided to get into the act again. Before she could answer, he said, "Well, typically, the operator sits in front of a computer terminal and/or keyboard, with a digitizing tablet, stylus, mouse, or whatever input device he's going to use—"

"Mouse?" McAdam interrupted, looking incredulous and puzzled at the same time.

Mary Nell hadn't liked it that Cal had tried to muscle in, so she said quickly, "A mouse is a small, hand-held device we move across an array of lines on a pad—the digitizing tablet Mr. Stewart referred to just now. The purpose of the mouse is to count the lines as it moves across them and to send information to the computer about how fast it's moving and how many times it has moved. The computer uses this information to move an indicator, like a cursor, around the screen."

"I see," McAdam said, but she wasn't sure he did. She hadn't, the first time it had been explained to her; she'd had to use it herself to fully comprehend what a mouse could do.

Cal stirred again. "Maybe you should explain why we need the mouse and the pad in the first place," he suggested.

She gave him a quick look. Was he laughing at her? Maybe he'd said that because he didn't think she knew. Well, she'd show him a thing or two!

"Yes, maybe I should," she agreed. "The key to CAD is computer graphics, or the use of the computer to display graphic images. The computer does this by utilizing mathematical coordinates, just like those points drawn on a graph for a geometry figure, for instance, except in CAD's case, we call those points digital electronic data. The computer stores or retrieves or processes this data so that it can be sent to the display screen as drawings."

"In other words," Cal said in that easy drawl that was beginning to get on her nerves, "CAD takes the pencil out of the hand of the operator and places it into the 'hand' of the computer."

"Is that right, Miss Barrigan?" McAdam asked, sounding impressed again.

Annoyed that Cal Stewart had stolen her thunder, she said coolly, "That's rather a simplified explanation, but yes, that's right."

"Well, it's good enough for me," McAdam said, and waved his hand. "As long as you understand what you're doing—and you both can use it to work up something for me, I'll take your word for it."

Cal looked at his fingernails. "Oh, I don't use CAD," he said. "I'm a simple man...like you. I still prefer Miss Barrigan's scorned drafting board and pencil." He looked up and smiled at the pudgy head of the company, a sort of man-to-man grin that immediately set Mary Nell's teeth on edge. "Sometimes the old ways are still best, don't you think?"

To her annoyance, McAdam beamed. "I do indeed, Mr. Stewart."

She didn't think that at *all*, but what irritated her even more was that Cal Stewart had sat here this whole time, egging her on to explain a complicated computer process, while he'd been laughing up his sleeve and just waiting for his chance to prove what a good old boy he was to Anson McAdam. Seething, she had to remind herself to rein in her redhead's temper. She was sorely tempted to tell them both what she thought, but she held her tongue. She wanted this contract. But more than that, after meeting this...this Cal Stewart, she was determined to take it right out from under his arrogant *ol' boy* nose.

"Well, CAD or not," McAdam said just then, "I'm hoping that one of you can come through for me. You see, I'm in a bit of a squeeze right now. For years my company has been Washington's biggest seller of camping and recreational gear, but this past year, SportsGear, a piddling little firm in Los Angeles, has been trying to take business from me. My people tell me that they're going to put out some new mail-order lines that'll do me a lot of damage, yessir, a *lot* of damage. I don't want that to happen."

"I can understand that," Mary Nell said.

"And now you want to update all your products?" Cal asked.

"Only a few," McAdam said. "In the future, I plan to introduce new lines, but right now, I want to concentrate on these." Opening the folder on the desk, he took out two papers and handed each of them one. "This here's a little list I want you to look over."

When Mary Nell accepted her copy, she saw ten typed items.

1. All-terrain helmet.
2. High-tensile fishing reel.
3. Arctic sleeping harness.
4. Multipurpose hunting knife.
5. High-optic bow sight.
6. Collapsible tent poles.
7. Quick-release trailer hitch.
8. Convertible backpacker's stove.
9. Ski sled.
10. Propeller for rubber raft.

When she finished reading, she looked up. "I don't—" she said, but he anticipated her comment.

"Those are a few of the new toys I want to develop this year," he said. "I'd like each of you to choose one of those ideas, take it back to the office, work up the drawings or whatever you do, have it built by my fabrication department, then tested and report back to me. On retainer, of course."

That didn't seem so difficult, she thought, and glanced at her rival, who looked up from his copy and shrugged. "You first," he said, glancing at her.

She looked over the list again, wondering which she should pick. Painfully aware that her selection and her handling of it could decide which of them got the contract, she quickly went through her options. She didn't know anything about motorcycle riding, so the helmet was out; the same with fishing, so she could eliminate the reel. Just the thought of the arctic sleeping harness made her shudder, and the hunting knife and optic bow sight were worse. Realizing that they were both waiting for her to choose something, she saw the next item on the list. How difficult could it be? she wondered. After all, she'd been camping...once.

"I'll take the collapsible tent poles," she said, quickly banishing the memory of that humiliating episode from her mind.

Her maddening opposition didn't miss a beat. "Then I'll take the propeller," Stewart said, grinning at her.

Pleased, Anson McAdam rubbed his hands together. "Good. Good choices, both. Now all we have to do is set up the field trial date so you can test the items yourselves."

She wasn't sure she'd heard right. He wanted *them* to test these things? But that was ridiculous. She was a designer, not a field supervisor! "I beg your pardon?" she said.

McAdam laughed—a tad paternalistically, Mary Nell thought—at her incredulous expression. "Oh, I know it's not usually done—asking designers to go out on field trials, but this *is* my company, and despite what my competitors do, I insist that the people who work for me are familiar with our products. If you test these things yourselves, you'll know how they work." He grinned slyly. "Besides, that way I'll be sure to get a fair evaluation from each of you. Then *I* can make up my mind."

As far as she was concerned, he could make up his mind when she submitted her design—on paper! But before she could refuse to participate in this outrageous charade, McAdam looked at her rival.

"Mr. Stewart?"

To her utter disbelief, he merely shrugged. "Suits me."

And now it was her turn. Practically choking with indignation, she started to say she wanted no part of the ludicrous scheme, but then she thought of how pleased this Cal Stewart would be if she backed out now, and her chin came up a fraction. No; she would not give him the satisfaction of beating her out of the contract before they'd even put pen to paper—or rather, she thought irately, mouse to tablet. Not only had he made fun of her CAD process during the interview; he'd done everything he could to make her feel at a disadvantage. So she wasn't one of the good old boys. She wasn't even one of the good old girls. But she knew design, and that was all that counted. She'd show this cocky, arrogant man—she and her computer.

"I accept," she said, her voice steely.

"Wonderful!" McAdam said, and beamed. "And naturally I'll make this worth your while."

The sum he mentioned was so generous that she almost forgot her outrage. Almost. Thinking that no amount of money was going to compensate her for this disaster, she knew she had to escape before she blurted that she'd made a terrible mistake. *What have you done?* she asked herself wildly, and got to her feet. Both men rose with her, and she somehow managed to hold her hand out calmly to McAdam. "It was a pleasure meeting you," she said. "I'll be in touch."

"I'll look forward to it," he said.

She made herself turn to her opponent. "And I'll be hearing from you?" she asked, referring to the absurd situation they'd been forced into.

There was no mistaking the challenge in his eyes. "Sooner than you expect," he said.

She gave him a cool nod. "Gentlemen," she said, and remembered by some miracle to take the unopened portfolio with her before she fled.

CAL WAS HALFWAY back to the office before he could appreciate the humor of the situation. Whoever this Mary Eleanor Barrigan was, he had to give her credit. She'd certainly taken the wind out of *his* sails, accepting the challenge McAdam had meted out. She looked like some demure, helpless little Southern belle, but she'd soon routed that impression. He shook his head. A temper to match that glorious red hair—and smart!

His expression changed, and he grimaced when he remembered the way she'd explained the CAD process to McAdam. He'd been too embarrassed to admit that his office didn't have a computer, so he'd been reduced to pretending disdain for the process. Thinking about it now, he felt his face grow red.

"How'd it go?" Brad asked excitedly when he walked into the office. "Did we get the contract?"

"Not yet. We've got to prove ourselves first."

"What do you mean, prove ourselves? How? What happened?" Brad asked.

"You're not going to believe it, Davy," he said, and started to tell him about that incredible office. "When I first walked in, I nearly ducked. I thought something was either going to swoop down from the ceiling or attack me from the corner. You never saw so much equipment in your life. I didn't know what half the stuff was."

Brad's eyes widened. "You're kidding."

"I wish I was. But it gets even better. Another firm was there. We're in competition with Barrigan Design."

"Who's that?"

Cal thought of the owner, cool and fiery by turn, and shook his head. "The company is owned by a woman named Mary Eleanor Barrigan. She's new—just opened last year."

"So that's why I haven't heard of it. What's she like?"

"Not so much," Cal said with a shrug, and quickly went on to something else. For some reason, he didn't want to discuss Mary Nell. "Don't you want to hear about the little contest McAdam drummed up?"

"Contest?"

"Yeah, contest," Cal said, and told him about the list of items McAdam had shown them and what he wanted them to do. "The best part is that he wants us to field-test the things ourselves," he finished.

"You're kidding. I've never heard of that."

"Yeah, well, neither have I. I guess when you own the biggest recreational gear company in the state, you can do that sort of thing."

"Did you agree to do it?"

Cal thought of how important this contract was going to be to both of them, how much McAdam had offered to retain them, how much they needed it...how much *he* needed it. He hadn't said as much to Brad, not yet. So he just said, as casually as he could, "Sure, why not?"

"What did you choose?"

"The propeller."

Brad sensed something, but he wasn't sure what. "And what do you think?" he asked anxiously.

Cal started toward his own office. Thrusting away images of mocking green eyes that rose again in his mind, he stopped at the door to look back. With a wink and a lot more confidence than he felt, he said, "I think it's going to be the proverbial piece of cake."

CHAPTER THREE

MARY NELL HAD anticipated Stacy's reaction to the competition for McAdam's account, and she wasn't disappointed. She had called her sister as soon as she got back to the office, and Stacy barely heard the story through to the end before she started to laugh. "You? *Camping?*" she said incredulously.

"It's not—" Mary Nell began, but was interrupted again by another merry gale. She broke off in pointed silence.

"I'm sorry, Mary Nell," Stacy said, trying to get herself under control again. "It's just..." Overcome by giggles once more, she had to stop.

Mary Nell had had enough of this unrestrained mirth. Telling herself she'd known her sister would act this way, she said severely, "It's not funny."

Stacy tried, but she still sounded a little choked when she said, "Honestly, Mary Nell, you have to admit it does have an element of humor. Don't you remember the one time you tried camping out?"

She didn't want to remember. She had never forgotten the humiliation, and she thought it tactless to remind her of that horrible experience now. After all, Stacy was the one who had talked her into going. Left to her own devices, she would never have done something like that in a million years. To make matters worse, once in the woods, Stacy seemed perfectly at home, while all she could think about were bears. It hadn't mattered that none had been seen in that area for years; she'd been convinced they were there, staring at her from behind the trees with their yellow, ferocious eyes as soon as it got dark. She'd been so terrified that she hadn't slept a wink the entire night, but had stayed rigidly in her sleeping bag, alert for the slightest noise.

She'd finally heard it, sometime during those long, endless, dark hours—a scraping sound that stood her hair right on end. Sure that they were going to be mauled and eaten on the spot, she'd screamed a warning and then tried frantically to get out of her mummy bag. The zipper had jammed. In a frenzy she'd jumped up and started hopping like a madwoman toward the car, screeching at the top of her lungs.

The car had been locked. She would have broken the window and launched herself in like a torpedo if her screaming hadn't raised the entire campground. People came running from all over, sure she was being murdered . . . or worse. Flashlights and lanterns and car beams had flared, pinning the culprit in the merciless light.

To this day, she'd never forgotten the mortification. The huge, monstrous, slavering grizzly she had envisioned had turned out to be a foraging raccoon, who had looked up with wide eyes from the pots and pans where he was sitting, obviously decided the area was getting too crowded and promptly waddled off.

Remembering, she felt red-faced all over again, and she muttered to Stacy, "It's not *camping*. I told you, it's a field trial. We just go out, test the designs and report back. Even *I* should be able to manage that."

The acid in her voice was impossible to ignore, and Stacy said contritely, "I'm sorry. I shouldn't have laughed."

"No, you shouldn't have," she agreed, still miffed. "This is a design test, not a contest in survival skills, remember?"

"Don't be too sure," Stacy said, stifling another giggle. "With you out there, anything can happen."

Annoyed anew by this lack of sisterly confidence, she retorted, "The only thing that's going to happen is that I'm going to pass this stupid test business with ease."

"I have no doubt," Stacy said soothingly. "When is this . . . test supposed to take place?"

"I don't know yet. As soon as we're ready, I suppose."

"I see. You haven't said very much about your . . . er . . . opponent in this. Who is it? Anyone I know?"

An image of a smug grin and amusement in deep blue eyes flashed into her mind. Irritably, she thrust it away and said coolly, "I doubt it. He's with Stewart-Davidson—a firm I've never heard of."

Stacy sounded amused again. "It doesn't sound like you're too worried."

"I'm not," she said, but despite herself, she thought of that maddening grin again. Haughtily, she added, "They're hardly competition, after all. They don't even have CAD."

"Well, good luck," Stacy said, and added hastily, "Not that you'll need it."

"Thanks for that much, at least."

"I said I was sorry for laughing," Stacy said. "Oh, and by the way, I've got to head back to school early today—a research paper I forgot about. We'll postpone the celebration until later, all right?"

"What celebration?"

"The one we're going to have when you get this account," Stacy said, making up for her earlier lack of support. "Bye."

Only slightly mollified, Mary Nell hung up. She sat behind her desk for a second or two, drumming her fingers against the top, wondering how best to tackle the project. At last, she stood and went to the door. Lucille was busy at her own desk, but she seemed to sense Mary Nell standing there and looked up expectantly.

"Did you get through to Stacy?"

"Yes, she was home," Mary Nell said, and thought grumpily that at least Lucille had been enthusiastic about the meeting this morning. Her secretary hadn't had any doubts at all about her ability to do this thing; she'd been thrilled that "they" had accepted the challenge. Which was more, she thought darkly, than she could say for her own sister.

"Well, what did she say?" Lucille asked.

The last thing Mary Nell wanted to do was launch into an explanation of why Stacy had found the situation so hilarious, so she said, "She was surprised when I told her about this little contest."

"You know, I was, too," Lucille said thoughtfully. "But then, I don't know very much about this business yet." She hesitated. "Is this kind of requirement...usual?"

Perching glumly on the edge of the desk, she shook her head. "Not really. But I wasn't about to argue—not with the retainer McAdam mentioned. Even if I don't get the account, that will tide us over for a while."

"Oh, you'll get the account," Lucille said confidently, pushing her glasses up on her long nose. "I just know you will."

"I wish I could be as certain as you," she said. Remembering Stacy's laughter, she fiddled with the pencil holder on the desk, forcing herself to add, "Recreational gear isn't really...my field."

"Then we'll make you an expert," Lucille said at once. Grabbing her secretarial pad, she looked up eagerly. "What do you want me to do first?"

Mary Nell had to laugh. "You know, the best thing I ever did was put that ad in the paper," she said.

Embarrassed and pleased at the same time, Lucille blushed, patted her pageboy and lifted her pen. "And the best thing I ever did was answer it," she said brusquely. "Now. Where do we start?"

A week later, Mary Nell was sure she had more information about tents and tent poles than she would ever want to know. Lucille had combed the library and brought back stacks of reference materials; she'd called different manufacturers; she'd sent away for brochures. She had even talked to the local Eagle Scout chapter! Then she had compiled a register of sporting goods stores Mary Nell was to visit—and a list of names of salespeople she was to talk to when she got to each one. The hardworking secretary had done so much preparatory work that Mary Nell couldn't refuse to go, but after listening to half a dozen salesmen rave about their various products, she felt her eyes glaze over. It was difficult to look interested in things like ventilation and daylight and rain and wind and weight and bulk and space, when all she really wanted to know about were the poles that held everything up.

"I never want to enter another sporting goods store as long as I live," she groaned to Lucille one day after she'd spent her lunch hour talking to yet another enthusiastic salesman. Throwing herself down in the chair behind her desk, she put her head back and closed her eyes. "I'm beginning to think the Great Tent Hunt is never going to end!"

Sympathetically, Lucille brought her a cup of tea and sat down in the chair opposite her boss. Mary Nell's desk was littered with drawings, glossy photographs, reference materials, magazines, books and all manner of promotional material from mail-order houses—all about tents and related equipment. "What happened this time?" she asked.

Mary Nell opened one eye. "You don't want to know," she said, and reached for the cup. "Thanks for the tea."

"You looked like you could use it. So—what did this one say?"

"Where do you want me to start?" she muttered. "With the fact that a lot of tent buyers get more tent than they really need? Or that no one really realizes the importance of a fly sheet—which isn't to keep out insects, as we might imagine, but is actually an extra outer layer designed to protect the tent itself from moisture."

"I didn't know that," Lucille said, marveling.

Mary Nell looked at her over the rim of her teacup. "Now your life is complete."

Lucille smiled her shy little smile. "What else did the man tell you?"

Rolling her eyes, Mary Nell deepened her voice in imitation of the latest salesman and pointed her finger. "We can't forget the importance of a good floor," she said. "Now a good floor is a tub-style—and more than just waterproof material on the bottom. A tub floor, you see, comes up the side of the tent at least several inches and should have as few seams as possible. And naturally, it should be coated with waterproofing."

"Naturally," Lucille said, laughing. "But what did you find out about tent *poles*?"

"Tent poles?" she repeated, raising an eyebrow. "Ah, but first we have to decide what kind of tent we're talking about, don't you see? Do we need the self-supporting A-frame, or the tunnel-style? Perhaps a dome or a geo-dome? Do we require a single-person or a two-person tent?

Or perhaps a heavy-duty one for three or four people? And then, there is always the basic bivouac sack.''

Lucille laughed again. They'd been through this before. "Tent poles?'' she prodded.

Mary Nell nodded briskly. "Oh yes, the tent poles. The original purpose of our investigation. Shall I treat you to yet another lecture?''

"Please do,'' Lucille said, her eyes twinkling.

"Well, most tent poles are made of one of three materials—rigid aluminum tubing, flexible aluminum tubing—often called 7075 aluminum, for those who want to know—'' she glanced at Lucille from under her eyebrows and received a giggle in reply "—or various forms of fiberglass. Now, rigid aluminum is good for A-frame tents, because the poles don't have to bend. But domes, geodomes and tunnel tents do better with flexible aluminum and Fiberglass.''

"Well, see—there you go,'' Lucille said encouragingly. "You're learning more every day.''

Wonderingly, Mary Nell shook her head. She'd once thought she was the incurable optimist, but ever since Lucille had come to work for her, she'd realized that wasn't true. She sometimes saw the glass as half-empty, but her secretary never did.

But then, Lucille didn't have to design these stupid tent poles—*she* did, and she was fast approaching the deadline. McAdam hadn't given them much time to begin with, but he'd called the other day to impress her further with the need for haste. The competition, it seemed, was gaining, and she couldn't—as he'd put it—dillydally.

Seeing her expression, Lucille tried to be even more supportive. "You have enough information to start, anyway, don't you?''

Glancing down at her cluttered desk, Mary Nell pulled a random file out. "Oh, yes, thanks to you. All I have to do is sort through it. Here, for example, is a debate about fiberglass poles versus aluminum. And here—" she lifted another one "—is a discussion about shock cord."

"Shock cord?" Lucille repeated. "What's that?"

"A cord used to string the poles together. If they're not lined up properly, you see, you have to stop to figure out which piece fits which and then try to thread the whole wobbly thing through another thing called the pole sleeve."

Lucille marveled. "Who would have thought this would be so complicated?"

"Not me," Mary Nell said glumly, reaching for her tea.

"About this string," Lucille said thoughtfully, "—or what did you call it? The shock cord. Couldn't you just leave it out, number the poles instead, have them collapse in on each other like a telescope and then ask them to pop up when you need them again? Isn't that much simpler?"

"Sure. But if it was that simple, McAdam wouldn't be paying me this kind of money to design them, would he?"

"No, I suppose you're right," Lucille replied, undaunted. "But maybe that's why he *is* paying you. He's confident you'll come up with something, and so am I."

"If I had your confidence in me, I would have solved this problem days ago."

"Oh, you'll do it," Lucille said, and stood. She paused at the door to glance back. "You haven't said much about the competition."

Mary Nell felt herself stiffen. "No," she said in a tone that indicated she didn't intend to. "I haven't."

"I see," Lucille said, and closed the door on her way out.

Annoyed that Lucille's comment about the competition had stirred memories of Cal Stewart she preferred to forget, she frowned as she finished her tea. But try as she might, she could still see his face in her mind, still picture that maddening smile. *Who does he think he is?* she asked herself irritably, and set the cup aside. Her glance fell on her cluttered desk, and she had to fight the impulse to sweep everything on it into the wastebasket at her feet. Wondering why she couldn't seem to put Cal Stewart out of her mind when she hadn't even *liked* him, she got up abruptly and went down to the computer room. Her deadline loomed like a dark cloud, and Lucille was right: she had all the information she needed, and more. It was time to get to work.

"'Have them collapse in on each other, then ask them to pop up when you need them again,'" she muttered, quoting her secretary. She frowned. It wasn't that simple, but still, Lucille had given her an idea, and a few minutes later her fingers were moving rapidly over the keyboard, her eyes intent on the changing figures on the monitor screen. She was still there when Lucille glanced in to tell her she was going home. Without looking up, Mary Nell waved goodbye and then was lost to the design forming again on the screen.

LUCILLE QUIETLY TIPTOED out. Smiling as she walked down the hall toward the reception area and her own desk, she murmured in satisfaction, "Now *that's* more like it." Then she took her purse from the drawer, glanced around to make sure everything was in order and locked the front door behind her.

The April air was soft and warm when she emerged from the office; she stood outside for a moment, appreciating the spring evening. Although she knew how to drive, she didn't own a car; her mother insisted that maintaining two vehicles when one would do for both of them was a waste of money. Having lived with Eunice all these years, she'd learned not to make waves; they got along so much better when she went along, and it really didn't matter. She didn't mind taking the bus; she used the time to read.

Tonight, as she started walking toward the bus stop, she glanced back at the office and thought how glad she was that she had seen Mary Nell's advertisement and had actually been brave enough to answer it. To this day she didn't know where she'd found the courage. She'd always been in awe of Mary Nell, had practically idolized her from afar when they were growing up. She'd always been so pretty, with those big green eyes and that cloud of red hair; so petite, so popular. Even now there were times when just standing next to her, Lucille felt all angles and hands and feet, awkward and graceless, and so...unfashionable. She would never have the fashion sense Mary Nell did—or even if she did, the boldness to wear anything other than the skirts and sweaters and blouses she'd worn for years. She didn't even have the daring to change her hair; she'd worn the same pageboy style since the seventh grade. Now she wouldn't recognize herself any other way. Sighing, she started down the street toward the bus stop. She was supposed to stop at the market on the way home and pick up a head of cabbage; today was Friday, and they always had stuffed cabbage for dinner. She hated stuffed cabbage.

The bus was coming, and Lucille automatically started to hurry to catch it, when a sudden thought occurred to her, and she stopped right there in the middle of the sidewalk. Remembering how Mary Nell had blushed when she'd mentioned that other firm, Stewart-Davidson, she suddenly wondered why. She'd never seen Mary Nell blush before. She stood there indecisively.

It wasn't any of her business, she told herself firmly, and started off again, only to stop once more. She knew the address of Stewart-Davidson; she'd looked it up one day, just in case.

No! This was ridiculous. She *couldn't* go over there; what would she say if anyone found her out?

The bus had stopped at the curb; it was about to pull away again. She had to decide; if she didn't run, she was going to miss it.

But she couldn't get that blush out of her mind. What was it about that place—or the people in it—that had made Mary Nell react that way? Wouldn't a good secretary find out?

The bus wheezed off while she stood there, and she stared after it in dismay. That decided it. But now what?

Her heart started to pound. She'd never done anything like this. She was astonished at herself for even having had the thought, especially when her mother was expecting her with the cabbage. All right; a few minutes wouldn't hurt. She'd take a quick look, hurry to the grocery and be home before she knew it. And just for penance, she'd walk.

Twenty minutes of hard walking later, she found the address she was looking for. Her heart started to pound as she walked toward the office. She felt like an inept spy in come campy movie—or better yet, Agent 99 in *Get Smart*. What was she doing here? What did she hope to find out? It was already after five—all sensible people were on their way home. Did she really think she was going to stumble upon something by peering into the darkened windows of an empty office? She'd been silly to come, and she still hadn't been to the market for the cabbage.

But as long as she was here, she decided cautiously, she might as well try to see what she could. And it did look as though someone was still there; she could see lights in the window as she came close. Maybe she should cross the street so she wouldn't look obvious, she thought, and then flushed. What a fool she was! Who knew she was here? Who cared?

But her steps still slowed as she neared, and her heart started to pound again. Five more steps, four . . . two. She walked casually by the front of the place, peering in quickly, disappointed that the only thing she could see was a reception area, similar to that in her own office. The room seemed empty, though the lights were on behind it. Well, what had she expected—someone to be standing out front with a sign that said, Hi, There. We're So Glad You've Come?

Feeling foolish again, disappointed that her attempt had yielded so little, she walked to the end of the block and casually turned and headed back the way she had come. This time she stopped in front of the big windows, pretending to search for something in her purse, trying not to be obvious about staring inside. Was that movement she saw? Her heart leaped to her throat and hammered there. What if someone was looking out just as she was looking in? Galvanized by the awful thought, she took a quick step back, felt something at the back of her knees and promptly lost her balance. Her arms flailing, she uttered a startled exclamation, and fell . . . right into someone's lap.

Someone's *lap*? She was so horrified she didn't know what to do. Instinct took over, and she whipped her head around to see what had happened. When a pair of amused gray eyes met hers, she wished that the earth would somehow open and swallow her up. Had she really fallen on top of someone sitting in a wheelchair? She was so mortified she wanted to die on the spot.

"Hello, there," the man said. His voice resonated with laughter. "Need a lift?"

Face flaming, she leaped up and immediately began babbling out of sheer nerves and painful embarrassment. "I'm sorry, so terribly sorry. I don't know what... I mean, I can't think what I... Oh, my. Did I hurt you? Please say you're all right...."

"I'm fine," he said, grinning, and slapped his leg. "See? Didn't feel a thing."

She couldn't possibly smile back; she wanted to crawl into a hole. "I'm sorry," she babbled again. "I didn't hear you. I mean... I didn't know you were there. Oh, this is awful—"

"Not as far as I'm concerned," he said. He had nice eyes, Lucille noted, and thick brown hair that grew back from his forehead. His shoulders and arms were muscular, and he was wearing jeans and running shoes. She jerked her eyes back to his face.

"You're being very kind," she said, still mortified. "But I'm so embarrassed. I've never done anything... like this before. I can't believe I was so clumsy!"

"Don't worry about it," he said, and winked. "In fact, I wouldn't mind if it happened again. It's not every day a woman falls for me. Or on me, as the case happens to be."

She couldn't help it; the joke was so awful she had to smile, and then he did, too. He really did have the nicest smile. His eyes crinkled at the corners, and she was so bemused that she didn't notice he was holding out his hand. "Brad Davidson," he said, introducing himself. "And you are...?"

"Lucille Hendershot," she said faintly, and put her hand in his. His fingers were warm and strong—and, astonishingly, callused—as they closed around hers. She looked down in surprise, only to redden again when he laughed.

"It's the chair," he said, as though reading her thoughts. "I thought the motorized version would make me lazy, so I opted for the manual model. Unfortunately, it doesn't do great things for the hands."

She was mortified again. Was she really as transparent as that? "I . . . see," she mumbled, and glanced around, wondering how to escape. Her eyes fell on the Stewart-Davidson logo splashed across the big office windows, and she stiffened. How could she have forgotten? In a panic, she looked back at him. What had he said his name was? Brad *Davidson*.

Oh, it couldn't be, she told herself, and wanted to die. His smile confirmed her worst fears, but she had to ask. Gesturing toward the sign, she said, "Are you . . . are you . . . ?"

"Right," he said cheerfully. "I'm the Davidson part. Did you want to see us about something?"

"No . . . no," she said weakly, and wondered what Mary Nell was going to say about this. Briefly, she closed her eyes. "I . . . was just passing by."

"Oh, that's too bad."

She wasn't sure why he sounded disappointed, but she didn't want to ask. In any event, she didn't have time to pursue it, for just then, to her horror, the office door opened and a tall man stuck his head out. "Davy," he started to say, and then he noticed her. "Oh, sorry. I didn't know you had company."

"Yes, well, we just ran into each other," Brad said with a grin. "Lucille, I'd like you to meet my partner, Cal—the Stewart part of the logo. Cal, this is Lucille Hendershot."

It took her a moment to acknowledge the introduction. Glancing at him in puzzlement, she said, "I thought you said your name was Brad."

"It is," he said with a laugh. "Cal just calls me Davy—a childhood habit."

"Oh," she said faintly, and turned to look at Cal. She wasn't so flustered now, and when she saw the tall man with the lean face, the intense blue eyes and the dimple in the cheek that flashed so briefly as he smiled, she suddenly knew why Mary Nell had reacted the way she had. Cal Stewart was certainly one of the most attractive men she had ever seen, and as she gazed up at him, all she could think of was how glad she was that she wasn't Mary Nell.

Then Brad said something, and as she looked at him again, she knew she had to get away. With him smiling at her like that, she felt all tingly—a new sensation for her, and confusing. Without knowing what she was saying, she muttered a goodbye and hurried off. There was something about Brad Davidson, something that made her want to blush as Mary Nell had blushed. She'd never felt that way before, and she couldn't resist a quick look back. Brad was still there on the sidewalk, and when he saw her turn, he raised his hand and shouted something. But a car went by just then, and she didn't hear. She couldn't go back. Hurrying on, she caught another bus and went home. She was so stunned at the extraordinary thing that had happened to her, she didn't realize until she walked in the front door that she had completely forgotten to stop at the store for the cabbage.

CAL WAS SITTING at the drafting table, his arms folded, a grin on his face, when Brad came inside. Cal had been finishing up a project for Tacoma Tool when he'd heard voices outside, and he'd gone to look. He was glad he had. He couldn't believe that his partner was talking to a woman; he couldn't remember the last time his friend had voluntarily talked to a female who wasn't a client—and then, very reluctantly. Before the accident, Brad hadn't been what he'd call shy, but ever since then—and since Beth walked out—he had avoided women entirely.

"Who was that?" he asked, trying to be casual. If Brad had started seeing someone, he didn't want to scare him off. He'd been trying to talk him into going out more for months now, to no avail.

"I don't know. I ran into her outside," Brad said, and then gave a rare grin. "Or rather, she ran into me. I think I startled her, and she . . . just fell into my lap."

"That's a neat trick, if you can manage it," he commented. "What were you doing—sneaking up on her?"

Brad looked indignant. "Of course not. I forgot that article I wanted to read tonight, and I came back for it. She was standing outside, looking in. At first I thought she was a client."

"This late?"

"Yeah, well, you never know," Brad said, giving a powerful shove to the chair and heading into his own office. "G'night."

"Wait a minute," Cal said, following. "Are you going to see her again?"

Brad had reached his desk; he pretended surprise. "I don't know. I hadn't thought about it." He shrugged and began moving papers around on his desk. "I don't know her phone number."

"You know her name," Cal pointed out dryly.

Brad glanced away. "Yeah, well..." he muttered again.

"She seemed nice," he ventured. "Kind of . . . cute."

Brad stopped rummaging through the clutter. He looked up, a faraway look on his face. "Yeah, she did, didn't she?" he said, and then shook himself. "No, forget it."

Cal had learned during the long months of Brad's recovery not to avoid the subject of the wheelchair. Because he'd been so intimately involved in the therapy, they'd both had counseling sessions, and he'd learned to approach any problems associated with Brad's disability head-on. Now he spoke bluntly. "Why? Because you think she'll be turned off by the chair? She didn't seem to be."

Brad looked away. "She was embarrassed."

He wasn't going to let his friend get away with that. "Maybe she was embarrassed at falling into your lap—not at the fact that you were sitting in a wheelchair when she did it."

Glaring, Brad said, "Are you trying to set me up?"

"Would that be such a bad idea?"

"Maybe you're just tired of me."

"Well, I have to admit that given a choice between your mug and that of a pretty woman, the woman would win out every time."

"Speaking of pretty women, you haven't said much about our competition in this recreational gear contract," Brad said suddenly. "Mind telling me why not?"

Feeling his face getting red, Cal said, "Don't try to change the subject. We were talking about you."

They'd been friends for a long time. Brad saw the tell-tale flush and crowed, "I knew it! Something's going on!"

"Nothing's going on," he said, and heard the weak protest with a grimace. He couldn't help himself. He *had* been thinking about Mary Nell Barrigan this week. For some stupid reason, he hadn't been able to get her out of his mind. But that didn't mean he had to admit it, and he started back to his own office.

Naturally, Brad followed him. "Isn't it?" he asked. "Well, if that's so, tell me this—why have you spent the entire week staring into space? If I'd known you were

going to take this long to design those pipe fittings for Tacoma Tool, I would have done it myself." Laughing at
Cal's expression, he went on slyly, "What does she look
like, my friend? You've really been closemouthed on this
one."

"She—" Cal started to say, and stopped. How could he
explain what Mary Nell looked like? It wasn't just her
physical appearance—that glorious cloud of red hair or
those green, green eyes; it was something in her manner—
in the tilt of her chin, the look on her face. He shook his
head. He sounded like a fool, even to himself. "I told
you," he muttered. "She's not so much."

"Okay," Brad said. "Then why haven't you called her
to set up a field test date? We're running out of time, Cal-
vin John, or haven't you noticed?"

Cal glared at him. Brad knew how he hated to be
pushed; how he disliked even more the use of his full
name. "I'll call her," he grunted.

"When?" Brad asked.

"What do you mean, when? When I feel like it, that's
when!"

Brad picked up the phone. "How about now?"

Exasperated, he took the receiver and slammed it into
the cradle again. "Are you nuts? I'm not going to call her
now! For Pete's sake, it's—" he glanced at the clock and
saw with relief that it was after six "—it's too late."

"All right. When, then?"

"Maybe I should call her at home," he said sarcastically, and then added on inspiration, "Maybe I'll just do
that . . . if you call this Lucille. Come on, Davy—what do
you say about that?"

Brad didn't have too much to say. Giving his partner a dirty look, he said, "All right. You made your point."

"Thank God. I was beginning to think we'd be here all night."

Brad shoved the chair toward the door. "But you will call to set up that test date, won't you?" he said, and grinned suddenly over his shoulder. "If you're afraid to talk to her, make an appointment with her secretary. She must have one."

"Why? We don't."

Brad just laughed. A second later, Cal heard the back door slam, and he waited for the sound of the van. Long ago Brad had been fitted for a special vehicle, so he didn't have to depend on others to drive him around, and Cal nodded to himself when he heard the toot of the horn a few moments later as Brad drove by. Throwing himself into his chair again, he glanced at the drawings on the board and decided he could finish them tomorrow. He was tired; it was time to go home.

Then his eyes went to the phone. *If you're afraid to talk to her, make an appointment with her secretary.* He grunted. It wasn't that he was *afraid*, he thought, and to prove it, he picked up the receiver. He had her office number around here somewhere—yeah, on the Rolodex. He flipped through it and dialed. As it rang the first time, he glanced in satisfaction toward the front door. Could he help it if she'd already gone home?

"Barrigan Design."

He hadn't expected anyone to answer; he didn't know what to say. Absurdly, once he recognized her voice, he nearly hung up. Then he pulled himself together. *Stop acting like a jerk,* he told himself, and said, "Mary Nell Barrigan, please."

"This is she."

Was that amusement he heard in her voice? Had she recognized him and wondered what kind of game he was playing? Wondering that himself, he said, more brusquely, "Ms Barrigan, this is Cal Stewart, of Stewart-Davidson. I'm sorry to call so late. I really didn't think you'd still be at the office."

Now she definitely sounded amused. "I see," she said. "Is that why you called?"

He could feel himself turning a deep red, and he tried to compose himself. He'd met this woman once; how could she be having such a devastating effect on him? He sounded like an idiotic schoolboy.

"No," he said. "I called because I thought we should discuss those field trial dates." Then, to vindicate himself, he added, "We're on a tight schedule, and I wanted to be sure you had enough time to prepare."

"How kind," she said while he frowned fiercely into the phone. She was definitely laughing at him, he decided, and who could blame her? He'd gone from sounding like an inane teenager to an insufferable chauvinist. What was *wrong* with him?

"I take it you're prepared with the—what was it? Oh, yes, the propeller," she said.

Propeller? What propeller? For a second or two, he didn't know what she was talking about, then his glance fell on the preliminary drawings he'd done. Oh yes, the *propeller.* Closing his eyes, he ran a hand through his hair. Why had he called? This wasn't going at all as he had anticipated. Why had she answered the damned phone?

"Look, maybe I'd better start over," he said, and then, in absolute horror, he heard himself add, "Maybe we could discuss all this over dinner."

"Dinner?"

He wanted to groan and curse at the same time. Now what had he done? He could almost feel her surprise, and he couldn't blame her. The last thing he'd intended to do was ask her out; all he had wanted was to set up the field test dates so he could get this ordeal over with as quickly as possible. And it *was* going to be an ordeal. If he'd made such a fool of himself over the phone, he could just imagine how he'd act when they actually got together to test their projects.

Telling himself not to think of that just yet, he tried to salvage the situation. "Forget it," he said quickly. "It was a stupid idea. Maybe we should just—"

"I accept," she said.

"I beg your pardon?"

"I accept your invitation to dinner," she said, sounding a little strange herself. "What night did you have in mind?"

He hadn't had any night in mind; he hadn't meant to ask her out at all. "Well, this is Friday.... Would tomorrow night be too soon?" he said, and put his head in his hands. What was happening here? He didn't even know if she was married or not. Galvanized at the thought, he stiffened.

"Tomorrow night is fine," she said. "About...eight?"

"Eight," he repeated, as though he'd never heard the time before. "Well...yes, that would be...just fine. If you give me your address, I'll pick you up."

"Oh, no, that's—"

He got it together at last. "I'll pick you up," he said firmly, and took down her address. He didn't notice until he got off the phone that his heart was pounding as though he'd just run a hard race.

CHAPTER FOUR

"SO, HOW'RE THINGS?" Stacy asked when she called from school on Saturday night.

Things weren't going well. In fact, as she glanced around the disheveled bedroom, Mary Nell began to feel a little frantic. Cal was supposed to pick her up in thirty minutes, and she wasn't ready. She had to decide what to wear soon, but nothing she'd tried on seemed right. Wondering why it mattered so much to her since it wasn't important anyway, she sat on the edge of the bed and blurted, "Oh, Stace, you'll never guess what I did!"

"From that tone, I'd say you either robbed a bank or accepted a date," her sister said dryly. "Since I doubt it's the former, you must be going out with someone." She paused a fraction. "It's not Robert, is it?"

Mary Nell couldn't remember for a second or two who Robert was. Then she shook her head impatiently. "No, it's not Robert. I told you, that's over."

"You've said that before," Stacy commented. "But if it's not Mr. Chili Pepper, it has to be someone else."

"It's no one! I mean, well, it is, but it's not a date. Not really. I mean—"

"For heaven's sake!" Stacy interrupted with a laugh. "You sound like you're about to come unglued!"

Mary Nell was too agitated to take exception. "Well, I am. I mean, I feel like it. Oh, I don't know why I said I'd have dinner with him in the first place!"

"Who?"

"Cal Stewart," she said, and heard her voice rising. With an effort, she controlled it. What was she so upset about? "He called last night just as I was leaving work and asked me to dinner. I...I was so surprised that I accepted." Despite herself, her voice rose again. "What am I going to do?"

Stacy didn't hesitate. "Choose a *very* expensive place and enjoy yourself, of course."

"This isn't funny, Stacy!"

"Yes, it is. Honestly, Mary Nell, you should hear yourself. You're acting as though this is your first date."

"It's not a date at all!"

"Then what do you call it?"

"A business meeting! What else could it be?"

"I don't know," Stacy said dryly. "The way you sound, maybe you'd better tell me."

"I don't know! I can't imagine why he asked me!"

"The fact that you're an attractive woman might have something to do with it," Stacy said, dryly again. "Why are you so panicked about this? Is he repulsive or something?"

"No, of course not. He's—" A picture of Cal flashed into her mind just then. She saw the look in his eyes, the quirk to his mouth when he was amused and the dimple that flashed so charmingly in his lean cheek. Red-faced at the thoughts that rose in her mind along with the images, she shut her eyes tightly. "No, he's not repulsive."

"Then what's the problem?" Stacy asked, and then paused. "Oh, I get it. This could be awkward, right? After all, he's competing for the same contract as you. Is that what's bothering you?"

Of course it was. This...going out...was awkward, and at the moment, she resented Cal for putting her into such an uncomfortable position. What was the matter with him? Why couldn't he just make an appointment at the office, like anyone else?

Because he isn't anyone else, that insidious little voice whispered at the back of her mind. Hearing it, Mary Nell tightened her lips and tossed her head. That was ridiculous. Of course he was. He was just like anyone else—only she didn't know why he'd asked her out. It wasn't necessary for them to meet outside business hours, so that indicated—

She didn't want to think what it meant. Because the truth was that despite all the rationalizing, she hadn't been thinking of Cal Stewart as a business rival; she'd been thinking of him as a man. As mortifying, as humiliating as it was, it was true.

But no more. She'd concentrate on him solely as a competitor, one she had to watch her step with, and that was all. That was *all.* And they weren't going out on a *date*; this was strictly a business meeting, nothing more than that. She might even learn something. She always did whenever she got together with colleagues.

"You've been a big help, Stacy," she said hurriedly after a glance at the clock. "But I really have to go now. He'll be here any minute, and I'm not ready."

"Anytime," Stacy said, sounding amused again. "Have fun."

"This isn't supposed to be *fun*," she reminded her sister. "It's a business meeting."

"Fine, just remember one thing."

"What?"

"You can discuss 'business' much better in a quiet French restaurant than in a noisy diner somewhere," Stacy said with a giggle, and hung up quickly before her older sister could reply.

"Very funny," she muttered, glancing around the cluttered bedroom after she'd replaced the receiver. Now that she was sure where she stood, she didn't have to worry about what to wear. She'd just choose the first thing that came to hand, which was...

A very boring, ultraconservative gray suit. It lay on top of the nearest stack of clothes, and she looked at it with revulsion. She hated gray; she couldn't imagine why she'd bought it. Grimacing, she pushed it away. There were limits.

In the end, she chose a pair of loden-green pants with a cream-colored satin blouse and then tossed a paisley scarf in bright tones casually over one shoulder for color. Satisfied that she looked calm, confident, in charge of things, she went into the bathroom to do her hair. She was still fighting with it when the doorbell rang, and she immediately felt panicked all over again.

"Calm down," she muttered, and counted to five, forcing herself to breathe deeply. Her hair was standing out all around her head, looking like an unmanageable fiery cloud, but it was too late to try to force it into a more appropriate style. Tossing the useless hairbrush down, she took another breath, turned out the light and went downstairs. She could see his shadow through the stained glass in the front door as she approached, and despite herself, her heart leaped. Steeling herself, she opened the door.

He was wearing slacks, loafers, a sport shirt and a corduroy sport coat. He was just as tall as she remembered, even more good-looking, and he seemed—her heart sank—utterly sure of himself.

"Hi," he said easily, and smiled.

Murmuring some kind of greeting, she stepped aside so he could come in. The foyer was small, and they had to jockey for position. She caught a whiff of his after-shave as he moved by her and closed her eyes briefly. He smelled so...*clean*, she thought, and tried not to think that this was going to be more difficult than she'd imagined.

Quickly, she gestured. "The living room is through there. We could have a drink if you like."

"I'm not sure we have time," he said, looking down at her. In the close, almost dim confines of the entryway, his eyes seemed nearly black, intense...striking. She had to force herself not to look away. "I made reservations at McNalley's for eight-thirty."

She forgot her discomfort in a rush of pleasure. "McNalley's! That's one of my favorite places!"

He looked at her in pleased surprise. "Is it? It's one of mine, too. I like the piano bar."

"Especially on Saturday nights when they play all those old movie themes!"

"Like 'Days of Wine and Roses'—"

"And 'Love is a Many Splendored Thing,'" she blurted, and immediately flushed crimson. Why had she mentioned that one? Hastily, she said, "Well, I guess we should go. I'll just get a sweater."

She took one from the hall closet, still embarrassed. Why did she feel so off balance with him? She usually had better control than this, even if she was attracted to someone—

Immediately, she checked *that* thought. She didn't even know him, she told herself. She didn't intend to. She didn't care how charismatic he was...and he was, she thought, closing her eyes briefly again. She shook her head quickly. Well, that didn't matter. She was immune to all charm. With everything else on her mind, she certainly didn't need to chance getting involved with a business rival—she could just imagine the complications. They were competing for the same contract; it would be awkward beyond belief. She didn't need any more problems. What she needed was that contract. If she remembered that, she'd be all right.

So, she thought resolutely, no more gaffes. No more blurting out schoolgirlish, silly things. She was a businesswoman; she owned her own firm. She was in control, in charge of her life. With a cool smile, she told Cal she was ready, and then she led the way out. She was on the porch before she remembered that she'd left her purse inside.

"Excuse me," she muttered, red-faced again, and went to get it. He was still waiting when she came out again, and she was surprised when he took her arm to assist her down the porch steps. She must have given him a quick look, for he shrugged a little.

"Sorry," he said. "An old habit my mother taught me."

"Don't apologize," she told him quickly. "I think it's a lovely gesture."

"You're not one of those fiercely independent modern women who view something like that as a threat?"

"No, I...I kind of like it," she said, flushing despite herself.

Smiling, he said, "Does that mean you're still fiercely independent and modern?"

"Aren't you?" she said, and then caught herself, adding quickly, "Fiercely independent and modern, I mean?"

"Touché," he said with a laugh, and then saw her looking at the car parked by the curb. Sounding a little embarrassed, he said, "Hope you don't mind riding in antiques."

She wasn't sure what he meant. The car didn't look old to her; it shone so that even in the streetlight, the hubcaps gleamed. It was obviously well cared for, and when she thought of her faithful little Honda in the garage, with its coating of dust, she winced.

"It looks fine to me."

"Well, it is ... for a '64 Impala," he said, opening the door. "I don't know why I don't get rid of it. Sentiment, I guess."

She'd never understood why so many men had a thing about automobiles. To her a car was just a means of transportation, and she said teasingly, "You make it sound like you'd prefer a Porsche."

"I used to have one," he said, and looked strange for a second. Hastily, he muttered, "Not that it matters."

Since she seemed to have inadvertently touched upon a sensitive subject, she was thankful when he opened the door for her and she could climb in. He came around and got in himself, looking sheepish. "Sorry," he said, and tried to laugh. "This old buggy gets me around, so I shouldn't complain."

Instinctively, she knew it was important to make light of it. "That's okay. I understand how sensitive men can be about their cars. I had a boyfriend once who was so proud of his classic '57 Chevy that he made me take my shoes off before I got in."

He laughed. "I was never that bad."

"Maybe you never had a '57 Chevy."

"No, this is as close as I want to get to that vintage, thanks," he said as they started down the street.

"Cars aren't your hobby, then?"

"No, I'm more into sports. Diving, skiing, that sort of thing."

Again, she seemed to have stumbled into dangerous territory. Well, she'd known he was a sportsman; why should that surprise her? "I see," she said faintly.

"What about you?"

Since she was competing with him for a recreational gear contract, she could hardly admit that she loathed exercise, that she was impossible at sports and that her sister teased her about the fact that her greatest exertion was padding out to the porch to get the morning paper. But she did have a big garden, and she did enjoy her relatively sedate hobbies, such as playing the piano and sewing. She could read by the hour and, of course, she never stopped being fascinated by the possibilities of computer-aided design. But these things seemed so tame compared to Cal's likes, and she muttered something about having her activities restricted because of allergies and a trick back.

"That's too bad," he said sympathetically. "Especially here in Washington. It seems like everybody is into some kind of outdoor activity."

"Yes, I know," she said, and crossed her fingers against the little white lie. "I used to enjoy things like that myself when I was a kid. But now..." She shrugged, hoping he'd let it drop.

He didn't. "I know a great sports medicine doctor," he offered. "Maybe he can help."

"Oh, that's all right," she said quickly. "It really doesn't matter right now. I'm so busy with the business and everything. I really don't have time to...enjoy myself."

"That's too bad," he said.

"Yes, well..." She let her voice trail away, feeling like such a fraud that she nearly confessed she'd made the whole story up. They arrived at the restaurant just then, and in the business of parking the car and then going inside and finding that they had to wait in the bar while their table was being cleared, the moment was lost. She told herself that it didn't matter, that he'd probably already forgotten the conversation by this time. But she was so unnerved at lying to him that she ordered a white wine she didn't want and was just leaning forward to confess all anyway when Mort, the piano player, looked up.

"As I live and breathe, is that Mary Eleanor Barrigan sitting over there?" he boomed. Mort was a trained singer as well as pianist, and his already powerful voice was amplified by the microphone attached to the piano. The sound easily carried over the noise of the crowd in the bar, and suddenly heads were swiveling their way. Cal looked at her in surprise.

"A friend of yours?" he asked.

She was so embarrassed, she wanted to crawl under the table. "Sort of," she muttered. "We knew each other in school." She didn't tell him that they'd been in chorus and glee club together, and she made a furtive gesture in Mort's direction, signaling him to pick on someone else. Naturally, he ignored her. Laughing, he fingered an introduction. She knew what he was going to do even before he did it, and she gestured with both hands, a definite *no*. He just laughed again. After all, he'd asked her to do this before.

"Ladies and gentlemen," he said in an even louder voice she was sure carried all over town, "you might not know it, but we have here tonight, in our midst, one of Tacoma's—no, one of *Washington's*, great pop piano players. You wanna hear what she can do?"

He was so enthusiastic that people started clapping and laughing and turning expectantly her way. Sitting beside her, Cal looked at her in amazement. "Is this guy serious?" he asked.

"Well, I—"

She didn't have time to finish, for Mort boomed again, "Hey, come on up here, Mary Nell, and play us a tune or two! What do you say, folks? You wanna hear how this little lady can play?"

When the clapping turned to applause and whistles and cries of "Yeah!" and "Give it a go!" she knew she had no choice. Cal was looking more stunned by the moment, and she knew Mort wouldn't let it go. "I'm sorry," she said faintly. "But I'd better…er…I'll just be a minute, okay?"

Looking dazed, Cal glanced around at the happy, laughing, clapping crowd, then at Mort, who was gesturing and doing another maddening rill. "Take your time," he said.

"Hey, Mary Nell!" Mort shouted just then. "These ivories are gettin' cold!"

This was getting worse and worse. Thankful that the dim light hid her red face, Mary Nell got up and made her way through the enthusiastic crowd. But once on the dais, she turned her back to the audience and glared at her old friend Mort. "I want you to know that you just embarrassed the hell out of me!" she hissed.

"What are friends for?" he said with a grin.

"Some friend!"

"Oh, you know you love it," he said serenely, and glanced over her shoulder toward her table. "Besides, this will give you a chance to impress that good-looking guy you came in with."

She was mortified. "I don't want to impress him! He's just a business associate!"

"Then you don't have anything to worry about, do you?" Mort said blithely, and slid off the piano bench with a gallant gesture.

She took her seat. "What should I play?"

"Anything you like, love. How 'bout something by Lerner and Loewe—or Sondheim. He's always good."

So she played something from *My Fair Lady* and then, encouraged by the applause and—although she didn't want to admit it—by the admiration in Cal's eyes, two selections from *Brigadoon*. She thought she was finished then, but the crowd wouldn't let her go, so she did two songs from *A Chorus Line*. Finally, despite protests, she finished with a rendition of "Send in the Clowns" that transfixed everyone. Before the applause erupted again, demanding another encore, she sprang up and dragged Mort back to the piano, where he belonged. Then she hurried through the enthusiastic crowd back to the table where Cal was sitting with that strange expression. Behind her, Mort did another rill.

"Ladies and gentlemen!" he cried. "Mary Nell Barrigan! You heard her here!"

Her face flushed with pleasure and embarrassment, Mary Nell grabbed Cal's hand and pulled him to his feet. She'd seen the hostess standing by, waiting to tell them their table was ready, and she wanted to get out of the lounge before Mort came up with another bright idea—duets, or something. Waving at him, she escaped, Cal in tow.

"Wow," he said when they were seated in a corner booth in the dining room. "You never said you could play the piano like that."

"You never asked," she said, but she flushed again, despite herself, adding, "Besides, it's just a hobby."

"You sounded pretty good for it just to be a hobby. Did you ever want to make it a career?"

"A career?" she repeated, before being alerted by something in his voice. She gave him a curious look, but he just seemed interested, and she shook her head. "No, never that. I was never dedicated enough—or good enough—to pursue it to that extent. Why?"

"Oh, no reason, really," he said, fiddling with the menu. "It's just that I used to know someone who...who was a violinist with the symphony."

There was definitely something odd in his tone. She wanted to ask, but didn't quite dare. Besides, she had other things on her mind. Now that the excitement in the lounge was over, she felt even more like a fraud. Their earlier conversation about sports hung over her like a cloud, and she couldn't just leave it at that.

"Cal, remember what we were talking about in the car on the way over? About my...my trick back?"

He'd started reading the menu; now he put it aside. "Yes."

"Well, I...I sort of exaggerated," she said, and took her medicine. "The truth is that I'm...I'm not really very good at athletics."

To her surprise, he simply shrugged. "If I could play the piano like that, I wouldn't waste time skiing, either," he said, and then smiled. "Feel better?"

She knew her face had gone red. "You knew it all the time!"

"No, but I sort of guessed."

"How?"

"The shifty look in your eyes," he said with a laugh, and then relented. Reaching for her hand, he turned it over, palm up. "Does this look like the hand of a woman who loves to play tennis or go bowling?" He squeezed her arm. "Are these the biceps of someone who lifts weights or casts fishing lines?"

She jerked her arm away, telling herself she had absolutely not been affected by his touch. "You don't have to be muscle-bound to enjoy sports!"

"That's true," he said easily. "But you just don't look the athletic type."

She knew it was ridiculous, but she was even more piqued at that. "I didn't realize there was a 'type'!"

"Of course there is."

"Well, if there is, I never heard of it!" she said, and grabbed her menu. Vexed that he'd pegged her so easily, she sat fuming behind the cardboard. Well, that was just great, she thought. She'd bared her soul, and he had suspected the whole time that she hadn't been telling the truth in the first place. She felt like a fool, and she knew it served her right.

"What are you going to have?" she muttered.

"How about a little humble pie?"

She lowered her menu and looked at him suspiciously. "Why do you say that?"

"Look, I'm sorry. I didn't mean to make you mad."

"You didn't make me *mad*," she said, although he had. She glanced away. "I just didn't like being told I wasn't the right type!"

"I said you didn't look like an athlete," he said quietly. "I didn't say anything about you not being the right type."

She was silent. They seemed suddenly to have navigated into dangerous waters, and because she didn't know what else to do, she picked up the menu again.

"Then I accept your apology," she said, pretending to have misunderstood him. But, safe behind the menu again, she shut her eyes, striving fiercely for control. She didn't want this to be happening; already she could feel herself perilously close to forgetting all those high-sounding resolutions and vows and promises she'd made to herself about not getting involved. His presence was like a magnet; she could feel herself being drawn to him against her will, and the feeling was getting more difficult to ignore. She had to control it—she had to. Too much was at stake for her to forget everything now.

Newly resolved, she set aside the menu and ordered something—she hadn't the faintest idea what—when the waitress came. But she welcomed the distraction, using the time Cal was talking to the woman to get herself in order again. By the time the waitress had gone, she was in control. She hoped.

"So," she said brightly, "tell me how you got involved in mechanical engineering."

He seemed a little surprised at her determined maneuver into mundane matters, but almost relieved. "The usual, I guess," he answered. "I've always been interested in how things work—you know, taking apart toasters and dishwashers and things."

Smiling, she said, "When you were younger, the scourge of your mother."

He laughed. "But I always put things back."

"The way they were supposed to be?"

"Pretty near. What was left over, I pocketed so no one would know. Davy was the same way—"

"Davy?"

"My partner. We've known each other for years, and after we both got engineering degrees, it seemed natural to open an office together. How about you? Why did you opt for the career? You'll pardon the observation, but we don't see too many women entering the mechanical engineering field."

She'd long ago accepted the truth of that, but it didn't make it any more palatable. "More's the pity."

"I agree. A female viewpoint would be refreshing."

She'd heard this before, too. "Especially in regard to domestic matters—redesigning kitchens and baths and closets, right?"

"Yes," he said without missing a beat. "Or making efficient use of space in space stations or designing practical engines for cars."

She looked at him. "You mean that, don't you?"

"Indeed I do. I've always thought we needed more women in the field."

Marveling, she sat back. "That's an unusual attitude, I must admit."

He grinned. "I'm an unusual person."

"You certainly are."

"So, come on.... What made you decide to make engineering a career?"

She owed him more than flippancy. "My father was an engineer," she said quietly. "When he saw I was interested, he encouraged me."

"He must be proud of you."

She smiled sadly. "He died before I got my degree."

"I'm sorry."

"So am I. He and my mother were killed in a plane crash. He loved to fly," she said, a faraway look in her eyes. She came back to the present with a mental shake. "What about you...? Parents, brothers or sisters?"

"My parents live on a houseboat in Florida."

"A houseboat!"

"Yeah, my dad always wanted a house on the water, and since my mother loves to fish..." He had a fond look in his eyes. "It was the perfect solution after they retired. As for siblings... my brother, Dan, owns a real estate business in Denver, and my sister is an editor at a publishing house in New York. We're sort of flung all over. How about you?"

"One sister—Stacy. She's studying nursing in Seattle." She smiled, too. "We're not so far-flung."

He hesitated, but finally asked, "Married?"

"Never," she said with a shrug, and hesitated herself. She hated to ask. "You?"

His face closed down briefly. "Once. A long time ago. We divorced."

"I'm sorry."

He shook it off. "I was, too. But it was inevitable, I guess. We were both pretty young, pretty full of ourselves. Or at least, I was. It was mainly my fault."

She wasn't sure what to say to that, so she said nothing at all. Fortunately, the waitress came with their meal right then, and the conversation passed on to other things—safe things, topics related mainly to their work. With relief, they discovered a mutual interest in industrial design and entered into a lively discussion. As though they both sensed they needed to pull back a little, they kept things light. And if she concentrated, she could almost forget how attractive he was. Almost.

Even so, time sped by, and she was surprised when the waitress returned to ask about dessert. Glancing around while Cal ordered some sinfully delectable chocolate delight for her despite her protest, she was astonished to see that they were the last people in the dining room.

Dessert came and went, Cal laughingly finishing most of it, and when finally the woman had returned to the table for about the tenth time, sans coffee carafe, to pointedly ask if they needed anything else, Mary Nell realized reluctantly that it was time to leave. Wondering where the evening had gone and why she'd been so nervous about it, she started to feel anxious again on the way home. Should she invite him in? She wanted to, she thought with a groan. Oh, she wanted to. At her front door, she held out her hand.

"I enjoyed tonight," she said, praying he wouldn't ask to come in. She didn't know what she'd say if he did. To her relief, he just smiled.

"So did I," he said, taking her hand briefly and dropping it again, as though afraid to hold on too long. "The best part was listening to you play."

She had forgotten about that part of the night. "It wasn't planned—"

"I still enjoyed it."

"Then maybe I'll do it for you again sometime," she said thoughtlessly, and realized too late how that sounded. "I mean, if we're ever at McNalley's again . . . at the same time, I mean."

He looked amused. Horrified, she realized that she was babbling because she was so nervous. His nearness was almost overpowering; she knew that if she waited a second more, she would invite him in, and then—

She couldn't allow herself to think about it. "Well," she said quickly, "good night."

"Good night, Mary Nell," he said quietly, and turned away.

She still had the key in her hand. He was halfway down the walk—all she had to do was say his name. She nearly did. Now that he was about to leave, she didn't want him to go. She wanted to ask him in for coffee, a nightcap, anything. She bit her lip. Then, before she could change her mind, she went inside and shut the door.

FEELING LIKE AN IDIOT, Cal turned to look back at the house. He'd heard the front door open and close, but he waited a moment, hoping she would change her mind and ask him in. She almost had; he'd felt it. But when the entry light went out, he turned and started toward the car again. Well, all right; it was for the best. He'd had to remind himself all evening of his promise not to get involved with any woman, especially Mary Nell, but even so, he'd been on guard the entire time against those eyes, that smile. He had no business going inside. God only knew what would happen.

Jerking open the car door, he got inside. Now was one of the times he wished he hadn't given up smoking. He would have given anything for a cigarette, just to steady himself. But his hand clenched on the steering wheel, and he wondered why it was that despite everything, he still wanted to take her in his arms. The urge to do that had been almost overpowering; he'd had to hold himself back. That's all he'd wanted—just to put his arms around her, to feel her against him, to...

Willing away the tantalizing images, he abruptly started the car. This was ridiculous. He had no business fantasizing about Mary Eleanor Barrigan; she was a competitor, a business rival, a...a *musician*, for God's sake.

Muttering a curse, he started off. He'd had his fill of female performers. If he doubted that, all he had to do was remember Miss Anna Maria O'Malley, right? When the chips were down, she'd chosen music over him, and that was that.

But Mary Nell isn't a musician, a little voice whispered. *She's a design engineer who happens to play the piano.*

Oh, was that right? He shook his head. He didn't care. A musician was a musician, piano player or violinist; they were all the same. *Women* were all the same. He'd never had any luck with them, and with this big account at stake—as well as his entire future—he didn't have time for this. He didn't have time for Mary Nell. The only thing he wanted to do was get these field tests over with and—

Groaning aloud, he jerked the car to a stop at the corner. He couldn't believe it. He'd completely forgotten to set a date for those stupid field trials. He'd spent the entire night with her, and he'd forgotten! Now he'd have to go back and—

No. He shook his head vehemently. He could not go back there, ring the doorbell and sheepishly admit that they still needed to settle one minor detail. He couldn't do it. He already felt like a fool; that would just cap the entire evening. No, he'd call tomorrow. Make it a business deal—as he should have done tonight. This dinner date had been a mistake; he knew that now. And once these field tests were over, he'd—

What? Never see her again? Never have the opportunity to watch that expressive face, to be fascinated by the intensity in those beautiful green eyes? Never touch that soft hair or listen to her laugh? He groaned again. He didn't know what he wanted. But right now, he thought, he could for damn sure use that cigarette.

CHAPTER FIVE

MARY NELL DIDN'T remember until she got to work Monday morning that she and Cal had never discussed the date for the first of the field test trials. "Oh, great," she muttered, rolling her eyes in exasperation. That was supposedly the reason they'd gone out in the first place. Frowning, she went to her desk and sat down. Now what?

She looked at the phone, debating about calling, then shook her head. She wasn't ready to talk to him. After spending the weekend in a fog since their date Saturday night, she wasn't at all sure how she felt about him.

But she couldn't ignore those field tests, and she was just reluctantly deciding she'd have to phone when Lucille, who had been in the storeroom making coffee, poked her head in and asked if she wanted any.

She was glad of any excuse to postpone her little chore. "Yes, thanks. That would be great."

"Be right back."

When Lucille returned moments later with two mugs, Mary Nell gestured her to a chair. "How was your weekend?"

Lucille made a face. "Like all the others, unfortunately. An endless succession of chores. Laundry, cleaning the house, going to the cleaners, the grocery store, the drug store. How about you? Anything exciting?"

Did she want to tell Lucille about meeting Cal? She hadn't yet decided when the phone rang. Lucille automatically reached out and answered.

"Barrigan Design," she said, and stopped to listen. Then, "I'll see if she's come in yet, Mr. Stewart. Would you hold please?"

As soon as she heard the name, Mary Nell tensed. She wanted to signal her secretary to say she wasn't here, but then she realized how silly that was. Cal wasn't some ogre she was afraid of; he was just a...a man. Gesturing, she indicated that she'd take the call.

"I'll be at my desk," Lucille whispered, handing the phone to her boss. Then she quietly exited.

Trying not to notice that her hand was suddenly shaking, Mary Nell forced herself to say pleasantly, "Good morning, Cal."

"'Morning," he said abruptly. "I hope I'm not interrupting anything."

She had to take a deep breath before she answered. Just hearing his voice made her heart skip a beat, and she told herself to calm down. But she couldn't help wondering dismally what it was about this man that could cause such a stir in her despite all her resolve, and she hoped she sounded more serene than she felt when she said, "No, of course not. I just got in. What can I do for you?"

He sounded even more strange than she did. His voice tight and clipped, he said, "I'm sorry to call you so early, but I...I realized something over the weekend that we never...that we didn't set a time for those field trials."

"Oh, yes," she said with a grimace. "Those."

"Yes, those," he repeated, and stopped.

There was an awkward little pause. As she gripped the phone, she thought for a minute that he probably felt as uncomfortable about this call as she did. Then she told herself to stop being absurd. She'd never met anyone with as much self-assurance as Cal Stewart. She was misreading him only because she felt so inept herself right now.

"Well," she said clumsily into the silence, "I guess we should set a time, then."

As soon as the words were out of her mouth, she despised herself. *Oh, great,* she thought. Now, instead of merely feeling like a fool, she sounded like one, as well.

He seemed too preoccupied to notice. To her relief, instead of making some sarcastic comment, he said simply, "Yes, that would be wise. We're pushing the deadline, so would you like to go first, or shall I?"

She just wanted to get this over with. Cursing Anson McAdam for rushing them in this fashion, she said, "I don't care. I will, if you like."

"That's fine with me."

"Good," she said, and took the plunge. "How about this coming weekend?"

"Will that give you enough time?"

She was so on edge, she nearly retorted that she'd be ready before him. But then her glance went to the computer printout of the tent-pole design she'd been working on so diligently Friday night when he called, and suddenly she wasn't quite so sure of herself. Things had been going so well until then; after she'd rashly agreed to go out with him, her concentration had been irretrievably lost. She hadn't thought about the stupid tent poles all weekend. Now she could see she had some catching up to do.

Even so, it was too late to retract. With more confidence than she felt, she assured him she'd have plenty of time—and then added a wary caveat. "That is, if McAdam's fabrication department can get to work right away on these specs."

"I'm sure that won't be a problem. Everybody there knows how anxious Anson is for these designs. My guess is that we'll have top priority."

Anson, now, was it? She could feel her suspicions rise. When had it become Anson, instead of Mr. McAdam? Was something going on here that she didn't know about? Her voice noticeably cooler, she said, "Fine. Then I'll get these drawings over to them right away."

Sounding a little cautious at her tone, he said, "All right, then. In the meantime, we'd better decide where we want to do this thing. How about Pine Meadows Campground? That's a nice—"

She couldn't help herself; the words were out before she thought. "A *campground*?" she exclaimed in horror.

He was clearly taken aback. "Well . . . yes. I thought . . . I mean, I didn't think . . . That is—" He stopped and tried again. "Where did *you* think we were going to conduct this test?"

She didn't know what she'd thought. Maybe that they would test these things at McAdam Recreation. Or in a parking lot somewhere. Or in her backyard. She certainly hadn't expected to trek into the *woods*!

"Mary Nell?" he said.

She tried to compose herself. Still shuddering at the idea of going out to some wilderness, she squeezed her eyes shut and took the plunge. After all, it did make some horrible sort of sense. Where else would they test tent poles except . . . on site?

"Pine Meadows is fine," she said, gritting her teeth. She hadn't the faintest idea where Pine Meadows *was*, but all those places were the same: they teemed with insects and snakes and all sorts of things. She shuddered again and forced herself to say, "Where do we meet?"

"Oh, there's no sense taking two cars, is there? Why don't I pick you up on Saturday morning?"

Relying on the theory that if she got the whole thing over with as quickly as possible she wouldn't have time to think about how awful it could be, she said, "All right, but let's do this early. When can you be ready?"

"Well...six?"

"In the *morning*?" She was appalled.

He laughed in genuine amusement, his nervousness forgotten. "Don't tell me you're one of those people who have never realized there are two six o'clocks in every day," he said teasingly. Then, "All right—you pick a time."

Embarrassed as she was, she was still cautious enough to say, "I might be able to manage it by...nine."

"Nine it is," he said cheerfully. "I'll see you then."

"Fine," she said, and put her head into her hands as she hung up. What had she gotten herself into? she wondered bleakly. Oh, why had she agreed to do these field tests in the first place? She'd never get through it in one piece—never!

That reminded her that she still had to finish designing the poles for the field trials. Galvanized by the thought, she pushed back her chair. Lucille was at her desk in the outer office, but instead of using the buzzer—something she'd always felt foolish doing, since only about ten steps separated her office from the reception area—she went out there.

"Lucille, I've got to work on this project for Mc-Adam," she said, trying not to sound as desperate as she felt. "So please hold any calls, okay?"

"Sure, but don't forget about your appointment this afternoon with Montezuma Hardware."

She wanted to groan. She'd forgotten all about that meeting, scheduled for two o'clock this afternoon, and she couldn't afford to cancel it. The small chain of hardware stores had contacted her last week about designing swivel mechanisms for one of their most popular items: a hammock, of all things. She'd remarked at the time that things had certainly changed; she remembered hardware stores as being places where you bought nails and paint and things. Still, she wasn't about to question any account. Business had picked up these past few months, but she wasn't going to let anything go by.

"No, I won't forget," she said, and glanced again at her watch. She seemed to be obsessed with time lately, she mused, preoccupied with how much she had to do, but spinning her wheels instead of doing anything. Forcing herself to think things through, she decided that if she put everything out of her mind and concentrated only on the computer, she might be able to edit those tolerances in the tent poles before noon. That decided, she took care of a few other details.

"I'll keep the Montezuma appointment," she said, "but would you please call the fabrication department at McAdam Recreation and make sure they can have my tent-pole prototypes ready by the end of the week? Tell them we'll deliver specs this afternoon."

Lucille's pencil was already flying over her secretarial pad. "Right," she said without batting an eye. She made another notation and glanced up expectantly again. "Anything else?"

She grimaced. "Pray for rain on Saturday."

"Rain?" Lucille repeated, looking surprised.

"Never mind," she said with a weak smile. "Bad joke. I'll be in the computer room if you need me."

"I'll call you at noon."

"Fine," she said, but she was already thinking of what she had to do. Moments later she was sitting in front of the computer, flexing her fingers and muttering to herself. She started, and within seconds she was lost in the fascinating world of CAD, feeling, as she always did, as if she'd stepped into a wonderland. The only thing missing was the feature that rendered the images three-dimensional. But the 3-D system was so expensive—the next step up. And up. And right now, she was lucky she had this. Getting to work, she concentrated on the screen as she manipulated drawings and figures. The swiftly changing images flickered across her intent face, and the only thing she thought of was doing it right.

WHEN LUCILLE TIPTOED in a while later to tell Mary Nell that she'd called McAdam Recreation and that the fabricators had promised to do what they could, she saw Mary Nell's intense expression and backed out again silently. But her shoulders, always so posture perfect from years of having her mother remind her to stand tall, slumped as she went back to her desk. She felt so guilty, and she glanced unhappily toward the computer room. She could hear the rapid click of the keys on the computer keyboard, and it seemed that every click reinforced what a traitor she was.

You should have told her, a voice nagged at the back of her mind. *You had chances. You should have said something.*

She knew that, she thought, slumping even more. It was just that she hadn't found the right moment to...confess? She shut her eyes. That sounded so awful. Maybe *admit* was a better word.

She shook her head. Why was she playing around with words? The truth was, she should have told Mary Nell about her little trip uptown, and she hadn't. She should

have said that she'd been curious about Cal Stewart and
that she'd gone to have a look and had run into Brad Davidson, instead. That was the truth. But it didn't matter
now: she hadn't confessed or admitted to anything. All
she'd done was spend the entire weekend thinking about
Brad—fantasizing about him, about what she'd say if he
called. She'd known he wouldn't, but she'd been unable to
stop herself from dreaming, all the same. No one had
called her; no young man, certainly. She was, she thought
with a heavy sigh, a terrible dud.

She gave another guilty look back toward the computer
room. And now, by not saying anything, she'd made
everything a hundred times worse. What would she do if
either Brad or Cal ever came here? They'd recognize her,
surely; if for nothing else than as someone who had been
clumsy enough to fall into Brad's lap. Even now her cheeks
burned with that mortifying memory, and yet...and yet...

Her flush increased when she remembered how Brad's
strong hands had steadied her, how broad his chest had felt
when she'd fallen onto him, how powerful his arms had
been. To think that those hands, those arms,
had...touched her. Squirming, she squeezed her eyes shut.
The only time a male other than her father had put his
arms around her was in dancing class in eighth grade, and
then reluctantly—only because the teacher had made him.
She was thirty years old, and she'd never gone out on a
date—not a real one, she thought hastily: cousins didn't
count. But she knew that if he'd asked, she would have
gone out with Brad Davidson.

Sighing again, she opened her eyes and concentrated on
her notepad. She had some letters to get out, a proposal to
type, other papers to file. But she sat there, thinking of
Brad Davidson. She couldn't get him out of her mind, and
she didn't know why. She didn't even know him, and yet...

And yet, she did. Dreamily, she thought that even though they'd met so briefly, she would never forget him. One glimpse had been enough to assure her that he was one of the most attractive men she'd ever met. It was something about his eyes, the look on his face—kind and compassionate, and marked with past suffering. Even though she knew it was absurd, she longed to reach out and smooth away those lines of remembered pain, brush his thick brown hair back, hold his head to her breast....

Blinking, she shook herself. *For heaven's sake,* she thought, and reached quickly for her notepad. Hold his head to her breast, indeed! What was she *thinking* of?

Embarrassed even though she was alone, she got up quickly and went to the file cabinet. An hour later when she couldn't find her notepad, she searched high and low and finally located it, indexed neatly in the files, under *B*.

A FEW MILES away, at Stewart-Davidson, Cal opened one drawer of the filing cabinet, rapidly riffled through the contents, slammed the drawer shut, opened another, riffled through that one, and slammed that one shut as well, this time with a muttered curse.

All right, he told himself. *Calm down.* He knew he'd put that research on motorized rubber dinghies somewhere; he had to check the tolerances on the motors before he could design the propeller for McAdam. But where was it?

Attacking the filing cabinet again, he tried a third drawer, then another, and felt like erupting when he still came up empty-handed. *Okay, that's it,* he told himself. He'd been saying for months now that they needed a secretary; this proved it. He couldn't find a damned thing.

"Davy?" he called in exasperation. "Where the hell are those files I asked you about? They've got to be around here somewhere, and I can't find anything in these crammed drawers!''

When there was no answer, he went out into the hall. ''Davy!''

Still no answer. Alarmed now, he went quickly toward Brad's office. Brad was at his desk—not on the floor, as he'd imagined—concentrating on something, oblivious to the world. Relief made Cal angry, and he banged on the half-open door. ''What are you doing? Didn't you hear me calling you? I need those damned files!''

Brad looked up blankly. ''What?''

''The files, the *files!*'' he shouted, waving his arms. What was the matter with Brad? He looked as though he were in another world!

''What files?''

He wasn't getting anywhere. Aggravated, he threw up his hands. ''Forget it,'' he said. ''What's wrong with you?''

''Nothing, why?''

''Why? I've been tearing the office apart for an hour now, and you're sitting here like a zombie, that's all! Do you mind telling me what's going on?'' Then he saw the telephone book sitting open on the desk. ''What's that?''

''The phone book,'' Brad said dreamily. ''Do you realize how many Hendershots there are? And how many of them only use an initial for the first name?''

Cal gave up. Dryly, he said, ''No, I can't say that I've wondered about either one.''

''I'm oblivious to sarcasm,'' Brad said, and glanced down at the book again. ''Do you think she's married?''

''Who?''

''Lucille, that's who,'' Brad said, looking at his partner as though he'd turned into a cretin. ''Who do you think I'm talking about?''

"Ah, so that's what this is all about!"

Brad flushed but held his ground. "It's not 'about' anything in particular," he said defensively. "I . . . I just thought I'd call her to see how she was."

"How she was," Cal repeated solemnly. "Well, that's certainly considerate of you, old buddy, since she's the one who fell on you."

"Yes, well . . . it didn't hurt me."

"I see. And you think it might have hurt her."

"You never know."

"That's true, you never know. But maybe you shouldn't have waited all weekend to call. Suppose she had to go to the hospital or something. Suppose—"

"All right, all right, knock it off. You made your point."

"I didn't know I had one," Cal said with a sudden grin. He reached for the phone book, thinking how glad he was that they could joke around again. Only last year, they'd both avoided words such as "hospital" like the plague. It was such a relief to Cal not to have to watch everything he said.

"Hendershot," he murmured, glancing at the page. "Hmm. I see what you mean." He glanced up innocently. "Why don't you just start at the top?"

"And say what?"

" 'Hello, I'm trying to locate the woman who tripped over my wheelchair last Friday night. Does she live here? If so, I'd like to talk to her. We can exchange insurance numbers or something.' "

"Very funny," Brad said, grabbing the heavy book. "I think I'll handle it my way."

"What *is* your way?"

"I haven't decided yet."

"Are you really going to call her?"

Suddenly glum, Brad closed the book. "No. She's probably married."

"Did you see a ring?"

Brad gave him an indignant look. "That's not exactly the first thing I look for, you know."

"Yeah, well, you have been out of circulation for a while, remember?" he said. "Maybe it's time you jumped back in—" he paused "—so to speak."

To his relief, Brad grinned. "Maybe I will," he said, and then looked dejected again. "What if she won't go out with me? What if she thinks—"

Cal wasn't going to get into that. "She won't think anything if you don't call her," he said firmly, and pointed at the book. "Now, start at the top and work down. And in the meantime, if you could spare a second's thought to the work we have around here, could you give me a hint about where I might find that research?"

"I don't know what your problem is about the filing system," Brad said smugly. "It's in the top drawer."

"Where? That drawer is crammed full of stuff. I can't make heads or tails of it."

"It's under *M*."

"*M*?" he repeated, raising an eyebrow. "I'm talking about the research on dinghies, Davy. Why would I want to look under *M*?"

"For 'mess,' of course," Brad said, and reached for the phone. "Now will you get out of here so I can start making these calls?"

Shaking his head, Cal left. But when he glanced fondly back at his friend before he headed toward his own office and saw Brad already absorbed, he grinned to himself. It had been a long time since his partner had felt confident enough to call a woman, much less ask one out, and he hoped Brad would find his Lucille. It was time things stopped being so grim around Stewart-Davidson.

Cal hadn't had much of social life since the accident, either; he'd been so preoccupied with getting them both through the aftermath that he hadn't had time to think about himself. But now, it seemed their lives were finally getting under way. It had been a slow process, but things were moving, at least. He hadn't wanted to say too much when he'd found Davy with the phone book, because he hadn't wanted to scare his partner off. But he'd been delighted all the same. Lucille seemed like a nice lady, and he crossed his fingers. A woman was just what Brad needed.

And what about him? he asked himself. What did he need? A vision of Mary Nell at the piano the other night, enthralling an entire roomful of strangers with her playing, came to him, and he frowned. He'd felt proud to be with her that night; he hadn't felt that way in a long time.

Thoughtfully, he wandered over to his drafting table. Final drawings for a pop-up sprinkler system stared at him, but he didn't see the meticulous diagrams. For some reason, he saw Mary Nell's house, instead. He hadn't seen much of it when he'd been there the other night, but it was like something out of a greeting card: a big, squat, sturdy clapboard structure, with wonderful dormer windows on a sloping roof, a big front yard shaded by huge old trees, even a swing on the front porch. They didn't make houses like that anymore, and when he thought of his own apartment, he suddenly saw it with new eyes. After he and Anna Maria had split up and she'd taken most of the furniture, he'd moved to a new, smaller place, supposedly one of those "swinging singles" complexes. Well, it was new and small, but there was nothing swinging about it—not these days, when everybody was being more than a little careful. But it didn't matter. At the time he'd bought it, he hadn't been interested in dating, only in finding a place to live that wouldn't kill him with rent. But he still hadn't furnished it properly, and when he pictured it, he grimaced in distaste. Mary Nell lived in this wonderful old place, with a banister that glowed from years of use and polish, while he hadn't even bought a couch. There was something to be said for a mind-set like that; he wasn't sure what.

"Forget it," he muttered. He didn't want to think about Mary Nell at all, but now that he had started to, he couldn't seem to get her out of his mind. She was a woman of contrasts, he thought, with one small foot planted firmly in the world of high-tech computer-aided design, and the other in a lovingly cared for house that looked as if it had been built at the turn of the century. She was the most modern of women, with an old-fashioned name. His frown deepened. Was it any wonder he was confused?

"For*get* it!" he muttered again, and sat down at the table. He couldn't spend all day thinking about some woman—

Some woman?

All right, *that* particular woman. He had work to do. Selecting a pencil, he positioned a new sheet of paper and started on the design for the propeller. He didn't have time to rummage through Brad's filing system for the research on those rubber dinghies. After years of participating in water sports—everything from skiing to rafting—if he didn't know how to design a propeller for a simple rubber boat, he was in the wrong line of work. That decided, he drew a line. The pencil lead broke. Muttering to himself, he selected another pencil. That one was too dull. A third wasn't right, either. He threw it down. This wasn't going well.

Maybe what he needed was a cup of coffee, he thought, and went to get some. The pot had about an eighth of an inch of sludge in it, and he looked at it in disgust. He debated briefly about making a fresh pot, then decided that what he really needed was to get back to work. Returning to his office, he sat down again. Throwing what he'd done so far—which wasn't much—into the waste basket, he took out a new pencil, a fresh sheet of paper and...stared at it.

"Damn it all," he muttered. He never should have asked her out in the first place. They shouldn't have gone. How could he compete with her on this contract, feeling the way he did?

And how did he feel?

He didn't feel *anything*, he thought angrily, and it was time to stop playing schoolboy games and get to work. He *had* to win this contract; he didn't have any choice. This...preoccupation with the competition was unprofessional, wasteful and absolutely ridiculous. He was acting as though he'd never seen a woman before, much less been around one. She was no different than any of the others. All he had to do was remember a marriage that had ended in divorce and an engagement that had gone down in flames. Both his ex-wife and that prima donna, Anna Maria, had flitted off and left him flat, without a thought. He'd sworn off women. How could he have forgotten that?

He hadn't forgotten. It had only been a momentary lapse, brought on by a brief fascination with laughing green eyes. After all, it had been a long time since he'd gone out—obviously too long. Telling himself he had to find a way to change that, he jerked the drafting table toward him and told himself he wasn't going to leave until he was done.

Realizing that might take a while, considering the less-than-creative mood he was in, he settled in for a long haul. Hours later he was still there, practically back at square one. In disgust he threw down the last of his sharpened pencils, waded through the sea of discarded drawings he'd crumpled and thrown to the floor and went home. Surely tomorrow would be a better day.

CHAPTER SIX

SATURDAY MORNING DAWNED bright and clear, with only the barest hint of cloud on the horizon—and still no tent poles. As Lucille drove to McAdam Recreation to meet the fabrication department supervisor, her hands tightened on the wheel. After making her extraordinary stand this morning to her mother about needing the car for an errand, she was determined to get those poles. Mary Nell was depending on her. She'd told her mother as much, and, for once in her life, she'd remained unmoved when Eunice had expressed cold disapproval. Saturday morning was the time they cleaned the house. After that they went to the grocery store. They *always* did those things. What had gotten into her?

"I have responsibilities, Mother," she'd said calmly, although under her Peter Pan collar, her heart had been pounding. She *never* defied her mother. But Mary Nell had asked her to do this.

"And what about your responsibilities to me?" Eunice demanded. She was a tall woman, solidly built, with long iron-gray hair braided in a coronet around her determined head. In her younger days, she had been what they called a handsome woman, but now she just looked bitter. She loved her daughter; there was no doubt about that. But, having been born into a strict household where discipline was regarded as a character builder, she'd raised her child that way herself. Until now, Lucille had never questioned it.

"The housecleaning can wait, and so can the grocery shopping," she replied bravely. "And I'll pick up the cleaning on the way home. But I have to do this, Mother. I promised Mary Nell."

"'Mary Nell! Mary Nell!' Those are practically the only words to come out of your mouth these days!" Eunice exclaimed. "Ever since you started work at that dingy little shop of hers, you haven't been the same!"

"It's not a dingy little shop, Mother. It's really a very nice office. I'm sure you'd agree if you ever accepted my invitation to come down and look."

"I wouldn't set foot across that girl's threshold!" Eunice stated haughtily. "*She's* the one who inveigled you to quit that wonderful job at the library to go to work for her. This is all her fault!"

She'd said nothing to that; in a way, it was true. If Mary Nell hadn't put that ad in the paper, she never would have quit her former job. She would have trudged along loyally until they had retired her with a tea, a little gold locket and a lemon cream cake. She shuddered, relieved at having been delivered from such a fate, glad that she had seen that ad. Now she had a *future*, she thought with an inward little glow; she had excitement . . . adventure!

Right now, in fact, she was in the process of doing an important errand for Mary Nell; she was on her way to get those tent poles. After a week of phone calls, two visits to the plant and finally an implied threat to the supervisor about having to mention the lack of cooperation on a project that the president of the company had ordered himself, Mary Nell—oh, she was wonderful, Lucille thought admiringly—had finally extracted a grudging promise from the manager just last night to have those damned—*pardon the expression, ladies,* she thought with another giggle—tent poles ready Saturday morning, if he had to stay all night and fabricate them himself.

Remembering that scene, Lucille shook her head. She'd been on the point of feeling sorry for the man when he'd said that; if she'd been by herself, she would have apologized profusely for putting him to all that trouble, but Mary Nell had just nodded briskly.

"Fine," Mary Nell had said, while Lucille had stood behind her petite boss, proud as could be. "I'll have my assistant here pick them up at—seven-thirty."

The man had grumbled, but no one could refuse Mary Nell. Not with that look in her eye, that confident, determined air.

So, with Mary Nell's example in mind, how could she not brave her mother's wrath and say she was taking the car this morning? It had seemed the least she could do... especially when she still felt so guilty.

That thought made her remember the exciting thing that had happened the previous night when she'd gotten home from work. Her mother had waited until they were sitting down to dinner to mention the call she'd taken just before Lucille had walked in the door.

"Do you know a Brad Davidson?" Eunice had said as she was passing the peas.

Lucille had nearly dropped the bowl. Instantly, a guilty flush sprang to her cheeks, and she quickly bowed her head. She hadn't mentioned that meeting with Brad to anyone; it had been her secret.

"Brad Davidson?" she repeated to give herself time. Carefully, she scooped some peas onto her dish. She didn't realize she'd added another big spoonful until she saw Eunice glancing at her plate with displeasure. She looked down. Peas spilled everywhere; there wasn't room for anything else. Embarrassed, she quickly set the bowl on the table. "Why do you ask?"

"Because someone of that name called tonight, right before you got home. He asked if a Lucille Hendershot lived here."

She hadn't realized she was holding her breath until it came out in a gasp. "What did you say?"

"Why, naturally, I demanded to know why he was calling."

She groaned. "Oh, Mother!"

Eunice looked at her in surprise. "You don't really think I should have handled it any other way, do you? After all, you've never mentioned this . . . person. For all I knew, he could be a . . . He could be after something."

"Brad?" she exclaimed disbelievingly, without thinking. Her mother saw her expression and tightened her lips.

"Then you do know him," she said. "Why haven't you mentioned him before?"

After her outburst, her protest was too feeble. "I don't really *know* him. We . . . met last week. It was nothing."

"Nothing? Then why are you blushing like that?" Eunice said. Her voice rose demandingly. "I want you to tell me what it is about this Brad person that makes you look like that!"

But she couldn't answer; she was suddenly tingling with the delicious thought that Brad had actually called. She knew her cheeks were pink, but she couldn't help it. *He'd called!*

Hard on the heels of that thought galloped instant panic. What was she going to do? She'd never been good with men; even when it didn't matter, she always felt tongue-tied and unsure of herself. She never knew what to say, and when she finally did decide on something, she sounded like a fool. She'd been like that the other night, tripping all over herself—in more ways than one. What would she do if he called again?

Then she realized it didn't matter. After the reception he'd received from her mother, he'd probably never call again. She slumped. Maybe it was for the best. She'd never had a . . . a beau before; she wouldn't know how to act.

"I really don't like the idea of strange men calling the house at all hours, Lucille," Eunice said stiffly.

"I don't think we have to worry about that," she said. "I'm sure it won't happen again."

They hadn't spoken of it again, and this morning, Lucille had resolved to put all thoughts of Brad Davidson out of her mind. She had a job to do, and as she drove grimly out to the McAdam plant, she reviewed what she was going to say. To her relief, the man met her at the door, poles in hand. Mercifully, she didn't have to say anything but a fervent "Thank you," then she rushed off again. Mary Nell was waiting, and she couldn't be late!

MARY NELL WAS pacing by the time Lucille drove up in a carefully preserved Ford that looked as if it could have been driven by Henry himself. At that point, she couldn't have cared if her secretary had arrived by chariot. As she flung open the door and flew down the walk, all she thought was that she had only scant minutes before Cal arrived.

"I thought you'd never get here!" she cried, taking the box from the front seat. "Will you help me set these up?"

"Sure!" Lucille said excitedly. "What do you want me to do?"

"Follow me!" she cried, and led the way into the house again at a dead run.

Because she hadn't wanted to go out to Tar Flats—or wherever Cal had said they were going—before she had a chance to test her design, she had planned to set up the tent once in her living room before they left. She had to know if these things worked; she'd die if they got all the way out there and something went wrong. She was not going to let that happen.

"Oh, my," Lucille said when she saw the living room.

"We have to have space," she said hurriedly, gesturing to Lucille to help her with the tent.

While she'd been waiting for Lucille, she'd pushed the living room furniture back against the walls. Now, as they began to wrestle the heavy canvas to the center of the floor, she blessed her secretary's efficiency. Lucille had found one of McAdam's company catalogs for her, and after checking the specifications of all the tents listed, she had selected a two-person dome tent around which to construct her new pole design. Now, seeing how much room this one took, she was glad she hadn't chosen one of the larger, family-size models.

"Boy, this is heavy," Lucille panted at one point.

Mary Nell sat back on her heels, wiping perspiration from her face. Was this supposed to be fun? She felt as though she were trying to inflate a rubber raft in a closet; there seemed to be canvas everywhere.

"Once this is over, I never want to think about camping again," she muttered. She looked around. "Where are the poles?"

Lucille found them under a flap of canvas. "How do they work?" she asked, taking one from the box. It looked like a foot-long length of aluminum tubing, with additional segments nestled inside.

"Like this," Mary Nell said, taking another out of its nest. Holding her breath, she pressed the little recessed button on the bottom and flicked her wrist. Instantly, exactly as it had been designed to do, the segments inside the tube extended out in a graceful curve, segment by segment. As each one hit the end of its arc, it locked, until the final result was a flexible, but fixed, length of pole. Pleased—and relieved—at her success, she grinned at Lucille. "You try it."

"Are you sure?"

"Go ahead. We have to know if they all work."

"Okay...." Still looking hesitant, Lucille pressed the little button on her tube, flicked her wrist and exclaimed when the pole instantly extended out, bobbing gently at the end. Delighted, she glanced up. "This is wonderful! Oh, Mary Nell, I knew you could do it. How clever you are!"

Pleased at the compliment, Mary Nell smiled. But she couldn't take all the credit, and she said generously, "You were the one who gave me the idea."

"Me? Oh, no. What did I do?"

"You told me to do away with that stupid shock cord, and—"

Interrupted by the sound of a car pulling up in the driveway, she broke off and looked out the window. She looked back at Lucille in sudden panic. "He's here!"

Lucille looked as panicky as she did. "You didn't say Cal was meeting you here!"

"Didn't I?" Mary Nell said, clearly distracted. "Well, we thought it would be easier that way."

"Oh, but—"

She hardly heard Lucille's faint protest; she was looking down in dismay at the sea of canvas at her feet. They'd spent too much time playing with the tent poles; they hadn't set up the tent itself. Now it was too late. Dropping to her knees, she started to wrestle with the heavy canvas again.

"Help me get this back into the sack, will you?" she grunted. Her cotton blouse had come untucked from her jeans in the struggle, but she didn't have time to worry about that now. She just wanted to get the stupid thing folded up and back into the bag before Cal saw it. She didn't want him to think she hadn't had enough confidence in her tent poles to test them on-site first.

With one eye on the door, Lucille hastily joined her, and together they managed to push and shove the tent into an untidy, thick roll that was never in a million years going to fit into the tiny little bag they'd taken it from. Wondering what magician had managed to stuff what seemed like acres of canvas into the minuscule pouch, she gave Lucille a stricken look.

"I guess we'll just have to take it like this," she said. She felt hot and sweaty and disheveled, and she hadn't even left her living room. Wondering how anyone could possibly think camping was fun, she jumped when the doorbell rang.

Lucille startled her by leaping to her feet. "Uh . . . er . . . Mary Nell, I think it would be best if I just slipped out the back way, don't you?"

She frowned. "Well, no. You don't have to hide. You can at least stay to meet him."

But Lucille was already edging her way out. "Oh, I'll meet him some other time," she said hurriedly. "I really do have to go now. Do you mind if I have a drink of water before I leave?"

What was going on? "Of course not, but—"

"Good luck, Mary Nell," Lucille said, and practically ran out of the living room when the bell rang again. "I'll think about you all day!" she called over her shoulder, and disappeared into the kitchen.

"Lucille!" Mary Nell called, and then blinked when she heard the back door slam. What was wrong with Lucille? She knew her secretary was shy, but this was ridiculous.

Then the bell rang a third time, and she wished she could run out, too. Nervously, she got to her feet and went to answer the door.

"I thought you'd chickened out," Cal said when she admitted him.

She had to put a brave face on. "Not a chance," she said loftily. "I was just making sure everything was ready."

"So I see," he commented, glancing into the living room.

She followed his glance, trying not to wince at the sight of the bulky bulge of the tent in the middle of the floor. Deciding to ignore his mocking tone, she gestured. "If you could carry that out to the car..."

"Your wish is my command," he said, and went to fetch the tent.

Sure she'd seen him smirk, she glared at his back while she gathered up the tent poles and put them back into the box. She tried to ignore him, but she couldn't help admiring the ease with which he hefted the heavy canvas over his shoulder. She'd had such trouble moving it, yet he handled the tent as though it weighed mere ounces. Realizing she was staring, she jerked her eyes away from the strong arms and broad shoulders under the plaid shirt and led the way out to the car. Silently, she waited while he stowed everything in the trunk.

"You know," he said as they started off, "we should have brought a picnic lunch or something. Made a day of it."

All too aware of him, she'd been staring tensely out the window. She turned to look at him, surprised. "A lunch? I...I really didn't think we'd be gone that long."

"That confident, eh?"

She wasn't confident at all—not where he was concerned, anyway. She'd spent the entire week assuring and reassuring herself that she could handle this...could handle him, but now that they were together again and she was feeling that high-voltage unconscious charm of his, she felt all her resolve dissolving away. What was it about him? she wondered, depressed. If she was to be critical, she'd have to say he wasn't the most handsome man she'd ever met or the smoothest or the most suave. And yet...

She shook herself. There was no *and yet*. No matter what she was feeling, she couldn't forget the real reason they were here—the thing that had brought them together in the first place. This wasn't a picnic, it was a competition, and they were rivals for the same account. That was all that mattered. All.

"Aren't you?" she said.

He seemed more at ease than she did, damn him. Shrugging, he switched lanes and said, "About your tent poles—or my propeller?"

She had to pretend confidence, even if she didn't feel it at the moment. "Either. Both."

He had the nerve to grin at her. "I know the propeller will work."

Piqued, she lifted her chin. "Then we're even. I'm just as sure of the tent poles."

"Well, we'll soon see, won't we?" he said with another grin, and turned off the main road onto a dirt track. "We're just about there."

There? Where? The only thing she could see up ahead was wilderness...nature at its most raw. Was this a campground? Did people really like to do this? What was wrong with cement?

She was still trying to adjust when he stopped the car in a cutoff at the edge of a small meadow. All around them were tall, stately pines. Birds were singing when she got out, the meadow grass was green, wildflowers were blooming, and ahead was a beautiful little lake, glinting the obligatory sapphire under the bright morning sun. A picture-postcard setting, she thought: romantic, lovely, serene. All she could think about was doing this test and getting away from here.

Nervously, she glanced at Cal, who had gone around to the trunk to get the tent. She felt so stiff and anxious, not at all like herself. *He* did that to her. The whole time they'd been driving, she'd been too aware of him, of his arm casually leaning out the window, of his hand gripping the wheel, of that grin. Now she knew that, for more reasons than one, it had been a mistake to come. She should have insisted on doing this test in a parking lot somewhere, with plenty of people witnessing. She never should have agreed to drive all the way out here, with no one around. Anything could happen.

But nothing will, she told herself fiercely, trying to get a grip on herself. This was ridiculous. *She* was being ridiculous. They were only going to put a tent up! He'd exclaim admiringly about her magnificent design for the tent poles, they'd take the thing down again, and then they'd both go home. Resolved again, she went around to the back of the car.

"Do you want some help?"

He was just taking the tent out of the trunk. Hefting the awkwardly folded canvas over one shoulder, he grunted, "Oh, no. I can...manage."

"I'll get the poles."

"That would be nice," he said, and heaved the tent to his other shoulder. "Where do you want to set this up?"

Where? Why not here? She didn't want to leave the car. Who knew what lurked out there in the grass? Pointing to her feet, she said, "This is a nice spot."

He gave her a you've-got-to-be-kidding look. "We come all the way out here, and you want to set the tent up by the car? If I'd known that was how you felt, we could have done this in a parking lot somewhere."

Great. Swell. Maybe they both should have mentioned that earlier. Exasperated, she said, "Well, where do you want to do this?"

He glanced toward the lake, which seemed an impossible distance away to her. "How about over there? We could at least enjoy the scenery while we're testing the product." He shifted the bulky tent again. "Besides, I have to take notes, and I always think better by the water."

She looked at him disbelievingly. "You're going to take *notes*?"

He grinned. "Just kidding. But let's decide something, all right? This thing is a little heavy."

She didn't seem to have much choice. She could insist on staying here and be a poor sport, or she could... Before she could think about it, she started off toward the lake. But she tossed over her shoulder, "I wouldn't think that would be any problem for a big sportsman like you. Aren't you used to carrying field packs, or whatever they are?"

"I've done my share of that, too," he said, following. "And believe me, I'd choose this any day. Anything is better than marching with a steel pot on your head, heavy boots and a forty-pound field pack digging into my back."

She stopped short and glanced at him. "Are you talking about the service?"

"Weren't you?"

"No, I meant—" she started, and tried again. "What branch were you in?"

He looked suddenly distant. "It doesn't matter. It was a long time ago."

She was silent. *Vietnam,* she thought, and started walking again. She felt his withdrawal and cursed her slip of the tongue. But how was she to know?

They trudged along in silence for a few yards, but finally she had to apologize. "I'm sorry," she said. "I didn't mean to—"

"Forget it," he said. "As I said, it was a long time ago."

She looked up at him, and their eyes held. She saw memories there, shadows she couldn't comprehend in those blue depths. Feeling worse than she had before, she started to turn away. To her surprise, he reached out and took her gently by the arm.

"It's not you," he said quietly. "I just don't like to talk about it."

She nodded, looking up at him. She hadn't noticed until now the slight bump on the bridge of his nose. It made him look...rakish. Feeling her cheeks redden, she glanced away. But she could still feel him gazing at her.

Then he gave a small laugh. "I'm sorry," he said. "I seem to be saying that a lot to you, don't I?"

"No more than me," she said, and saw with dismay that the lake didn't seem any closer than it had before. To distract herself, she glanced down at her loafers. They weren't made for trekking, and because she just wanted to get this over with, she said hopefully, "We don't have to walk all the way to the lake. I know how heavy that tent is."

"I don't mind," he said. "Besides, we're almost there."

Almost there? She could still hardly see the water. As she followed in his wake, she began to understand why people lost in the desert began to see mirages. She was starting to see one herself. Thirsty from all this exercise, she was imagining storm clouds gathering on the heretofore flawless horizon. But that was her fevered imagination, which seemed to have gone into overdrive lately. No rain or storm had been predicted for today; she'd scrutinized the weather reports all week, hoping for a miraculous reprieve in the shape of a hurricane or something. The only thing that had been forecast had been blue skies.

"Cal," she said suddenly, "does that look like rain?"

He squinted and looked up. The clouds that had been lingering on the horizon all morning, a cottony backdrop to an otherwise serene blue sky, seemed to be on the move. Just as he spoke, the sun was momentarily obscured by a scudding drift. "I believe it does."

She tried to hide her dismay. "What are we going to do?"

He laughed. "What are you—made of sugar? Afraid you'll melt?"

"Of course not," she said indignantly. "It's just—"

"What? We've got a tent, remember?" he said, grinning that grin. "We'll be safe."

Safe? In a tent, during a rainstorm, out in the middle of nowhere? Hurriedly she looked around. Mercifully, they had finally reached the shores of the lake. She was so obsessed with getting the test over with before the storm broke that she hardly waited for Cal to drop his burden to the ground with a relieved sigh before she knelt down to unwrap the tent poles. With one eye on the growing clouds and the other on the instructions for erecting the tent, which she'd stuffed into her jeans pocket, she calculated that if they hurried, they could get the thing set up and taken down again and be on their way back to town long before the rain came.

If they hurried. When she glanced up again, she saw Cal strolling down toward the water, and she let out an exasperated sigh. What was he doing? They didn't have time for this!

"Where are you going?" she demanded shrilly.

Hands in his pockets, he turned to her. "Just checking the lake."

Feeling more riled by the second, she put her hands on her hips. "For what?"

"I don't know," he said with a casual shrug. "To see if the fish are biting, I guess. To find out if it's warm enough for swimming."

"*Swimming!* You don't have time for that!"

He gestured upward with his chin. The clouds were marching right along. The sun peeped in and out, losing the battle more often than not. The wind had risen a little. "We're going to get wet anyway. Might as well enjoy ourselves."

He couldn't be serious, she thought grimly. If he thought she was going swimming, he had another thought coming.

"That's not funny, Cal," she warned him. "Aren't you going to help?"

"Why?" he asked innocently. "This is your test."

In horror, she glanced down at the untidy pile of tent. Was he actually going to let her struggle with the heavy horrible thing while he dipped his toes in the lake? Maybe he planned to dive right in. For all she knew, he planned to go skinny-dipping. Galvanized by the thought, she cast a quick look over her shoulder and jumped. He was standing right behind her, laughing.

"You didn't really think I'd let you do this by yourself, did you?" he said, his eyes twinkling. "Besides, I have to help. I'm the field supervisor."

To her chagrin, he didn't need the instructions she'd hoarded so carefully. In seconds, the tent she'd thought an impenetrable puzzle at home was spread out on the ground, awaiting the introduction of her tent poles.

"How did you do that?" she asked.

"Years of practice," he said, grinning yet again. He put out a hand. "If you'll give me the tent poles, we'll get this done."

Now that the moment was at hand, she was reluctant. Hesitantly, she handed one over. "You have to press that little—"

But he had already figured it out. At a flick of his wrist, the pole unfolded beautifully—a shining, flexible rod. He tested it, and when it refused to give, he shot her an admiring glance.

"Not bad."

She gave what she hoped was a casual shrug. "Thanks."

He held out the pole. "Do you want to do the honors?"

She just wanted to get out of here. Glancing up at the rapidly darkening sky, she shook her head. "Go ahead. I'd like to do this before the flood, if you don't mind."

"No worry. We'll have this up in a minute."

With that, he inserted the pole he was holding into the first canvas sleeve. She had another one ready for him when he finished, then a third. She wanted to think it was her design that was making the process go so quickly, but she had to admit with an envious twinge that he really did seem to know what he was doing. By the time he was ready to insert all the poles into the clamp at the top of the tent, she was almost beginning to believe they were going to make it before the storm. Clamped together, the poles bowed out, and instantly the tent puffed into a dome, exactly the way it was supposed to. She was so proud she wanted to strut. She was still admiring her work when she felt the first drop of rain on her face. In her euphoria, she'd forgotten about the coming storm. Looking up, she saw with dismay that the sky was an ominous blackish gray.

"Cal . . ." she started to say, but the rest of her sentence was drowned out by a loud roll of thunder. *Oh, no,* she thought, *not that.* She hated thunder—always had, even as a child. Hunching her shoulders to her ears, she wondered if she could leave him here and make a dash toward the car.

"What?" Cal said from inside the tent, where he was testing the strength of the poles.

"I said..." Another roll. She looked quickly toward the car. It was a little dot at the far edge of the meadow.

Cal stuck his head out from inside the tent and grinned. Holding the tent flap up, he said with a bow, *"Mi casa es su casa."*

She was about to refuse when the skies seemed to open. There was no choice but to duck inside, so she ran for the doorway and stumbled in, to the accompaniment of another loud roll of thunder. Squeezing her eyes shut for an instant, she told herself not to panic. Cal was right: they had shelter, and they could wait out the storm. But why now?

Despairingly, she glanced around. She hadn't realized the ceiling was so low—or the space so puny. With both of them hunched over, the tent seemed seven sizes too small, and as she backed away to make more room, her foot brushed against something. Even before she heard the shushing sound of the pole segments retracting—just as she had designed—she whirled around, anticipating the worst.

"Oh, no!" she cried.

"What . . . ?" Cal exclaimed as a section of the tent collapsed.

She whirled back around. Just before the canvas fell on her, she saw him step back, exactly as she had done. "Don't . . . !" she shouted.

It was too late. Just as she must have, his foot hit a retract button, and with that same fateful shush, another
pole retracted. The remaining three poles weren't strong
enough to stand up under the entire weight of the tent, but
again, she had done her research too well. Instead of
breaking, the last poles simply bowed to the ground; in
seconds she and Cal were enveloped in a sea of bobbing,
weaving yellow canvas.

"Mary Nell?" Cal called. She could hear him fighting
his way out from under the canvas on the other side of the
tent, but she was too mortified to answer. How could this
have happened? First the rain, now this! She was so embarrassed she wanted to find a hole and crawl into it.

"Mary Nell!" he called again, this time more anxiously.

She knew she had to answer, but her voice wouldn't
work right. "I'm here," she said faintly. She wanted to die.
She wasn't even trying to get out; the weight of the collapsing wall of the tent had pushed her down, and she just
crouched there, listening to the rain drumming on the
canvas, hoping that she would somehow disappear or that
Cal would never find her in this five-foot space.

It was too much to hope for. The rustling sound came
closer, and she cringed when he lifted up the section that
had fallen over her. "Are you all right? Why didn't you
answer me?"

Wondering if anyone had ever died from sheer embarrassment, she forced herself to sit up. "I'm fine," she
mumbled, brushing herself off so she wouldn't have to
look at him. "Are you?"

"Yes, I'm okay." He glanced around from under the
temporary roof he'd made over them. "What happened?"

She made herself say it. "Two of the poles collapsed."

"I see," he said, laughter in his voice. "A slight miscalculation?"

"Nothing I can't fix," she muttered.

He was all innocence. "Soon?"

She glared at him. "I'm glad you think this is funny."

He tried to smother his smile. "Hey, the same thing could have happened to me."

She wasn't going to fall for that. "Yeah, well..."

"Hey, it could have." He paused. "Any suggestions?"

Yes, she had a suggestion: she wanted to disappear from the face of the earth and never be seen again. Failing that, she wanted to be transported instantly back to her house so she could pretend this had never happened.

"Yes," she said. "I want to go back to the car and get out of here."

"It's still raining," he observed.

She glared at him again. "So? Are you afraid you'll melt?"

He did laugh at that. "Touché. Did you know you've got a streak of dirt on your cheek?"

He reached out to wipe it off, but she didn't want him to touch her. Rearing back, she scrubbed at her face, thinking that she was probably covered with dirt. She felt as though someone had dumped her in a sack of coal, she who hated to have a spot of anything on her clothes. That, on top of everything else made her want to burst into tears. Oh, how could this have gone so wrong?

"Hey," Cal said, seeing her miserable expression. This time when he reached out to touch her cheek, she didn't flinch; she was too startled by the gentle note in his voice. Unwillingly, she looked at him. They were so close she could see tiny flecks of black in his blue eyes, and she thought fleetingly that that was what made them look such a dark blue. She was still bemused when he kissed her.

His lips were soft and warm, almost hesitant at first. It was as if he wasn't sure what her reaction would be. She wasn't sure herself. Things had turned out so horribly that she hadn't been expecting this at all; she was so unprepared that she just sat there.

Then the pressure of his mouth increased, and she closed her eyes, giving in despite herself to all the sensations flooding through her. She forgot they were both half-buried under the tent; she forgot the storm. Even the thunder seemed to have receded. There was only the beating of the rain, a sweet counterpoint to the beating of her heart. Without her realizing it, her arms came up and encircled his neck, and she didn't resist when she felt him move closer. Another second or two, and his weight would push her down to the ground, and that would be all right, too.

I could get lost in him, she thought dazedly.

And then she pulled back. Cal looked at her in surprise.

"I—" he said, and stopped. The rain drummed overhead, and she looked away.

"I think we'd better leave," she said.

He didn't answer for a moment. Then he said, "Maybe you're right."

Absurdly, she was disappointed—and angry with herself. What had she expected, an argument? She'd already ruined the moment by pulling back like that, and if she didn't know why she'd done it, how could she expect him to understand?

"Cal..." she said, but he had already found the tent flap and had climbed out. He was holding it up for her, and she had no choice but to follow. In silence, they quickly took down the rest of the tent, rolled it into an untidy sausage and carried it back to the car in what had become a driving rain. Both soaked, neither spoke, and it was a quiet, tense, disturbing drive back to town. When they got to her house, Cal unloaded the tent into her garage and then drove away. She stood at the window for a long time after he'd gone, watching the rain stream down the glass, not seeing anything but the look on his face.

CHAPTER SEVEN

MARY NELL LEFT for work Monday morning after spending part of the weekend working out the glitch in her tent pole design, and the rest of it thinking about Cal. After what had happened, she hadn't wanted to think about either again, but while she couldn't get one subject out of her mind, she realized she could do something about the other.

Solving the design flaw hadn't been difficult. After playing around with the poles for a while, she had decided that reversing the play of the reset button would eliminate accidental retraction of the poles. All of which supported, she thought irritably, the necessity for field tests. But why had she been the one to make a fool of herself?

The only comforting thought was that the new specs would pass. After all, the poles *had* worked—they'd just worked a little too well. She shuddered. She'd heard that ominous shushing sound in her head all weekend.

So, one problem was solved. The competition between her and Cal was a different matter. She'd gone around and around about it all weekend until she thought she would scream, and she still hadn't come up with a solution. One thing was certain: she didn't want to see him again. The more she thought about it, the less she liked her passionate response to that kiss. Even now, the memory of it made her burn, and she couldn't quite convince herself that if she hadn't been so upset about the tent falling in on them like that, it never would have happened. The truth was, she couldn't be sure.

Then she shook her head. No, the truth was that despite all her denials, she had been attracted to Cal right from that first day at McAdam's office. And if she was to be brutally honest, she would have to admit she'd wondered what it would feel like if he kissed her.

Well, now she knew. Furthermore, she knew that to continue like this would not only be foolhardy, but emotionally dangerous. She had vowed not to get involved again—at least until the business was financially on its feet; she'd made that her priority. She knew from bitter past experience how easily things fell apart when she scattered her energies, and she had made a big commitment here. She couldn't afford to fail.

Feeling beset on all sides because she couldn't find a solution to this dilemma, she blamed Anson McAdam. *He* was responsible for this mess! If he'd been like any other businessman instead of the madman he'd turned out to be, she wouldn't have this problem. She and Cal could be in contention for the account and never even have to lay eyes on each other. They probably wouldn't even be aware that they were both competing for the same contract. But now?

She wondered if she shouldn't just give it up and withdraw from this stupid contest. But the more she thought about that, the more irritated she became. It was so unfair! In any other circumstances, she wouldn't even *have* a problem. If Cal had been someone else, for instance—*anyone* else—they'd do this thing and that would be that. But not now; oh, no. Now, despite everything, she'd developed this maddening attraction to the opposition. What was she to do? *Was* withdrawal the answer?

She still hadn't decided when she got to work. Feeling even more depressed than when she had left the house, she

parked in her space behind the office and went inside.
Maybe she could call McAdam and sort of feel him out.
Maybe he'd change his mind about this stupid field-testing.

As always, no matter how early she seemed to get there
herself, Lucille was already at her own desk. Mary Nell
could smell fresh coffee brewing as she came in. Thinking
how glad she was that she was still friends with Lucille, at
least, she went into the reception area to say good morning. They'd already talked about the disaster with the tent
poles on Saturday night, but Mary Nell had still been so
upset about what had happened that she hadn't remembered how Lucille had run out that morning until now.

"Why did you leave like that on Saturday?" she asked.

Lucille had trouble meeting her boss's eyes. Her voice
small, she said, "I thought I'd be in the way."

"That's silly! After all the help you gave me, you should
have at least stayed around to be introduced!"

"Oh, Mary Nell, I've never been good with people, you
know that," Lucille said anxiously. "Maybe some other
time, all right?"

Thinking that she might as well tell Lucille right now,
Mary Nell said, "I don't know about that. I'm thinking
about withdrawing from the competition."

Lucille was dismayed and shocked at the same time.
"But why? You said you could fix the poles—"

"I know, but . . ." She really didn't want to go into it.
Waving her hand, she finished vaguely, "There are—other
problems."

"Oh, but—" Lucille seemed ready to cry. Wringing her
hands, she blurted, "Mary Nell, I've got to talk to you
about something."

Surprised at this sudden intensity, Mary Nell said,
"Well, sure. What is it?"

"Someone—a man I met—called the other night and . . . and asked me out for a date!"

So that was what the problem was, Mary Nell thought. Forgetting her own difficulties for the moment, she smiled. "That's great. Who's the lucky guy?"

Lucille looked ready to faint. "Oh, I . . . I don't think you'd know him," she said quickly, and then seemed to grow even more desperate. "But that's not the problem."

"Oh," her boss said, nodding in sudden understanding. "That's right. You said you've never been out on a date."

"That's true, I haven't. But—"

"Well, don't worry about it. You'll have a good time."

"Oh, I don't know—"

"Trust me," Mary Nell said confidently. "If this guy liked you well enough to call and ask you out, you'll get along just fine."

"But that's not—"

Deciding it was time for a little heart-to-heart, Mary Nell put her briefcase on the desk and sat beside it. "If you said yes, you must like this man," she said encouragingly.

Distracted from what she'd been trying to say, Lucille twisted her hands again. "You make it sound so easy. But you've always been so popular! You don't know what it's like to stay home, Mary Nell!"

"You'd be surprised," she said dryly. "I can remember quite a few times I stayed home and cried because some boy I liked hadn't asked me out."

Lucille looked shocked again. "I don't believe it."

"It's true," she said with a shrug. She didn't say she'd exaggerated a little. "So, tell me—where are you going?"

"He wants to go out to dinner!"

"What's wrong with that?"

"At Marlin's?"

Mary Nell raised an eyebrow. Marlin's was the newest hot spot in town: luxurious, expensive, with a waterfall in the main dining room and roses given to all the ladies upon departure. "Wow. This guy must really like you. I think that's great. Why don't you?"

"Because I don't have anything to wear!" Lucille blurted. She gestured at the skirt and cotton blouse she was wearing. Her sweater was hanging primly on the chair behind her, the dangling sweater guard glinting in the light. "I can't wear something like this. I know how fancy that place is, but I . . . but I . . ."

She was so shaken that Mary Nell reached out and shook her arm a little. "Don't get yourself all upset!"

Lucille looked up plaintively. "Wouldn't you be upset if you were me?"

"When is this date?"

"Saturday."

"Then one day this week, we'll go shopping. You tell me how much you want to spend, and we'll spend it in style. How's that?"

Lucille sat back, her mouth agape. "You mean it?"

"Of course."

"You'd really do that for me?"

A little embarrassed by such obvious adoration, Mary Nell said, "After everything you've done for me? Absolutely. It'll be fun."

"But—"

"No 'buts,'" she said decisively, and then decided to take the plunge. She'd been wanting to suggest this for months now, and this seemed the perfect time. "And since this is such a momentous occasion, I'll even spring for a session with my hairdresser. What do you say?"

Lucille's eyes widened even more. Longing was evident in her face, but she reluctantly shook her head. "No, I can't let you do that."

"Yes, you can. I want to. Consider it a bonus."

"A bonus?" Lucille said. "But I thought you might withdraw from this big new account."

"Well, I might. But what if I do? Other things will come along, so we'll just consider it an advance."

And with that, she went to her office. As soon as she closed the door, her confident air disappeared, and she slumped again. Despite her bravado just now, she really didn't know what she would do without that account. Her expression glum, she wondered if she'd have to start pounding on doors again. The prospect filled her with gloom. She'd hoped she was done with that.

Well, it couldn't be helped. And the sooner she made this call to McAdam the better. Thankfully, this was Stacy's last year at school; if she managed things carefully, they could squeeze through until the end of the school year. After that, they wouldn't have the school fees to worry about, and Stacy would start to work. They could manage—if everything went according to plan.

Trying not to think that in her experience, at least, that didn't happen very often, she sat down behind the desk and looked at the phone. But it was ten minutes before she could drum up the courage to reach for the receiver; she couldn't rid herself of the depressing feeling that she was slamming a door to the future. Telling herself it was now or never, she was just putting her hand on the phone when Lucille came to the door and said, "Stacy's on line one, Mary Nell."

She'd been so preoccupied that she hadn't even heard the phone ring. Glad to postpone the distasteful chore even a few minutes longer, she punched the blinking line and said, "Stacy?"

"Where have you been?" Stacy cried without benefit of a hello. "I've been trying to get in touch with you all weekend!"

"I tried to call you at the dorm," she said defensively. "And I did leave a message."

"Well, I didn't get it," Stacy said. "And I called and called and *called!* Why didn't you answer at home?"

Remembering how the phone had rung repetitively all day Sunday, she flushed. She hadn't answered because she'd thought Cal was trying to call. After the tent fiasco, she just couldn't talk to him, and she said weakly, "I'm sorry. I just wasn't in the mood to talk to anyone."

"Oh, swell. If I hadn't gotten through to you today, I was prepared to drive down. I was worried about you, Mary Nell. How did the test go?"

"Not well."

There was a silence. "Oh. I'm sorry to hear that. Do you want to tell me what happened?"

She didn't, but she knew she had to. Briefly, she recapped the entire embarrassing experience for her sister, grateful that Stacy didn't laugh, not even when she got to the part about the tent falling down on them.

"Lord, how awful!" Stacy exclaimed sympathetically. "You must have been absolutely mortified."

She sighed. "That doesn't begin to describe it."

"So what happens now?"

"Well, I redesigned the tent poles this weekend—"

"That doesn't surprise me. I'll bet they work perfectly now."

"They worked before!"

"You know what I mean."

She was sorry she'd snapped at her sister. "Enough of that. What's up with you?"

Instantly diverted, Stacy laughed. "How did you know I had great news?"

"You do?"

"I do. I hope you're ready for this. I want you to know that your humble little sister has been selected to participate in a special graduate program next year. Can you believe it? Me! It's really a great honor, and I'm so excited I could die! What do you think? Aren't you thrilled, too?"

Thrusting away instant thoughts of additional school fees and the accompanying question of how she was going to pay for the extra year, Mary Nell willed enthusiasm into her voice. She was happy for Stacy, she was. It was just...

"I think that's great. I'm so proud of you."

Stacy knew her too well. "You're worried about the money, aren't you?"

"Of course not!"

"Yes, you are. I can tell. Come on, be honest. Can we afford it?"

She wasn't about to step on her sister's dreams just because she'd had to abandon a few of her own. "Of course we can," she said stoutly, thinking that she'd find the money somehow. "Don't worry about that."

"But I do worry about it, Mary Nell. I know how hard you've been working to build up your business, to get some good accounts. I know how expensive it's all been, especially with my school fees and everything."

She couldn't insult her sister by pretending it hadn't been difficult; Stacy knew the score. But she could say, "Well, we've managed so far, haven't we? We can certainly manage another year."

"I could get a part-time job—"

"Absolutely not! We've talked about that before, and we agreed—"

"All right, all right," Stacy said hastily. And then she pleaded, "But at least let me apply for work-study, Mary Nell. After all, this will be a graduate program. It'll be different than the past four years."

"Are you trying to say that it's going to be easier?"

"Well, no, but—"

"Then there's nothing to talk about," Mary Nell said firmly.

"But—"

"No! End of conversation," she said. But then, because she knew how responsible and guilty Stacy felt, she added, "Besides, don't think I'm not writing all this down in my little ledger. Once you get your cap, things are going to be different."

"Are you saying I'm going to support you for a change?"

"In style," she said. "How do you feel about that?"

"I can hardly wait," Stacy said fervently. Then she paused. Her voice suddenly soft, she said, "Thanks, sis. One day I hope I'll be able to show you how much I appreciate all you've done."

Touched, Mary Nell replied, "You've already done that, Stacy. I know you're going to be a wonderful nurse."

"Just like you're going to be the best industrial designer Tacoma ever had!"

Mary Nell's smile faded as they hung up. She knew Stacy had meant that last remark to show her admiration and support, but she wondered now if such a thing would ever come to pass. She'd taken her engineering degree knowing she wanted a career in industrial design, but that took time. Now, glancing around her little office, she felt more depressed than ever. How was she ever going to graduate to the big leagues if she couldn't even rise above this?

Give yourself time, Mary Nell, a voice whispered at the back of her mind. Her mother used to tell her that. *You're always in such a rush.*

With a sad smile, she had to admit that was true. She'd been in a rush since she was a little girl. There had never seemed to be enough hours in the day or days in the year or years in a lifetime to do everything she wanted to do. She'd always felt time to be more an enemy than a friend, and she'd never felt that more keenly than now.

Her glance fell on the phone again, and she shook her head at the irony. If she had phoned Anson McAdam when she'd gotten in, as she'd intended, or if Stacy had called ten minutes later, her situation really would look hopeless. But since she hadn't formally withdrawn yet, she at least had a chance—a minute one, she had to admit, since Cal still had his field trial to conduct.

Trying not to think that she wasn't sure she wanted one, she told herself, instead, that since she had to continue on, she would just have to put Cal Stewart out of her mind, except as a business rival—something she'd intended doing from the beginning. The fact that she hadn't been successful thus far in doing that was beside the point; she had no choice now. She'd have to work that much harder to make ends meet this coming year. She couldn't withdraw now just because she was afraid of getting involved with her rival. With Stacy's additional expenses, she needed every edge she could get.

Firmly, she told herself she could do it if she had to. And she had to. Too much was at stake here to be derailed by this...schoolgirl infatuation. So she was attracted to Cal; so what? She could overcome that attraction; she could handle it. From now on, she would concentrate solely on business. She had a job to do, and she'd do it. She could win the contract if she really put her mind to it; she knew that. She might be shaky on personal relationships, but if she wasn't sure of anything else, she knew design. All she had to do was remember that.

And when she and Cal set up the date for the next field trial, she'd be all business. They'd go out, do the test, come home again, and she'd submit her report. It would be out of her hands then; Anson McAdam would decide. But at least she would have given herself a fair shake. She couldn't ask for more than that.

Couldn't she? Suddenly even more depressed by the thought, she pulled her briefcase toward her and got to work.

"I THOUGHT YOU SAID this was going to be a piece of cake," Brad said on Monday morning. He'd come in to find Cal looking, as his mother once would have said, as though he'd been dragged through a bush backward. "If I didn't know better," he added, "I'd think you were hung over."

Sitting at his drafting table, a cold cup of coffee by his elbow, his head in his hands, Cal turned bloodshot eyes on his partner. "I haven't been drinking."

"From the looks of it, you haven't been sleeping much, either," Brad observed, pushing the chair closer so he could see what Cal had been working on. The pad was blank. "That looks good," he said mildly.

"I can do without the sarcasm," Cal muttered, glaring at him. "What are you so happy about, anyway?"

Nonchalantly, Brad did a wheelstand with the chair. "I've got a date this weekend."

Forgetting his own problems for a minute, he stared at his friend. "A date? As in . . . with a lady?"

Brad grinned. "Yes, indeedy—as in woman, female, member of the opposite sex, that sort of thing."

He sat back. "I'll be damned. Who with?"

"Who do you think? Unlike you, I haven't exactly been swamped with women lately, remember?"

"Don't look at me," he said, his jaw tightening. He was still furious with himself about what had happened on Saturday; he'd thought of about a dozen different ways he could have handled it—should have handled it—since then. He never should have kissed Mary Nell, for one thing. If he hadn't acted like some overeager teenager, if he hadn't rushed things . . .

Then he shook his head. It wouldn't have mattered. He'd been doomed from the start. He just wasn't himself when he was with her; he still didn't know what had happened. The furthest thing from his mind had been making a move on her like that, but when the time came . . . when he saw her looking so vulnerable and upset and so damned beautiful, he couldn't help himself: he'd had to kiss her.

In some ways, it had been worth it. Her lips had been so soft, and her perfume had filled his nostrils. He'd wanted to bury his hands in that glorious hair, press that slender body down to the ground and cover it with his. All sorts of tantalizing visions had risen in his feverish mind, and the thought that he could have imagined all those things in that situation, with the storm beating down and the tent collapsing around them, made him cringe. No wonder she'd been angry. He'd acted like a fool.

He didn't want to think about it anymore. The idea that he still had to get through his own field test, somehow, made him wince. He just wanted to forget the whole thing. What was he going to say to her? How would he act?

"Still thinking about Saturday?" Brad asked, jerking his attention back to the demeaning present.

"No," he said shortly. He didn't want to talk about it. He'd had to tell Brad what had happened, but he hadn't told him the whole story—not by half. Deciding he didn't like the grin on Brad's face, he opted for attack. "No, in fact, I was thinking about your date. Don't tell me you tracked down your Lucille."

Instantly diverted, Brad grinned. "I did indeed."

"And?"

"Remember how nervous I was?"

Did he remember! He'd thought Brad was going to collapse from sheer nerves. "Just a touch."

"Nuts to you," Brad said mildly. "Anyway, after I got through with the mother, asking Lucille out was easy."

Relieved to think of something besides his own problems, Cal leaned back. "What's with the mother?"

"You wouldn't believe it. From the way she acted when I asked if Lucille lived there, you'd have thought I was a heavy-breathing pervert or something. I'll tell you, meeting her is going to be ver-ry interesting."

"And all this takes place on Saturday?"

"Yeah. I'm taking her out to dinner—without the mother, hopefully."

"Where?"

"Well, I thought that new place—Marlin's."

Cal whistled. "You're really out to impress this girl, aren't you?"

Brad wouldn't be drawn. "Yes, well, it's time for me to...to break out a little, don't you think?"

"I do indeed, buddy," Cal said with a grin, and meant it. He'd waited a long time for his friend to show an interest in...anything. He was delighted that Brad had found someone he wanted to date, and glad that she didn't seem the type who'd go out with someone like Brad out of pity and then drop him when she got bored—or the going got a little tough. Reaching over, he gave his friend a companionable punch on the arm. "You want a driver for the night?"

Brad looked at him indignantly. "Absolutely not," he said. "I'll take the van."

Even more pleased, Cal laughed. "Well, I'd suggest you clean it up first. You don't want to scare her away on the first date by taking her out in what could pass for a cave."

"Very funny. As a matter of fact, I'm going to spend all day Saturday giving it the cleaning of its life."

"You want some help?"

"Oh, I don't think so," Brad said innocently. "You're going to be pretty busy yourself, aren't you?"

"Me?"

"Didn't you plan to hold your propeller field test this Saturday?"

Cal frowned. "When did I say that?"

"Well, you didn't, actually. But I was looking at the calendar and thinking you'd better get it done, or you'll run out of time. Remember the deadline?"

"You attend to your deadlines and I'll see to mine, all right?"

"No need to get testy," Brad said blithely. "Weren't you the one who said this was going to be a piece of cake?"

"When did I say that?" Cal retorted, although he remembered saying it very well. It seemed a million years ago. How could he have been so confident?

"You did indeed, my friend," Brad said, starting to wheel himself out. He glanced over his shoulder. "But don't forget to call her, will you?"

After dithering around for an hour, Cal finally called. He'd prayed she wasn't there, but when a vaguely familiar voice answered the phone with a "Barrigan Design. How may I help you?" he was caught.

"This is Cal Stewart," he said crisply, telling himself that no matter what happened, he was going to hold it together. "Is Mary Nell there?"

"Just a moment, Mr. Stewart," the voice said. Where had he heard it before? "I'll see if she's in."

Hoping she'd gone for the day—or the year—he waited a few tense seconds until he heard another click. Fully prepared to give a message, he was taken aback when a voice he recognized very well said musically, "Hello, Cal. This is Mary Nell."

This was it. *Just do it right,* he told himself, and said, "Hi. I just thought I'd call and tell you I went over the specs you sent over this morning. It looks like you solved the design problem on those tent poles all right."

"Thanks," she said. "I was hoping you'd say that."

Trying not to think how sexy her voice sounded over the phone, he told himself to remember the objective. "I also wanted to set up a date for this propeller test of mine. If we're still on for it, that is."

"Why wouldn't we be?" she asked.

Why, indeed. Maybe he'd made more of that kiss than she had, he thought, and stiffened. Well, fine. If she'd forgotten all about it, he could, too.

"No reason," he said tersely, feeling like a fool.

She seemed more composed than he did. "Since this is your test, I think you should set the date, don't you?"

"Right." He couldn't seem to think. Remembering that Brad had said something about this weekend, he seized on that as a good time. "How about Saturday morning, same time?"

"Fine," she said. "Where would you like to go?"

She was being so businesslike, so...so businesslike, so...*cool,* that he couldn't resist. "I had thought about

Pine Meadows, since it has that little lake, but if you'd prefer someplace else—"

"Pine Meadows will be fine," she said.

Now he was sorry he'd tried to needle her into a response. Was he trying to get a reaction because he felt so foolish himself? Until this moment, he was sure he hadn't imagined her reaction to that kiss, but now he didn't know what to think.

He also didn't know what to say next. Cursing the effect she had on him, he said awkwardly, "Okay, then. I'll see you Saturday morning."

"I'll be ready," she said, and added, "with my clipboard."

Somehow he managed to hang on to his composure until he hung up. But as soon as the receiver clattered into the cradle, he put his head in his hands. What was she doing to him? He'd never felt like this. He'd never acted like this around a woman. Not even Donna or Anna Maria had tied him up in knots like this. This was madness. He should get out of this situation right now, before it was too late.

Raising his head, he gave a short, mirthless, hopeless laugh. The way he felt, he knew it already was.

CHAPTER EIGHT

MARY NELL SPENT all week dreading Saturday, the day she'd see Cal again. Even though this was going to be his field test, and she knew she didn't have any reason to be nervous, she was. Well, not *nervous*. Apprehensive, maybe. Tense and anxious, definitely, and not eager to test her once-again-found resolve about not getting involved.

Fortunately, Stacy came home Friday night, and they went out to dinner and a movie. It was a good distraction, but not good enough. Halfway through the meal, Stacy asked her sister in exasperation what she was thinking about. Mary Nell only looked blankly at her. Then Stacy wanted to analyze the movie when it was over, but she couldn't remember what it had been about.

"Well, this has been a real fun evening," Stacy muttered on the way home.

"I'm sorry, Stace," she said, her mind on other things. "I'm afraid I haven't been good company tonight."

"No kidding."

"I'll make it up to you, I promise."

"You want to tell me what it's all about?"

No, she didn't want to do that. Instead, she muttered something about problems at work and, mercifully, Stacy left it at that. But now it was Saturday morning, and the day she'd dreaded all week had arrived. Remembering that she hadn't called Lucille to wish her luck, she put on a pair of jeans and a floral-patterned, fine cotton blouse and phoned right before Cal came to pick her up.

"Oh, Mary Nell!" Lucille cried when she heard her voice. "I'm so nervous I could die!"

"Oh, come on now," Mary Nell said soothingly, wondering how she could possibly sound so calm when she felt like falling apart herself. "We talked about this, remember?"

"Yes, yes, but that was earlier in the week! Now, it's Saturday, and ... oh, why did I accept this date, anyway? I'll never get through it without making some dreadful mistake!"

Thinking that she felt exactly the same way, Mary Nell tried to be encouraging. "You've got to stop this," she said firmly. "You're getting yourself in a state for nothing. This is supposed to be fun, remember?"

"Fun! It's going to be one of the most nerve-racking nights of my life! Assuming that I can even get up the courage to go out in the first place. Maybe I should call and cancel! That way—"

Wishing she could do exactly that with Cal, she said, "You can't cancel. We spent all that time shopping for your dress."

"Yes, and it's beautiful, and I do appreciate all the time you spent with me, Mary Nell, but I ... I—"

She broke in again. "And you have to keep that appointment with my hairdresser. Annette gets very annoyed when people cancel at the last minute."

"I know, but—"

"No, I won't hear it," she said. "There's no reason why you shouldn't enjoy the company of a nice man. You said he was nice, didn't you?"

There was a short silence. Then Lucille said faintly, "Oh, yes. He's very nice."

"Then you go and have a good time," she said. "And on Monday morning, I'll expect to hear every wonderful detail."

She hung up feeling better because she'd called and talked Lucille into keeping her date—until she looked at the clock and realized how close she was to hers. Her palms suddenly clammy, she rubbed them together and was just pouring another cup of coffee when Stacy came into the kitchen. Mary Nell was so nervous she jumped.

"What are you doing up?"

Stacy looked at her in surprise. "That's what I usually do in the morning—get up."

"Yes, but now?" she said unreasonably. "You're never up before noon on weekends!"

"Not true. What's with you? You look as nervous as a cat."

Was it that obvious? Knowing it was, she still tried to deny it. "I'm not nervous. Do you want a cup of coffee?"

Looking cautious, Stacy nodded. "Sure. You want me to get it?"

"No, of course not!" Mary Nell said irritably, and almost dropped the cup when she took it out of the cupboard.

Accepting it warily, Stacy sipped and said, "Something's up. Are you sure you don't want to talk about it?"

"Yes!"

"All right, all right, you don't have to bite my head off."

Feeling badly that she'd snapped at her sister, she decided she might as well confess. Stacy knew her too well. "I'm sorry, Stace. I guess I'm just a little nervous about this field test with Cal."

Nodding as though she'd known it all the time, Stacy asked calmly, "Any idea why?"

"Yes—no...oh, I don't know!" she exclaimed, exasperated with herself. "It's silly, really. This is his test, not mine. But I'm acting as though I'm the one who has everything at stake here."

Stacy regarded her silently for a moment or two. Finally, she said neutrally, "Maybe you do."

Mary Nell had gone to the sink to rinse her cup. Whirling around, she demanded, "What does that mean?"

Stacy shrugged. "Just what it says. Maybe this means more to you than you're willing to admit."

"That's ridiculous!"

"Okay, have it your way."

She really didn't want to pursue this, not when time was running out. She glanced at the clock and wished Cal would arrive so they could get it over with. She didn't care about the success or failure of the field tests anymore; the only thing that mattered to her in this high-strung state was getting through the morning without making a complete fool of herself.

"I'm going to have something to eat," Stacy said. "You want anything?"

The thought of food made her nauseous. "No, thanks. You go ahead."

Shrugging, Stacy took out a loaf of bread and popped two slices into the toaster. "What time does the man arrive?"

Mary Nell glanced nervously at the clock again. "Nine." It was ten minutes to.

"I'm glad I came home this weekend."

Mary Nell turned around. She'd been trying to peer casually through the kitchen archway to the living room windows that looked out on the street. "Why?"

"Well, for one thing, I'm looking forward to meeting this Cal Stewart. He must be quite a guy, to put you in a tizzy like this."

"I'm not in a tizzy!" Mary Nell denied hotly, and then jumped again when the front doorbell sounded.

Stacy saw her violent movement and grinned. "Oh, yeah? What do you call that? Do you want me to answer the door?"

"Absolutely not," she said grimly. "In the mood you're in, you're liable to say anything."

"I'll be purely circumspect, I promise."

"Just stay here."

Naturally Stacy followed. Mary Nell didn't know it until she heard a swift intake of breath behind her as she opened the door.

"Ah," Stacy murmured in her ear. "Things become clear..."

She turned warningly, but it was too late. Grinning, her sister stepped out from behind her and said, "Hi. I'm Stacy, the little sister. You must be Cal Stewart."

Cal didn't miss a beat. "Hi," he said. "Pleased to meet you."

"Likewise," Stacy said with another grin. "Mary Nell has told me so much about you."

"She's mentioned you, too."

Since she didn't like being discussed as though she weren't there, Mary Nell deftly stepped between them. Flashing a what-are-you-doing glance at Stacy, she said to Cal, "I'm ready if—"

"Aren't you going to invite Mr. Stewart in?" Stacy asked innocently. "It's still so early. We could at least offer some coffee."

Glaring at her sister again, Mary Nell spaced every word carefully. "We don't have time for coffee, Stacy." She looked up at Cal, daring him to contradict her. "Do we, Cal?"

He hesitated, but then he saw the look in her eyes and decided to go along. Shrugging at Stacy, he said, "I'm afraid not. Another time, maybe."

To Mary Nell's disbelief, Stacy actually winked at him. "I hope so. I can see that my sister hasn't told me nearly enough about you."

Mary Nell closed her eyes. What was her sister *doing*?

"Goodbye, Stacy," she said heavily, glaring at her sister again when she cheerfully waved them off. They'd have to have a little sisterly chat when she got home. . . .

"Your sister is a kick," Cal said when they were on their way.

She was still embarrassed. "More like a kook," she muttered.

"You don't look alike."

That wasn't news; she'd heard the same refrain for years. When she was younger, Mary Nell had been envious of Stacy's blue eyes and blond hair, but she had long since come to terms with that. But because she was still annoyed with Stacy, she said, "No, I look like my mother. Stacy looks like she was found in the cabbage patch."

Cal laughed. "Spoken like a sister."

"Do you and your brother look alike?"

"Not really," he said with a grin. "I'm the handsome one."

"And modest, too."

He laughed. "I'm kidding, actually—envious, maybe. Dan has always been pretty hard to live up to."

"Why is that?"

"Oh, he always seemed to have things more together, I suppose. Always first, always best. Maybe that's the benefit of being the oldest."

"I don't know about that," she said dryly. "I'm the oldest, and I think it only seems better from the younger brother or sister's point of view. Sometimes it's pretty scary being first."

He looked at her in surprise. "I never thought of it that way."

She smiled. "Ask Dan. I'll bet he agrees."

"Yes, but knowing Dan, he probably wouldn't admit it."

"That's another curse of being the oldest—you always feel that you can't let the younger ones down."

"Is that how you feel with Stacy?"

Fleetingly, she wondered how they'd gotten onto this subject. But it seemed safer, more neutral, than so many other things they might have discussed, and so she said, "Yes, I do. But then, Stacy and I were left on our own pretty young, and so I've always felt responsible for her. I guess I always will—at least until she finishes nursing school."

"And when will that be?"

Without realizing it, she sighed. "Another year. She was just admitted to a special graduate program. I'm proud of her, of course, but it does mean all those extra school fees."

"That must be expensive."

She didn't want to discuss dwindling finances, especially with this recreational gear contract on the line, so she said, "Yes, but it's worth it. She'll be a wonderful nurse."

"Yes, I imagine she will be."

It was time to change the subject. Realizing that the scenery passing by wasn't familiar, she leaned forward and said, "Aren't we going to Pine Tar Lake again?"

"Pine Tar...?" he repeated, looking confused. Then he started to laugh. "You mean the lake at Pine Meadows?"

She flushed. "I knew it was Pine something."

"Yes, that's close, all right," he said. "I can tell you're really familiar with all these campgrounds." Grinning, he looked across at her and saw the stony expression on her face. Quickly he amended, "That's why I...er...thought we'd try a lake farther on ahead, if you don't mind."

"Why?"

Despite himself, his eyes twinkled. "It's a little easier to get to. We can park the car nearer to the shore."

"Are you implying that I held you back last time?" she asked.

"Not at all. I just didn't want to have to carry the dinghy all that distance."

She gave him a careful look, not sure whether he was being serious or not. He returned her gaze solemnly enough, but she still didn't trust that twinkle in his eyes. Sitting back, she crossed her arms and muttered, "Yes, well, don't worry about me."

"Oh, I don't," he said. "I'm sure you can take care of yourself...in any situation."

She wasn't sure how to take that, either, but she told herself it didn't matter. She just wished they'd get there. She'd been all right when they'd talked about inconsequential things, but now she was feeling tense again, all too aware of Cal sitting across from her. Wondering how she was going to get through the next few hours, she stared fixedly ahead, praying for a glimpse of the lake. When she finally saw a glint of blue through the trees, she felt faint. Thank heaven! They were almost there.

She was out of the car almost before he stopped at a gravelly area not far from the edge of the water. Now that the moment was at hand, she told herself not to think about how inept a swimmer she was or how cold the water might be. Glancing resolutely away from the sight of gentle waves lapping the sandy shore, she asked what she could do to help. Cal was already half-buried in the trunk of the car.

"You can carry this," he said, holding up a basket.

"What's that?"

"A picnic lunch," he said, his face reddening slightly.

"What?"

"It's not much—a few soft drinks, some sandwiches." He gave an embarrassed laugh. "I wasn't sure what to bring, so I called my sister. She said, whatever I did, to leave the Twinkies and barbecue chips at home. So I . . . I brought some fruit, instead." Mary Nell was too astonished to say anything, and he went on anxiously, "I hope that's all right . . . ."

She still didn't reply; she couldn't help it. She was beyond speech. No man had ever done something like this for her before, and she was so touched and amazed and taken aback by the gesture that she didn't know what to say.

"It's . . . fine," she managed finally, taking the basket.

"You don't sound like it is."

She made the mistake of looking up at him. He was gazing down at her with those startling eyes, looking so anxious that she wanted to reach up and touch his face. She didn't dare. She felt so emotional that one little gesture in return from him would be her undoing.

"It is," she said. "It's just that this . . . this is the nicest thing a man has done for me in a long, long time."

He kept gazing down at her; she couldn't look away. Finally, he said, "It's just a picnic basket."

But it was more than that, and she knew they were both suddenly, achingly, aware of it. As she stood there, she could feel the spark of attraction she'd always felt for him warming into flame, and she didn't know how to dampen it. A glow began to spread inside her, and she felt faint and breathless and very confused. He was so close, and it was so quiet all around them. A gentle breeze brought with it the spicy fragrance of the pines surrounding the lake. The scent mingled with a whiff from his after-shave, and she knew that forever after, she would always think of him when she smelled pine. Her pulse started pounding, and a quick musical snatch of bird song from somewhere over their heads underscored the rapid beating of her heart. She could see something happening to him, as well, and in the space of the heartbeat between the time he hesitated and the time he took a step toward her, she was faced with two choices: stay, or back away.

She backed away.

"I think," she said, "that we'd better get on with this, don't you?"

She saw the look of surprise on his face and wanted to call back her words, but she wouldn't let herself do it. She couldn't afford to let this get out of hand; already she was so attracted to him that it was an effort not to throw herself into his arms and beg for his kiss. She looked down at the picnic basket and felt a pang.

What would it hurt? she wondered, and she squeezed her eyes shut, trying to remember all those promises to herself, all her resolve. He was a *rival*, she reminded herself; she *couldn't* get involved. She had to think of the office, of Stacy, of Lucille, the debts she had. She couldn't weaken.

"Are you ready?" she asked, knowing the question sounded stupid, insipid, inane. But at least it broke that tension between them, and when she saw him take a breath—as though he were coming up for air—she felt some of the strain drain out of her body, as well. She'd done it. She'd passed. But at what price?

"Yeah, sure," Cal said, and turned back to the car. But he stood there for a second or two, as if trying to remember what he'd been about to do, before he reached for the inflatable dinghy he'd put in the trunk. With a grunt and a heave, he pulled that and two life jackets out of the trunk. Handing her one to put on, he took the other and dropped the boat on the ground.

"Do you . . . do you want some help?" she asked in a small voice.

He didn't look at her, but shook his head. "No, I can get it," he said, and pulled a cord that inflated the little craft. With a whoosh, it puffed up to the size of an elongated doughnut, and he spent the next few minutes attaching the motor with the shiny new propeller he'd designed to the craft—and ignoring her.

Feeling she'd done enough to ruin the morning, she waited in silence to one side, toying with the pull tab on the jacket until she remembered that it might inflate if she tugged hard enough. Since she already felt stupid and ridiculous with the thing on—and even more unnerved after that scene just now—she dropped her hand. All she needed, she thought miserably, was to inflate the thing. Then she'd look as foolish as she felt. Glancing away when she felt tears come to her eyes, she tried to tell herself that she'd done the right thing. But it didn't help, and when she looked down at the picnic basket once more, she wondered dismally why she had to meet Cal *now*.

Relieved when he finally finished attaching the motor and started dragging the boat toward the lake, she followed. Maybe they could get to get this over with before they were faced with another impasse, she thought hopefully, and then felt deflated again when he turned grimly and held out his hand. "Come on. I'll help you in."

His expression seemed set in granite, but she felt so badly that she couldn't let things go on this way. "Cal—"

"Look, let's just get this done, okay?" he said, his voice harsh. "Hand over the basket. We'll eat once we get to the opposite shore, if that's all right with you. Since we're here, we might as well give this thing a real test."

Wondering how she was going to choke down any food at all, she silently handed over the basket. She didn't dare argue; he looked too grim. Ignoring his outstretched hand, she climbed into the boat alone. Her courage nearly deserted her when she felt the raft shift under her unsteady foot, and she plopped ungracefully onto one of the slatted seats. He followed, immediately shoving off before jumping in himself, turning to start the motor with just the barest glance in her direction to make sure she was seated.

The little motor sprang to life. The instant the craft started moving, she forgot her distress about Cal and remembered instead that boats always made her seasick. Even though she knew by the little put-put sound of the motor that they couldn't possibly be going quickly, she felt as though they were speeding along, and she surreptitiously clutched the slippery rubber sides of the little craft, praying Cal would do as he already was and stay fairly close to shore. They rode in silence for a while, and she didn't realize her face must be getting green until Cal started looking at her strangely. Finally he leaned forward.

"Are you all right?"

She swallowed. "I'm fine."

He frowned. "You don't look it."

She'd die before she told him how she really felt. "No, honestly, I'm okay."

"I think we'd better head back," he said, and started to turn the dinghy around.

She wasn't about to argue. She wasn't sick yet, just queasy. "Well, if you think that's best...."

The motor made a funny sound just then, and he called over it, "What?"

"I said—"

But then there was another strange noise from somewhere near the motor, and she forgot what she'd been about to say. Instead, clutching the sides of the boat, she looked around fearfully. "What was that?"

He'd heard it, too, and with a frown, turned to look. Just as he did, there was an even more ominous sound, something that sounded forbiddingly like a rip.

"Cal!" she cried.

"What the—"

He didn't have time to complete what he'd started to say. The ripping noise was followed by an even more ominous whoosh, and Mary Nell exclaimed as, before her startled glance, the propeller suddenly took flight, like a wildly spinning aluminum projectile. At first she didn't know what it was. Wide-eyed, she stared as it emerged from the water, then spun away from them over the surface. It looked like a...like a Frisbee, she thought dazedly.

"Cal," she started to say again, but then she realized her feet were wet. Startled, she looked down and saw the bottom of the boat rapidly filling with water. *"Cal!"*

He was already on his feet. "I think we'd better get off," he said quickly. "This thing is going to sink."

"What?" she cried.

He didn't have time to answer. His end of the boat collapsed abruptly, throwing him over the side. He disappeared into the water, arms flailing, uttering an indignant squawk before he sank.

She was so horrified she couldn't move. *This isn't happening,* she told herself, squeezing her eyes shut. She could feel the water lapping at her legs now, and the sensation was so awful that she popped her eyes open again. Now the water was at her waist; the picnic basket was actually floating beside her. She couldn't see the boat, which she supposed was a couple of feet under the surface. The water reached her shoulders. She was going to die, she thought; she was going to drown right here, in Pine Tar Lake.

A few yards away, Cal's head broke the surface. "Oh, Lord!" he cried when he saw her sinking, just sitting there. "Get off! Get away from there! Can't you swim?"

"No," she said, and reached for the picnic basket as it started to float by.

"*What!* Why didn't you tell me?"

"I didn't think it would be necessary," she said. She wasn't really worried, now that the worst had happened. She couldn't swim, but she'd always been able to float. And she did have the life jacket.

"Hold on!" he shouted, and started churning frantically toward her, arms windmilling, feet kicking wildly.

She didn't need to be rescued. When her feet touched bottom and she realized that the water on her side of the boat was only a few feet deep, she simply stood, took the picnic basket and started toward shore. The dinghy had deflated on some kind of underwater shelf, and when Cal reached the place where she'd been and didn't find her there, he began to tread water frantically. "Mary Nell!" he cried, looking wildly around. "Mary *Nell!*"

"I'm here," she said from shore. Setting the picnic basket down, she started wringing out her hair. Cal was still in the water, staring at her disbelievingly.

"How did you . . . ?" he sputtered.

"You can walk," she said, pointing. "The water's only a few feet deep right there."

He came to shore, his hair standing on end, his face crimson. "God, I feel like a fool," he muttered. "Are you all right?"

"I'm fine," she said. She couldn't be angry with him; he looked so crestfallen. Still trying to dry her hair, she looked up. "What happened?"

The propeller had landed not too far from them on shore. He gave it a savage glare. "I think I cut the tolerances too fine. It must have...sheared off."

"A slight miscalculation?" she said innocently. Now that it had happened to him, she saw the humor in the situation and tried hard not to laugh.

"This isn't funny!"

She tried to sober. "I know," she said, biting her lip. "It could have happened to anyone."

"Are you laughing at me?"

He looked so outraged that she couldn't help it. Unable to stifle her amusement any longer, she burst into laughter. "Oh, Cal, you should have seen your face!"

"I'm telling you, it's not funny!"

"I know, I know," she said helplessly. When she saw how embarrassed he was, she tried to stop. But every time she thought of that propeller rising from the water and spinning off like a flying saucer, she started to laugh again. Clapping her hand over her mouth, she looked up at him with merry eyes and said, "I'm sorry, Cal. It's just..."

When he glared at her, his hair still in spikes, water trickling down his chin, she had to laugh again. It *was* funny. Here they both were, soaking wet, hair and clothes dripping, with the dinghy somewhere at the bottom of the lake and the propeller resting serenely on shore beside them. Could anyone not laugh?

Cal could. His eyes blazing, he glared down at her. "You didn't think it was so damned amusing when it happened to you."

"I know, but—"

He didn't wait to hear her out. His jaw clenched, he turned and went to fetch the culprit. Snatching up the propeller from the sand, he seemed to debate sending it to a watery grave, but with a curse, he just threw it down again in disgust. Wiping his face with the back of his arm, he narrowed his eyes and stared out at the lake.

"Cal?" she said tentatively. He ignored her. But when she saw his shoulders stiffen, she felt contrite. "Cal, I'm sorry."

When he still refused to acknowledge her, she knew what to do. Penitently, she picked up the dripping picnic basket and brought it to him. Holding it up, she said in a small voice, "All is not lost. I saved lunch."

There was a tense moment when she was afraid he would take the basket from her and fling it as far as he could into the lake. But then he looked down at the sorry contents and then into her eyes, and suddenly his eyes crinkled.

"You know what was really funny about all this?" he asked.

"What?"

"Seeing you going down with the ship. If you thought *I* had a strange expression, you should have seen *your* face!"

She couldn't help it. She started to laugh again, and when this time he joined her, they really started in. Soon they were practically hysterical with mirth, holding on to each other for support, going off again every time one looked at the other. She laughed until she cried.

"Oh, Cal," she begged, moving away from him, holding on to her stomach. "Stop it! You're making me hurt!"

"I can't—"

And then, suddenly, the laughter was gone, and another emotion, much stronger, stepped into its place. They looked at each other at the same time, and in a flash, something changed. She caught her breath. She couldn't look away.

"Mary Nell," he said.

When he first put his arms hesitantly around her, as though afraid she might break, she marveled that it didn't seem to matter how tall he was. She had thought it would, but they seemed to...to fit. It was almost as though they'd been made for each other, and in wonder she looked up into his eyes. When she saw the longing there, the desire—the passion—that mirrored the sensations churning inside her, she acted without thinking. Raising her arms, she wound them around his neck and pulled his head down to hers.

They had kissed before, but not like this. After the panic they'd shared, the laughter, the disaster, his lips were hard on hers, demanding, seeking, burning with hunger. She opened her mouth, and their tongues met, and she felt a thrill all through her. She'd never felt this way before, and she wanted more. Much more. Moaning, she pressed her body into his.

His response was instantaneous. His arms tightened around her, almost lifting her off her feet—but gently, as if he were still anxious he might somehow hurt her. She felt the hard rise of his erection against her thighs, and she pressed her hips into him shamelessly, delighting in the arousal she could feel.

"Oh, Cal," she murmured, wanting to fall down on the sand, to feel his bare skin against hers, to touch him in places that made him want more. The pressure of his lips increased; one hand came to her breast. She felt so weak at the sensation that flooded her, she would have fallen if he hadn't been holding her so tightly. She felt him begin to tremble, and she wanted him to go on and on....

And then she knew what would happen if they did. Things could never be the same; they'd never be able to go back to the way it had been. She'd have to choose: him, or her work, and she'd already done that. She'd promised herself that *this* time nothing was going to deflect her from her vow, and she couldn't go back on that promise, no matter how tempting. She *had* to make a success of her design company. Stacy was counting on her, and Lucille. She'd even mortgaged the house to pay for all those expenses. She couldn't afford to be distracted—not now, when so many other things were more important than this ungovernable attraction. Wondering if she truly knew what she was doing, she pushed him away.

"What is it?" he asked. He looked blank, his expression dazed.

She was so miserable she could hardly speak. "I'm sorry, Cal. I...can't."

"Can't? What? What are you talking about?" He reached for her blindly once more.

She couldn't allow him to touch her. Already she could feel herself weakening, and she wanted to throw herself into his arms and forget everything else, to take up where they'd left off, to explore each other, to make mad, passionate love right there on the sand. But she couldn't, and so she stepped quickly back.

"I'm sorry," she said again. "But I think...I think we'd better get back to town."

He looked at her uncomprehendingly. "I don't understand."

"I don't, either," she said, holding up her hands, as though that gesture alone could protect her and explain everything. "I don't, either. I just know this isn't right. I . . . I can't do this, Cal. I can't get involved."

"Can't get . . ." He shook himself. "What are you talking about?"

She didn't know what she was talking about. She knew she wasn't being fair, but there was no help for it. She still wasn't in control of herself, and she knew that if she tried to explain, she'd be lost.

"Please," she said helplessly. And then, barely a whisper, "Please."

The ride back was a tense and silent one, and she didn't invite him in. He drove off as soon as she was safely inside. To her relief, Stacy had gone out with friends, and she was alone in the house. Grateful for this time by herself, she crept upstairs to shower and change. But she still hadn't pulled herself together by the time her sister came home, and even though she deliberately made Stacy laugh with her amusing story about what had happened, she could tell her sister wondered if something else had taken place.

Something had, but—she vowed shakily and in utter misery—it never would again.

CHAPTER NINE

LUCILLE SPENT the week not knowing what to do. She was still on cloud nine after her date with Brad, but every time she thought about confessing all, she'd see how depressed Mary Nell was and decide to wait for a better opportunity. She knew things hadn't gone well with Cal's field test on Saturday, and even though she and Brad had had a wonderful time, she didn't feel right to crow about it when Mary Nell was so down. It seemed so... so disloyal to be so happy when Mary Nell looked so glum, and yet she couldn't help herself. Saturday night with Brad had been one of the best nights of her life. *The* best.

She still had to pinch herself at times to make sure it had been real. The only thing that convinced her the entire night hadn't been a dream was that she still had a new hairstyle. After wearing the same dull pageboy all these years, she'd let Mary Nell's hairdresser, Annette, talk her into a feathery layered style that made her feel light and free and—she blushed just thinking about it—attractive for the first time. Her mother had been outraged at the change, but it had been worth every snip when she saw the light in Brad's eyes. Now she was dissatisfied with her glasses; the frames she'd worn forever suddenly looked dowdy and out of style, and she'd been thinking of contact lenses. She would ask Brad on Saturday night when they went out.

Brad. Even his name seemed right. He'd looked so handsome in his tie and sport coat when he'd come to pick her up; she'd been so proud to introduce him to her mother. She giggled. Despite Eunice's determination not to like him, he'd won her over. It was like a miracle. She'd had a few anxious moments when they had all realized there was no way for him to get his wheelchair up the four steps to the front porch, but he'd been just wonderful. He'd told them problems like this weren't new, and he simply asked if he could get in the back door. Relieved, she'd raced around to the back, where there were no steps, and he'd wheeled the chair around the side of the house and come in through the kitchen. She'd felt so humbled— and so awed—at the way he'd handled that awful moment that she had resolved the next day to have a carpenter come out to the house and put a ramp up the side of the porch. She had expected an argument from her mother, but after meeting him—and being charmed—Eunice had been the one to suggest it.

"If you're going to be seeing that young man again, that is," her mother had said, avoiding her eyes. "It will be easier for him, I suppose."

Lucille had been so touched that she'd given her mother a quick hug before running to get the phone book so she could look up the name of a handyman. She did intend on seeing Brad again, and to her grateful amazement, it seemed he felt the same way. They'd had a wonderful time on their date; conversation hadn't lacked. She'd been so impressed upon finding out that he invented things, and the ride in his specially equipped van had been so exciting. She'd never ridden in a vehicle like that, with a hydraulic lift to get the chair inside and hand controls that Brad had let her try. She hadn't realized until then how strong his hands had to be to get himself around, and she'd been awed again.

But she still hadn't told Mary Nell who she was dating, and as the week dragged by, she felt more and more guilty. She'd have to tell her soon, but when? And how? Brad had laughed when she'd finally gotten up the courage to tell him where she worked, but she didn't think Mary Nell would be so amused with the situation. Hoping Brad would have a suggestion about what to do, she tried to cheer up the obviously depressed Mary Nell while she waited anxiously for Saturday.

MARY NELL WAS just worried about getting through the week to Friday morning—the day she was due to go out to McAdam Recreation to find out who had won the account. By then, she was almost too depressed to care about the outcome of the contest. She'd waited all week for Cal to call, but as the days dragged by and she didn't hear from him, she realized she had to face facts. *She* had called his office—twice—and left messages. When neither one had been returned, she knew it was time to put all this behind her and get on with things. But that didn't make her feel any better—only more despondent.

The one bright spot in the entire week had been Lucille, who had come in Monday morning with a new hairstyle, talk of contact lenses and a twinkle in her eyes that couldn't be denied. From what Mary Nell gathered, the date had been a big success. She was glad, but that only made her own situation seem more bleak. With Lucille going around the office humming to herself all the time, she couldn't concentrate.

But she couldn't blame her state of mind on her secretary. She had only herself to blame when Cal didn't call— or even include a note with the new propeller specs he sent over. If she'd been in his place, she probably would have done the same. How could she censure him for not wanting to pursue a relationship when she'd made it clear she didn't know what she wanted in the first place? First she advanced, then she retreated. Was it any wonder he was confused? She was confused herself. And frustrated. He seemed to have put her out of his mind. Why couldn't she do the same where he was concerned?

She waited until Friday. When he hadn't called by then, she decided she'd given enough time and energy to Cal Stewart. Besides, it didn't matter anymore. She only had to get through the day, and she'd never have to see him again. McAdam would award the contract to one or the other, and that would be that. Even more depressed by that thought, she went to meet her fate. Naturally the first person she saw when she entered McAdam's office was Cal. He'd been reading a magazine, and when he heard her come in, he looked up. There was an awkward moment when they just stared at each other, then she made herself nod coolly.

"Hello, Cal," she said, proud that her voice didn't shake. She'd been sure it would.

"Hello, Mary Nell."

Out of mere politeness and nothing more, she was sure, he half stood to acknowledge her. She knew then that this was going to be more difficult than she had anticipated, for her mouth went suddenly dry, and without warning her heart started to pound. He looked so handsome, dressed today in slacks and a pale blue shirt with a red-striped tie. A beige linen sport coat was tossed casually over the arm of the chair, and even his loafers shone. Quite a change from when she'd last seen him, she thought, with water dripping down his chin and his hair standing up in spikes. But then, she looked different, too. Wishing bleakly that she *felt* different, she took a seat as far away from him as possible. She was just reaching for some periodical she had no intention of actually reading when he put his own magazine aside.

"I'm sorry I didn't return your calls this week," he said.

She looked at him over the pages of the magazine. "That's all right. It wasn't important."

He seemed to feel a need to pursue it. "I meant to," he said. "But things got a little hectic."

Did they? she thought. She didn't believe him. But she wasn't going to let him know that it mattered, so she said matter-of-factly, "I told you, it wasn't important. I just called to see if you'd worked out the glitch in your propeller design. Of course, when you sent over the new specs, I saw that you had."

He reddened. "Yes, as I said, it was a minor problem."

She said nothing to that; she knew they were both remembering the previous Saturday when he'd dived into the lake to retrieve the boat. Once she'd seen the long tear in the rubber by the motor, she'd known what had happened, but she hadn't wanted to point it out; he was too good a designer not to see it himself. His propeller had simply been too efficient for the older motor he'd been forced to work with. The shaft couldn't keep up with the rotation, and when, inevitably, both had gotten out of phase, the propeller had sheared off. As he'd said, easy to fix, but embarrassing, nonetheless.

"You don't agree?" he said when she remained silent.

She hadn't anticipated how difficult this would be, and because she was feeling so off balance, she said, "As you said, it was a minor problem. Of course, it might not have happened if you'd used CAD."

"You used CAD for the tent poles, and it didn't help you."

Stung by his deliberately hurtful remark, she was about to make a sharp reply when she realized she'd deserved it. Annoyed with both of them for sniping at each other, she was deciding whether or not to drop it when the secretary tripped in, smiled brightly and announced, "Mr. McAdam will see you now."

The office was just as it had been the last time they'd been there, but she was too irritated by this time to be overwhelmed by the onslaught. Anson McAdam was just hanging up the phone when they came in. He didn't look pleased.

"Good, I'm glad you're finally both here," he said. "I've got a problem. Sit down, sit down, and let's talk about it."

Thinking that already she didn't like this, she cautiously took a seat in front of the desk. She was trying to think of something diplomatic to say when Cal just jumped in. Taking the chair beside her, he asked casually, "What's the problem, Anson?"

McAdam frowned. "I've just been on the phone with one of my people in Los Angeles, and he tells me that that damn SportsGear company down there is launching a new camping line."

Since he'd told them earlier that the SportsGear competition was the reason he had been thinking of hiring new designers in the first place, Mary Nell wasn't sure why this was supposed to be news. "But you expected that, didn't you?" she asked.

McAdam waved a pudgy hand. "Oh, yes, I knew about it. I just didn't know when they planned to do it." His scowl deepened. "Now that I know, it puts me in a little bit of a bind. According to my man down there, SportsGear plans to launch by the beginning of the year, which means—" he paused, giving each of them a significant glance ''—that I'm going to have to up my own timetable a little. To do that, I'm going to need the top two items in my own line reworked—and soon.''

''If you mean the tent poles—'' she started to say.

''If you mean the propeller—'' Cal began.

''No, not those two,'' McAdam said, and paused. ''By the way, good job on those.'' He nodded in Mary Nell's direction. ''Especially that tent pole design—very ingenious.''

Feeling a glow at this praise, she couldn't prevent a satisfied glance Cal's way. Her victory was a little premature, however. McAdam added, ''And Cal, that propeller design is going to work just fine. That's not the problem.''

Not sure she wanted to know what the problem was, she turned slowly back to McAdam. She'd thought this was going to be the moment when he told them which one he'd chosen, but she knew she'd been mistaken. Clearly, he was preoccupied with this other thing, and suddenly she had a feeling of impending disaster.

''I really hate to ask you to do this,'' McAdam said. ''But if you'll bear with me just a little longer, I promise, I'll make it worth your while.''

He'd already made it worth her while, she thought, just as he'd already promised to make a decision based on their performance with the tent poles and the propeller. What new game was this? Cautiously, she said, ''What exactly are you asking us to do?''

''Redesign the top two bestselling items in my current camping line,'' McAdam said. ''I'd intended to refurbish those when I had a little more time, but with SportsGear pressing me like this—'' he shook his head ''—I'm afraid I can't wait. I'm going to have to hit the stores with everything I've got . . . before they do.''

"Redesigning will make that much difference?" Cal asked.

"I'm sure of it," McAdam said.

Mary Nell was silent. Oh, this was just great. She could feel the circle closing in on her again, and she knew she didn't want anything to do with this. Then she glanced at Cal, saw his expression and stiffened. He was sitting there looking like the cat who planned to steal the cream, but she had no intention of giving up the dish without a swipe or two in return. Her mouth set, she turned to McAdam again. She'd made a study of the equipment the company manufactured, and she knew his camping line was fairly extensive. Right now she was too upset to remember what his top two bestsellers were, and she thought she'd better find out before she committed herself.

"Which two items are we talking about here?" she asked warily.

"The easy-release pop-up trailer hitch, and my back-packer's convertible stove to oven," McAdam said, beginning to rummage around in his desk. "The trailer has developed a little problem with these new hitches on cars, and the stove is too bulky for hikers these days."

Glancing up, he smiled. "Used to be we could just load one of those cast-iron goodies onto the back of a pack horse and away we'd go into the hills. Come nightfall, the cook would have biscuits light as a feather and a cake or pie or two. Nowadays, with all this physical fitness business, people prefer to walk places instead of riding like civilized folks." He shook his head. "Don't know what they're missing, but it can't be helped."

He paused again and seemed to find what he'd been looking for. With a grunt of satisfaction he handed two glossies across the desk, one to Mary Nell, the other to Cal. She looked down. She was holding a picture of what was identified as a pop-up trailer tent. It looked to her like a rectangular box on wheels, with a hitch in front to attach it to another vehicle. Trying to remember if she'd run across anything like it in her study of tents, she glanced covertly at Cal, who was staring down at his own glossy.

"Go ahead, trade 'em back and forth," McAdam said. "I want you both to see what we're dealing with here."

Silently, Mary Nell handed hers to Cal. She refused to let him know how unsure she was of herself at this point; she gave him a cool smile as she took the page he handed her. But she couldn't help wondering what she was getting into. She wasn't sure what McAdam had meant when he'd told them he'd make this worth their while. Had he already decided which one of them would get the account, but that in order to win it, one of them would have to agree to redesign both these items? Wondering how she felt about that, she looked down at the page Cal had given her. She was so unnerved at this new situation that she nearly laughed. *This* was one of the bestselling items in the camping line? It looked like a plain aluminum box.

Sure it couldn't be just that, she examined it more closely. Ah, yes. Now she could see the hinged door in front and another round cut-in on top. The box was supported by four little pegs of legs, which made it look low and silly and squat. She was still studying it—or pretending to—when McAdam spoke.

"As I was saying," he said, "now that SportsGear is breathing down my neck, I'm going to need these two items redesigned in a hurry. Since you two worked so quickly last time, I'd like you to consider taking on these new projects, just like you did last time—under the same conditions, I mean. I promise, once they're ready for production, I'll decide who gets the account."

She couldn't have been more appalled if he'd said he'd decide the winner of the competition after seeing which of them would dive off the Space Needle in Seattle into a net. She heard a strange sound from Cal, but she didn't dare glance his way; she was trying too hard to retain her own composure. Was the man serious? He couldn't really be asking them to do this all over again—this time with two different designs. *Oh, no,* she thought. She couldn't do it. She *wouldn't* do it. Once had been more than enough!

"As I also said," he repeated, glancing from one to the other, "I'll make it worth your while."

She didn't care how worth her while he made it, she would not participate in another of his unorthodox contests. It was cruel to ask them—inhuman! "Mr. McAdam..." she started to say.

"Before you decide, perhaps I should be a little more precise about the retainer I intend to pay this time," McAdam said. "Just to prove how important this is to me, I intend to offer..."

The sum he mentioned made her gasp. Even Cal sat up.

"You've got my attention," he said.

Unwillingly, she had to admit that he had hers, too. With a feeling of impending doom, she knew she couldn't refuse. The sum was even more generous than it had been the first time. It would be folly to pass up an opportunity like this. Win, lose or draw, she'd still have the retainer, and she could—

Then she remembered the conditions of the competition and nearly groaned. Could she do it all over again with Cal? She glanced at him. He seemed to be studying the tent trailer glossy with much more interest than necessary, and she wondered if he felt as reluctant about the situation as she did. Then her chin lifted. She hoped he

did. In fact, she hoped he'd refuse to participate alto-
gether. Then the account would be hers by default.

But just then, Cal looked up. Tossing the glossy on the
desk, he said, "Sounds fine to me." He looked over at her
and grinned. "How about you? You game for a second
round?"

She couldn't believe it. From his expression only seconds before, she would have bet anything that he'd refuse
to go along with this new proposal. Her chin lifted again.
Well, fine. She'd already made her decision; she didn't care
what he planned. She was not about to let Cal Stewart get
this account—not without a fight. Two more field tests,
that was all, she thought. She could do that with her eyes
closed.

"I'm game," she said.

"Excellent, excellent." McAdam was beaming. "I'd
hoped you'd both accept the challenge. Now, which of the
projects would you prefer? Miss Barrigan?"

She hadn't thought about which she'd do until now, but
glancing down at both glossies, she instantly made her decision. She knew Cal expected her to take the stove, so just
to prove him wrong, she pointed to the picture of the pop-
top hitch.

"I'll take the trailer hitch."

Cal ignored her smug expression. "Then I guess that
leaves me with the oven," he said. "Okay by me."

"Well, that's just fine," McAdam said, rising to shake
their hands on the new bargain. "Just fine."

Thinking it wasn't fine at all, she made her escape a few
minutes later—but not before agreeing to a timetable she
knew even at best was going to be a scramble to meet. But
she had committed herself now, and she wouldn't back
out. Not, she thought blackly, after being treated to an infuriating wink from Cal before she left. He called out to

her when she reached the parking lot, and because she was too proud to ignore him, she whirled around.

"What?"

"What's your hurry?" he asked.

Glancing back at him, she told herself she would absolutely not think about how good-looking he was. Sunlight glinted in his black hair, every wave of which was in place today, and his pale blue shirt made his eyes seem even more blue. He looked handsome and appealing and aggravatingly confident of himself as he propped one arm casually on the top of her open car door.

"I've got work to do, don't you?" she said. She just wanted to get away from him, go somewhere alone so she could regain her crumbling composure. She couldn't rid herself of the feeling that she had made a terrible mistake.

"Don't you have time for a cup of coffee?"

Was that his way of apologizing for not calling her this week? She gave him a suspicious look. Maybe it was another attempt to disarm her, get her to forget he was a rival and cause her to make some fateful design error that would guarantee him the account. Well, it wasn't going to work. *This* time she wasn't going to get involved. *This* time she was going to be strictly business. The way she should have been the first time. No one could say she didn't learn from her mistakes.

"I'm afraid not," she said coolly, and reached for the car door.

He seemed disappointed, but again, she couldn't trust herself to judge his reactions. After all, she had misjudged him before. "Maybe another time," he said.

"I doubt it. We'll be seeing more than enough of each other with these new field trials, don't you think?"

He looked as if he didn't know what to think. Before she could change her mind—which she wouldn't she told herself—she started the car and drove away. She didn't even look in the rearview mirror. It was over, done with, finished, she thought with relief. She was no longer susceptible to his charms. They were business rivals again, nothing more. She could handle that, she was sure of it.

She was almost at the office before she remembered that in all her self-congratulatory effusion about being immune to him, she'd completely forgotten to set a date for the first field test.

"I don't be*lieve* this!" she muttered furiously as she parked. Now she'd have to call him, after all. Or wait for him to call her. Either way, she'd have to talk to him again. This was terrible.

Even worse was the demeaning thought that despite everything, a tiny, shameful, dishonorable part of her was looking forward to seeing him again, to—

Irritated and totally out of sorts, she got out of the car and went inside.

"I TAKE IT things didn't go well again?" Brad said when Cal stormed into the office later that morning.

Cal glared at him. "What was your first clue?"

"Probably the look on your face," Brad said. "You want to discuss it?"

In answer, Cal tossed the glossy of the backpacker's stove at his partner. Brad looked down. "What's this?"

"The new project," he said, and threw himself into a chair. He was still furious with himself for agreeing to participate a second time in this absurd contest. If he hadn't wanted the account so much, he would have just walked out. He should have walked out. His jaw tightened. He couldn't have walked out, not with Mary Nell looking at him like that. Every time he thought of the challenge in those green eyes of hers, he—

He didn't want to think what he could have done. He didn't want to think of Mary Nell Barrigan at all. But he kept picturing the tilt of her chin, that damned self-assurance of hers. She looked like an exquisite little magnolia, but underneath that fragile exterior beat the heart of a...an Amazon. Now, just when he'd come close to getting her out of his system, they had to do this all over again. What a fool he'd been to agree to the mad scheme! Nothing was worth this aggravation, not even a big account that was supposed to brighten up his future.

"New project?" Brad said, and then looked up in sudden comprehension. "Uh-oh. Not again!"

"Yeah—again," Cal muttered. He didn't want to talk about it, but he couldn't avoid relating what had happened during the course of the morning.

"Aren't you leaving something out?" Brad asked when he'd finished.

"What?"

"Well, like Mary Nell, for instance."

Cal did not want to talk about Mary Nell. "What about her?"

Brad hid a smile. "Why do you always puff up like that whenever her name is mentioned?"

He was outraged. "I don't do that!"

"Oh, yes, you do. In fact, if I didn't know any better—"

He wasn't going to listen to this. Springing up from the chair, he snapped, "You don't know anything! Your imagination is working overtime, that's all."

"I know one thing."

"What?"

Brad shrugged. "That you haven't been yourself lately. That if you had been, you wouldn't have made a mistake like that with the propeller."

"Anyone can make mistakes!"

"That's true. But not like that, not someone who's as good at design as you are."

"So, it was a bad day!"

"Was it?"

He'd had enough of this. He knew that once Brad got started, he'd never hear the end of it. And he was having enough trouble trying to adjust to the situation as it was. But at the thought of having to meet with Mary Nell at least twice more, he nearly groaned aloud. What was he going to do?

"So, what about her?" Brad asked.

"What about who?"

"Mary Nell," Brad said patiently. "She was at the meeting this morning, wasn't she?"

"Of course she was there! And she's going to continue to *be* there if we don't forget about her and concentrate on this new project!"

"All right, all right, calm down."

"I'm not—" he started to shout, and suddenly realized how he sounded. With an effort, he controlled himself and sat down again, muttering, "If I'd known it was going to turn out like this, I never would have applied for the account! It's not worth the aggravation!"

"So, why don't you withdraw?"

He was upset, but not too troubled to see that the conversation was moving in a dangerous direction. He didn't want to talk about the real reason he so desperately wanted the account; he hadn't planned on talking to Brad about dissolving the partnership until he could present something in its stead. So he said, "It's the principle of the thing."

Brad hesitated. "Is that all?"

He definitely didn't like the way the conversation was going. Telling himself Brad couldn't possibly suspect anything, he said gruffly, "No, that's not all. We need the money."

"We've been worse off than this—much worse."

What was happening here? "I don't know about you, but I'm getting a little tired of living hand-to-mouth."

Brad still wouldn't let it go. "Are you sure that's all it is?"

Pretending he'd had enough, Cal made a dismissive gesture. "Yeah, that's all. Now come on, all right? I've got work to do, even if you don't. You're like some bored hausfrau, with too much time to imagine things and not enough to do." Grabbing the glossy Brad had put on the desk, he tossed it over again. "Here. Here's something to do. Start the research on that, will you? I've got to get that designed and prototyped by—"

He stopped, struck by a sudden awful thought. Brad saw the look on his face and said, "By when?"

Cal cursed. Once again, he'd forgotten to set up a time to field-test the things with Mary Nell. Wondering what was wrong with him, he looked up.

"Just get me the research so I can design the damn thing, will you?" he growled, and did his best to ignore Brad's knowing smile.

CHAPTER TEN

WHEN MARY NELL CALLED Stacy the next week to tell her about the latest development, her sister groaned, "Oh, no, not again!"

"I'm afraid so," she said grimly. She still couldn't believe she'd agreed to the outrageous scheme Anson McAdam had proposed a second time—nor could Lucille, who had sounded just as dismayed as Stacy when she'd found out.

"I don't believe this!" Stacy said. "Once was bad enough. Why didn't you just tell him no?"

Remembering the amused challenge in Cal's eyes, Mary Nell lifted her chin. "I couldn't do that. I was already committed."

Stacy seemed to accept that. "Okay, so what's the project this time?"

"A trailer hitch for a pop-top."

"It sounds like a can opener for a soda," Stacy said with a giggle, and then sobered when she didn't hear an answering laugh. "I'm sorry. I know this is serious. I shouldn't be joking."

"I don't know why not," Mary Nell said crossly. "As far as I'm concerned, this entire contest is a joke."

"Well, but you did just fine last time," Stacy said encouragingly.

"No, I didn't."

"All right, so you made a slight miscalculation. But so did Cal, remember? Maybe that's why this McAdam is giving you another chance."

"He's giving us another chance because he wants to beat the competition," she said, and then glanced at the clock. She'd called Stacy from the kitchen, where she'd been fixing a quick bite to eat. In a few minutes, she had to leave to pick up Lucille. Incredibly, they were going to an RV show. She hadn't even known what that meant until Lucille had shown her the advertisement in the paper. Since it definitely looked like something she'd be glad to bypass, she'd been trying to think of a tactful refusal when Lucille announced that she'd already sent for tickets.

"It says in the ad that the show is going to have on display every kind of recreational vehicle imaginable," Lucille had said enthusiastically. "You should be able to get all kinds of ideas for the trailer hitch!"

She hadn't had the heart to refuse then—not after Lucille had shyly asked if she could come along. "To take notes," she'd said. "Or just to keep you company. Please, Mary Nell. I've never been to an RV show."

Wondering how her secretary could possibly be viewing this outing with such zeal, she had reluctantly agreed that they should both go. Tonight, as she got ready, she was glad she wasn't going alone. If she had to *pay* to wander around and gaze at acres of cars and trucks and campers and trailers and heaven knew what else, at least she'd have company.

"I've got to run, Stace," she said, realizing she had to leave soon or she'd be late. "When are you coming home next?"

"What's the rush?" Stacy asked. Then, alertly, "Do you have a date?"

"No, I'm going with Lucille to an RV show."

There was a pause. "I'm sorry. I thought you said you and Lucille were going to an RV show."

"I did."

Another pause. "Are you feeling all right, Mary Nell? I mean, is this competition getting to you? Until this minute, I would have bet you didn't even know what an RV was, much less that shows existed for them."

"Very funny. You know I always do my homework when I'm involved in something."

"Yes, but not like this."

"Exactly like this," she insisted, but as she hung up, she couldn't help wondering if Stacy was right. Maybe this *was* getting to her. Even though she'd tried to immerse herself in other projects all week, she kept thinking about that meeting at McAdam Recreation. As irritating as it was, she couldn't seem to get Cal Stewart out of her mind. Nor could she forgive herself for running off like that, leaving him flat-footed in the parking lot. She wanted to call and apologize, but her pride wouldn't let her do it.

And it's a good thing, she thought. She didn't need to stir up that particular hornet's nest again. She'd vowed to put him out of her mind; if she couldn't do that, the very least she could do was refuse to call on such a flimsy pretext. This was supposed to be a business arrangement— hadn't she told herself that again and again? She would not contact him until she had the trailer hitch prototype ready, and that was that.

But to her extreme irritation, several times that week she caught herself gazing longingly at the phone. She knew why she wasn't calling, but why was he so silent on his end? The only explanation seemed to be that he just wasn't that interested. Obviously, his invitation to coffee that day had been an attempt to find out what kind of plans she had; it certainly hadn't come about because he cared about her. He'd proved just how much he cared the previous week by ignoring her messages, hadn't he? Oh, she knew what he was thinking, all right. It had been obvious from his attitude at the meeting Friday morning that he was sure he had the account wrapped up. But she had surprised him. It turned out that not only was she still very much in the running, she was more than equal to any challenge Anson McAdam meted out.

She lifted her chin. Cal hadn't expected her to choose the trailer hitch as her project; she'd seen the surprise on his face, even though he'd tried to hide it. The hitch was much more complicated than the oven, and having been given the first selection, she could easily have chosen the simpler project. Her mouth tightened. Obviously, he didn't know her very well. Now she was so angry with him that she couldn't even believe his previous assertion that he approved of women in engineering. She was sure that, too, had been a ploy to get past her defenses. Well, she'd show him. She'd design the trailer hitch to end all trailer hitches, and get McAdam's account in the bargain. With that thought, she went to pick up Lucille.

The Hendershots had moved from the old neighborhood years ago; now they lived in a house on the other side of town. She hadn't been in the area for years, and as she got out of the car, she glanced around and was glad she and Stacy hadn't sold out. The houses on her block might look as if little old ladies gathered for Sunday tea after service in them, but at least they had character. The homes here all looked the same.

Mrs. Hendershot answered the door, looking just as Mary Nell remembered her: tall and fierce and over-powering. Even the coronet was in place. As she politely introduced herself, Mary Nell had to fight the feeling that she was a little girl come to ask if Lucille could play.

Nothing had changed, she thought when she was stiffly admitted, not even the antimacassars on the furniture nor the plastic on the lamp shades.

"Of course I remember you," Mrs. Hendershot said, looking her over. "Hal and Marion's daughter. You had a sister, too...."

"Yes, Stacy," she said. "She's at nursing school in Seattle now."

"Is she?" Eunice said, sounding surprised. "Well, how nice. I remember her as a little girl, always stealing pansies from my flower beds."

Amused and exasperated at the same time, Mary Nell hid a smile. "Well, she has changed quite a bit."

Eunice gave her a curious look, but Mary Nell just smiled sweetly and glanced around. The heavy living room furniture was just as suffocating as she remembered from her childhood, but she said, "My, this room is lovely."

"Thank you," Eunice said. Her narrow glance warmed slightly as she looked around the room, and she couldn't hide a nod of satisfaction when she added, "I've done my best to make it look like home."

"It reminds me of the old house on Bentley."

Eunice looked pleased. "Yes, it does, doesn't it?"

She had run out of small talk. "Er... is Lucille ready? If we don't leave soon, we'll be late."

A frown. "She'll be right along. Although why you two girls want to spend your time wandering around a used car lot is beyond me."

She was spared the necessity of a reply, for just then Lucille appeared. Hoping she didn't sound as relieved as she felt, Mary Nell said, "Hi. Are you ready?"

"Yes, I'm—"

"You're not going out like that, are you?"

Lucille turned to her mother. "What do you mean?"

"Why, your hair, of course!"

Lucille immediately looked stricken. Her hands flying up to her head, she said, "What's the matter with it?"

"It just doesn't look like it used to," Eunice said, and without warning turned plaintively to Mary Nell. "I can't imagine what possessed her to have it cut," she said mournfully. "Her hair used to look so neat and nice. Now it looks..." She shook her head. "What do you think?"

Mary Nell thought it looked great. But she sensed that Eunice was bewildered at the change in her daughter—and understandably so. Even Mary Nell had been surprised a few times these past weeks by her once-shy secretary. Kindly, she said, "I think it looks wonderful, Mrs. Hendershot. Maybe it was time for a change."

Eunice looked uncertain. "I'm not sure," she said, and gave her daughter a confused glance. "Lucille has changed since she started seeing that young man of hers. She's just not the same girl."

Seeing Lucille's pink face, Mary Nell decided she didn't want to get into the middle of a family squabble. Hastily, she said, "I think we'd better go now, Lucille. We don't want to be late."

"Yes, you're right," Lucille said with a quick glance at her mother. "I'll just get a sweater."

She was only gone a few seconds, but it seemed endless to Mary Nell, who was left alone with the obviously unhappy Eunice. She wanted to say something to break the silence, but all she could think of when Lucille finally came back was an awkward, "It was nice seeing you again, Mrs. Hendershot."

Still wearing that bewildered look, Eunice lifted a hand and waved as they headed toward the car. Once the door shut, Lucille let out a breath. "I'm sorry, Mary Nell," she said as they started toward the car. "Sometimes she..."

Smiling at Lucille's helpless gesture, Mary Nell shrugged. "Don't worry about it. Mothers are like that sometimes."

"But she—"

"Don't *worry* about it," she said again as they drove off. She was smiling as she glanced across the seat, but when she saw Lucille's solemn expression, she sobered. "What's the matter? Doesn't she like your new boyfriend?"

"Yes, I think she does," Lucille said with a sigh. "I guess what she's having a hard time with is the idea of my having a . . . a beau."

Smiling at the old-fashioned term, but thinking how appropriate it was for Lucille, Mary Nell said encouragingly, "Maybe she doesn't think any man is good enough for you."

"Brad is."

"You're really stuck on this guy, aren't you?"

Lucille gave her a small smile. "I guess you could say that."

"After only one date?"

Looking uncomfortable again, Lucille reluctantly admitted, "We've seen each other since then."

She was surprised. "You never told me that."

"Well, you've been so busy," Lucille said lamely. "I didn't want to bother you."

She glanced across the seat again, shocked. "It wouldn't have been a *bother*! I thought we were friends!"

Distressed, Lucille said quickly, "I didn't mean it that way. Of course we're friends!"

"Then why didn't you say anything?"

Lucille looked away. "Well, there were . . . complications."

"What kind of complications?"

Lucille didn't answer for a moment. "Mary Nell, can I ask you something?"

"Of course. What is it?"

"Have you ever gone out with someone who was...disabled?"

They'd reached a red light. As she braked, she turned slowly to look at Lucille. She'd expected some innocuous question about dating etiquette, and this took her aback. "Disabled?" she said, and added cautiously, "How do you mean?"

Lucille glanced down at her hands, clasped tightly in her lap. Her voice low, she said, "Brad is...in a wheelchair, from an accident a few years ago. He hasn't been able to walk since."

The light turned green. Mary Nell didn't notice until someone behind her gave an impatient toot of the horn. Quickly, she shook herself and started off. She was dazed; this announcement had taken her completely by surprise. Deciding to be honest, she said, "I don't know what to say, Lucille. I'm sorry."

"Don't be—for Brad, that is," Lucille said admiringly. "He isn't sorry for himself at all."

Mary Nell gave her a quick look. "He's not?"

"Oh, he says that in the beginning he was bitter and full of hate, but not now. He's...he's learned to adjust."

Mary Nell pictured herself in that situation, and she knew that she probably would have drowned in self-pity. This Brad had to be a very special man, she decided. Struck by another thought, she glanced at Lucille again. Imagining the problems involved in dating someone in a wheelchair, her admiration for the other woman increased.

"No, I've never dated anyone with a disability," she said, and then suddenly remembered a boy in college long ago. "No, I take that back. I did date someone with a badly broken leg once, but that's not the same thing."

"No, it isn't," Lucille said. She smiled. "But you get the idea."

Recalling how difficult it had been for this boy—Jim Arvinson, she remembered—to negotiate even slight obstacles mobile people took for granted, like staircases and curbs, she shook her head. She hadn't thought of Jim in years. But she remembered his frustration, his fierce need to feel independent and his anger at having to accept help. And the cast had been temporary; after eight months, he'd finally been free. From what Lucille had said, Brad never would be.

"Why did you want to know?" she asked curiously, and then hesitated. Finally, she decided just to ask. "Are there... er... problems?"

"You mean with Mother?"

"Well, yes, your mother. But I was thinking about others. Sometimes people can be thoughtless, or... unkind."

Lucille nodded. "Yes, I know what you mean. But as I said, that's not the problem with Mother. And as far as anyone else is concerned, Brad says that ignorance is a kind of armor, and it's up to him to educate. He never minds answering questions, especially from children."

She hated to ask. But Lucille had brought it up, after all. "Then are there... other difficulties?"

To her surprise, Lucille said unhesitatingly, "Physical problems, you mean?"

Now she was the one who was uncomfortable. "Well, no, that's not what I—"

"It's all right," Lucille said. "I wondered about that, too. But Brad told me that his legs might not work, but when the time came, he'd... manage."

Mary Nell was glad they were in a dark car; she could feel the heat on her face. "That's not what I meant!" she said, flustered. "It's none of my business."

Lucille turned to her quickly. "I'm sorry. I didn't mean to embarrass you. It's just that Brad is so honest about everything, so open, that I'm afraid I've learned to be that way about him, too."

"I see," she said, and didn't have time to add anything more. The line to the stadium was up ahead, and as they joined the long row of cars jockeying to get into the parking lot, she had to pay full attention to her driving. But when they finally pulled into a parking space, she turned again to Lucille. "I think you're wonderful," she said simply. "I don't think I could handle something like this as well as you are."

Lucille blushed. "You could, if you knew Brad."

"I'd like to," she said as they locked the car. "But so far you've been doing a great job of keeping him to yourself. I was wondering if you'd ever offer to introduce us."

"Oh, I want you to meet him," Lucille said. "I think you'd like him."

"I'm sure I would," she said. They joined the throng surging toward the wide stadium doors. Music poured out into the night, and Mary Nell had to raise her voice to be heard. "You know, you've never even told me his last name."

Lucille suddenly looked distracted. "I . . . haven't?"

"No, you haven't," she said teasingly. "Now, come on, what gives? He has one, doesn't he?"

"Yes, he—"

But before Lucille could answer, they were suddenly propelled by the press of the crowd behind them through the big stadium doors. At the sight that greeted her, Mary Nell was so astounded that she forgot everything else. An attendant took her ticket from her unresisting hand, and as the crowd undulated her forward again, she grabbed frantically for Lucille's arm. She didn't want to lose her in this melee; she wasn't sure she would be able to find her again. Assaulted by noise and confusion and people and vehicles everywhere, they looked at each other, their eyes wide.

"Are you sure we're in the right place?" Mary Nell asked.

Lucille looked around at all the gleaming recreational vehicles: the self-contained motor homes, some an awesome forty feet long; the campers and camper shells; the off-the-road vehicles; the Jeeps; the snowmobiles; the trailers and dirt bikes and motorcycles; and all the accessories and paraphernalia and equipment necessary to equip and maintain and run the incredible things, and turned to Mary Nell with a delighted, excited smile.

"This is the right place, all right," she said. "Isn't it wonderful?"

Mary Nell didn't have time to answer. Right behind her, it seemed, a series of cymbals and gongs and whistles and sirens and bells exploded. The noise was so sudden, so loud and startling, that she jumped and whirled around, sure they were about to be run over by an out-of-control machine of some kind. Lucille grabbed her arm, and when Mary Nell looked wildly back, she saw by her expression that Lucille was actually enjoying all this.

"What's going on?" she asked, hoping she didn't sound as frantic as she felt.

Laughing delightedly, Lucille looked around. "I don't know, but it's very exciting!"

Sure it was life threatening instead, Mary Nell started to say something. Her first word was lost in another frenzied eruption of sirens and bells.

"Ladieeeeees and gentlemen!" an unseen announcer shouted over the cacophony as Mary Nell and Lucille clapped their hands over their ears. "Welcome to Tacoma's annual RV show!"

There was another roar, this one from the spectators, who had started running to congregate under what was obviously the announcer's booth, high above their heads. Mary Nell looked up and flinched at the sight of the boxed stage right over them. How could she have missed it? The suspended booth was draped in red, white and blue bunting, and as she watched, it started to... *gravitate* was the only word, she thought dazedly, across the huge expanse of domed ceiling, like a ship under sail.

"Let's follow it," Lucille whispered, looking upward, her amazed glance tracking the moving stage.

"Not on your life!"

Lucille dropped her eyes to Mary Nell's face. "Come on," she teased her. "Where's your spirit of adventure?"

Wondering where her once-timid secretary had found hers, Mary Nell had no choice but to follow. Lucille grabbed her arm and plunged in amid the shouting, cheering, delighted mob, who were moving en masse after the undulating, airborne stage. Hoping they weren't going to be trampled to death in the fray, Mary Nell closed her eyes and let Lucille lead the way.

In the end, they didn't win the all-expense-paid trip to Houston for the annual gathering of the national RV tour group; nor were they awarded the tour of Executive International, the premier manufacturer of self-contained motor homes, based in Indianapolis. They missed out on the white-water rafting trip down the Rogue River, and failed to take home the Jeep Cherokee that held a place of honor, rotating on a raised dais under brilliant floodlights in the center of the stadium. Even the deck chairs and the year's supply of septic powder were denied them—as were tickets to the next year's show. Sounding more like an auctioneer than a show announcer, the man high in the booth overhead called out all the winning numbers of what seemed like an endless array of show-sponsored prizes, each one greeted with an equal roar of enthusiasm from the jubilant, in-the-mood-to-celebrate crowd. Mary Nell couldn't believe it when the lights finally dimmed in the booth, concealing the gaily-waving announcer and signaling the end of the prizes presentation; she'd started to think she'd stepped into another time zone and this would go on forever.

"Wasn't that thrilling?" Lucille exclaimed as the crowd around them began to get down to the real work of examining and testing the thousands of items offered by the show.

"Fantastic," she muttered, holding her head. She had a headache from all the noise, and someone had fired up some kind of engine or generator. Now, in addition to the clamor, she could smell oily smoke. It competed none too gracefully with the greasy smell coming from the numerous hot dog and hamburger stands set up, and when she spotted someone with a fistful of cotton candy, her stomach rolled.

"Can we go home now?" she asked plaintively. Somehow she'd lost her enthusiasm for researching her trailer hitch. Gathering her design information from books didn't seem like such a bad idea anymore; she just wanted to leave.

"Are you sick?"

"No, just—" When she saw Lucille looking at her with concern, she suddenly realized that she was being a poor sport. She didn't like that image; she liked even less the vision of Cal's face that flashed into her mind. She could practically see him grinning that superior grin of his and winking at her. Her spine stiffened. "No, I'm fine," she said, changing her mind. Resolutely, she took Lucille's arm. This time it was she who led the way. "Come on, we've got work to do. Let's try to find one of those pop-top tents in this mess."

The crowd was immense; people clogged the aisles, stopping abruptly whenever they found something of interest and jostling whoever happened to be in the way. After twenty minutes of that, Mary Nell thought if one more person bumped into her, she'd turn around and at least glare at him or her in return. When she finally spotted an item that resembled the picture McAdam had given her, she wanted to cheer. Forging their way through the crowd, she and Lucille arrived, gasping, in the center of a small island of pop-tops.

"Can I help you?" a tanned young man said.

"I certainly hope so," Mary Nell panted, and as Lucille watched in admiration, she caught her breath and proceeded to grill him on every last detail about his product. When they fought their way back through the horde to the outside again and were finally on the way home, she was sure she knew everything there was to know about trailer hitches—of any kind. When she dropped Lucille off at her house, she thanked her profusely for having had the sense to insist they go to the show. Promising her a bonus if things worked out the way they should, she started the car again. She couldn't wait to get to work; already designs were shaping themselves in her head, and she wanted to rush home and put them down before she forgot.

"I'll see you Monday!" she called out gaily as she started down the street.

"Yes, Monday," Lucille said in a small voice, and waited until Mary Nell rounded the corner before she turned slowly and started into the house. She felt terrible. She'd promised herself that this was the night she would tell Mary Nell about Brad. But when the time came, she just hadn't been able to make herself do it. She felt like a traitor, a Judas, a . . . a turncoat. Mary Nell had been so wonderful to her—giving her a job, including her in her work, making her life so exciting. Take going to the RV show. She'd never done anything like that before, and she never would have, if it hadn't been for Mary Nell. In a way, Mary Nell was even responsible for her meeting Brad. And how had she repaid her?

She had to talk to Brad, she decided, and hurried into the house. Her mother had fallen asleep in front of the TV, and she tiptoed through the living room and into the kitchen, where the second extension was. Should she call him? Her heart started to pound at the thought. Except for business reasons, she'd never called a man before; her hand was already beginning to shake.

But Brad had told her to call. He was just as concerned about the situation as she was, thank goodness for that. They'd talked about it the other night, in fact—her face grew warm at the memory, because she'd been sitting in his lap at the time—and he'd said that if he had imagined that their initial meeting would grow to something more serious, he would have been honest with Cal right from the beginning. She felt the same way about Mary Nell.

"But now what are we going to do?" she'd asked him then.

He'd taken a strand of her hair and wound it around his finger. He'd told her he loved the silky feel of her hair, and he always wanted to touch it. She'd never had a man tell her such things before; she'd never had a man even notice her. He could make her feel weak even by such a simple gesture, and normally she would have been lost in sensa-

tion. That night, though, she'd been too concerned to pay
attention to her own rush of feelings. She hated keeping
things from Mary Nell; she felt her friend deserved better.

"Brad, please," she said quietly, "what are we going to
do?"

He'd taken her chin in his hand and looked into her face.
"We'll tell them," he said simply, and removed her glasses.
"Do you know you have beautiful eyes?" he said, and
then he kissed her.

It was the memory of that kiss that decided her. She had
never expected to feel that way; in fact, until that moment, she hadn't known what to expect. But the instant
she'd felt his lips on hers, she'd thought that she would
never ask for anything more than to be with Brad always.
With a passion that astonished her, that she hadn't even
known she'd possessed, she'd clung to him and answered
that kiss, and when his powerful arms had gone around her
and crushed her to him, she'd thought she'd die of pure
bliss. She forgot the wheelchair and all the difficulties it
entailed; she forgot that she was sitting in his lap and that
they were fully dressed. So strong was the power of that
kiss that she was transported; nothing existed in her world
at that moment except Brad. She'd never thought she
would love a man, but she'd known then, with a fierce-
ness that hardly surprised her—it seemed so right—that
she would never stop loving him. The miracle was that he
felt the same way. She knew that together they could conquer everything, anything, all things.

Tonight, her thoughts once again flying to Mary Nell,
she saw that her hand had stopped shaking. Long ago,
she'd memorized his number, and she dialed it without
hesitation. He'd told her that whatever problems they met
along the way, they'd work them out together. She didn't
doubt him. She never would.

When he answered, she said, "Brad, I need you."

He didn't ask why or how or what was wrong. Quietly, simply, calmly, he said, "I'll be right there."

Her heart sang.

CHAPTER ELEVEN

MARY NELL COULD hardly wait until Lucille came to the office Monday morning. As soon as she heard the front door, she poked her head out of the computer room and gestured frantically. "I've got it! Come and take a look!"

Lucille was startled. It was just eight-thirty; Mary Nell usually didn't come in until nine. She hadn't even had a chance to make coffee.

"Come on! I can't wait to show you!" Mary Nell cried, and ran back to the desk, where the computer was humming away merrily. The new design was on the video display, and the printer was droning to one side, awaiting further instructions. Already folds of printed paper were hanging down the front of it. Lucille stopped in surprise on the threshold. It was obvious that Mary Nell had been in for some time.

"When did you get in?" she asked.

Mary Nell glanced up from the computer. "I don't know—hours ago. I had to get this going. Come and take a look. I want to know what you think."

Lucille didn't want to come in. This room made her feel uncomfortable, and she never entered if she could help it. Even though Mary Nell had laughingly assured her it couldn't happen, she was always afraid she'd break something, and she glanced around hesitantly as she took a step in. All the machines happily whirring away made her even more nervous. Suppose she tripped over something?

Mary Nell glanced up again. She knew how much Lucille dreaded coming into the room, and she grinned. "The computer won't bite, I promise."

"Are you sure of that?"

"I'm positive. Now, come on. I want your opinion. I've been working on this trailer hitch since Saturday morning, and I'm sure I've got it."

"You've been here since Saturday morning?"

She laughed. "No, I didn't mean that. I still have a drafting table at home." She stopped, frowning, when Cal's face flashed into her mind. *He* still worked on a drafting table, too. But she didn't want to think of Cal, and she continued quickly, "I was so buzzed from that RV show Friday night that I couldn't sleep. I started fooling around with ideas until I came up with . . . this!"

Tiptoeing over, Lucille peered at the computer screen. "Is it . . . finished?"

"Yes, that's what I'm trying to tell you! What do you think?"

"It's very . . . nice," Lucille said.

She had to laugh. "You don't have the faintest idea what you're looking at, do you?"

"Well, I . . . no," Lucille admitted. But she added an earnest, "But it still looks nice."

Mary Nell shook her head. "Oh, Lucille, what am I going to do with you? Here, let me show you."

Quickly, she got up from the chair and went to the two side-by-side printers. One was a line printer, used for quick graphic copy. It produced dump prints that took the place of preliminary drawings. But she'd already gone through that process, so she ignored the several dozen drawings spilling down from it and went to the hard-copy printer, instead. This printer produced electrostatic acetate transparencies that were exact copies of whatever drawings were on the screen. She'd done many of those, too, and she took a handful, then crossed to the pen plotter. This machine was used to actually plot the drawings, detail by detail, and after glancing over what she had, she ripped the finished schematics off the role of fan-folded paper. Then she went to the big table in the center of the room and spread it all out.

"Now, is that better?" she asked, stepping back so Lucille could see.

Cautiously, Lucille approached the table. Ignoring the schematics—they always seemed like mere squiggles to her—she studied the drawings, instead. These showed exactly what the trailer hitch would look like from all angles, and when she realized what she was looking at, she glanced up in astonishment.

"This is amazing! How did you ever think of it?"

"That's what I do, remember?" Mary Nell said modestly, and then, because she couldn't contain her elation, she grinned again. "You think it's good?"

"I think it's wonderful! Tell me how it works!"

"I thought you'd never ask!" Quickly, she sorted the drawings and schematics into order and pointed to each one in turn as she explained. "Remember the man at the RV show who talked to us about the pop-tops? Well, when he showed us that you had to screw in a balancing wheel under the hitch before you could separate the pop-top from the towing vehicle, I knew right away that the problem wasn't the hitch—it was inserting the wheel."

Lucille nodded. "You know, I thought the same thing. It seemed so awkward."

"Exactly. So, after playing around with a few ideas, I decided the best approach was to redesign the hitch so that the balance wheel tucks up under it. I also added a gas lift to make things easier still. Now, with a touch of the button, the wheel drops down into place, balancing the trailer and lifting the hitch off the towing ball at the same time. Voilà! The easy-lift trailer hitch!''

Lucille looked at her in wonderment. "And when you want to hook everything up again?''

She waved a hand. "Just reverse the process. Back up the hauling vehicle to the hitch so that the towing ball is right under it, press the button, and like butter, the wheel retracts, gently lowering the hitch right onto the ball. A plain lock-down clamp to hold it on, a chain for added safety and away you go! What could be simpler?''

Lucille's admiration was undisguised. "I knew you'd think of something wonderful!''

Grinning again, she said, "It's all due to you.''

"Me!''

"Yes, you. You were the one who told me about the RV show and said we should go. If I hadn't talked to that man and experimented with those other hitches myself, I never would have thought of this. And so, remember that bonus I told you about? Well, this is the first part of it. I want you to take the rest of the day off—with pay.''

Lucille gasped. "Oh, no, I couldn't!''

"Yes, you could. You can. You will.'' Gently, she pushed Lucille toward the door. "I wish I'd thought of it before you came in, but I got too wrapped up in this. So, go. Enjoy yourself.''

"But . . . but what will I do?'' Clearly, Lucille was unprepared for such largess.

"I don't know. Do anything.'' She tried to look stern, but smiled instead. "But do something fun. Promise!''

"But this is so unexpected.''

"All the more reason to go out and enjoy yourself. I know. Call your fellow. Tell him you got an unanticipated day off and you want to play hooky. What man could resist that?"

Lucille shook her head. "Oh, I don't think—"

"I do," she said firmly. "No, go. I've been so busy with this trailer hitch thing that I've neglected my other work. For a change, I've got plenty to keep me busy. I won't even know you're gone."

"Well, thank you."

"Oh, you know what I mean. Now go—before I change my mind. You don't want to miss an opportunity like this, do you? A whole day, just you and your man!"

Two bright spots of color bloomed on Lucille's cheeks. "Mary Nell, about my . . . my man—"

Just then the phone rang. Lucille reached for it automatically, but Mary Nell got there first. "Barrigan Design," she said, and waved her hand at Lucille in a now-get-out-of-here gesture. When Lucille hesitated, she pushed her a little, grinning into the phone. "Of course I remember you, Mr. Withers," she said. "You'd like to set up an appointment? Well, of course, that would be just fine. When would you like to get together?"

She was just making an appointment for later that afternoon when she heard the front door close. She lifted her head. The office was quiet. Lucille had gone—reluctantly, but she had gone. Good. She was glad she'd been able to do that for her loyal secretary. It was little enough, considering all that Lucille had done for her. Smiling to herself, she started collecting the papers she'd spread out. Then she realized she wasn't alone, as she'd thought. Startled, she whirled around. To her amazement, Cal was lounging in the doorway.

"Cal!" she exclaimed. Without realizing it, she put the papers she'd just gathered behind her back. Then she realized how silly that was. Red-faced, she put them back on the table. "I'm sorry. You startled me."

"I didn't mean to. The waiting room was empty when I came in, so I called out, but I guess you didn't hear me."

"I was on the phone."

"I'm sorry, I didn't mean to interrupt."

"You didn't interrupt. I was just surprised to see you. What are you doing here?"

When he smiled, she flushed again. That sounded so ungracious, but it was too late now. "I had an early appointment in the area," he said, "and I thought I'd stop by. We still have to decide on the times of the next field trials."

"Oh, that's right." Why was she disappointed? Deciding it didn't matter, she went on quickly, "When did you have in mind?"

But instead of answering, he glanced around the computer room. "I've never seen your office," he said. "Do you mind if I come in?"

What was the matter with her? Where were her manners? Embarrassed again, she gestured. "I'm sorry, please do. I . . . I was just about to make some coffee. Would you like some?"

He was looking around with undisguised interest. When his glance came to the computer screen and the drawing there, he shook his head. "Maybe I'd better not. I see you're working."

Reaching out, she pressed a key and the design disappeared. She wasn't sure why she didn't want him to see what she had done. Since he wasn't working on the same project, what did it matter? But she couldn't help herself, and when she saw his expression, she felt like an idiot. "Oh, that," she said nervously. "I was just fooling around with some designs. Would you like that coffee?"

He took his eyes away from the computer. "If you're going to have some. Would you like some help?"

"No, no, I can manage," she said quickly. She had to get away from him, cool down her hot cheeks. She was making a fool of herself, and she didn't know why. What was he to her? A rival, that was all. "How do you like it?"

"Oh, black is fine."

"All right," she said uneasily. "I'll be right back."

She returned in record time with two mugs and saw that he was bending over the computer, gazing at one of the CAD menus she'd left on the screen. Hearing her come in again, he straightened and said, "That looks like some system you've got."

Because she still felt embarrassed about protecting her design, she handed him one of the mugs and replied, "One day it will be better."

"With 3-D, you mean?"

"Yes, with 3-D," she said, avoiding his eyes. He was having that effect on her again, and she began to wish she hadn't given Lucille the day off. She needed another person around, someone to break the tension she was already starting to feel—the same tension she always felt whenever she and Cal were together. What was it about him, she wondered despairingly, that made her want to drop all the pretense, stop playing the game that hid how she really felt? But she couldn't just admit how attracted she was to him, how much she wanted to step into the circle of his arms and have his head slowly bend to hers....

"That's quite an investment," he said.

Blinking, she jerked her thoughts away from the tantalizing images that were filling her mind. *An investment?* she thought, trying to remember what they'd been talking about. She saw him looking at the computer, and it came back to her. Oh yes: 3-D CAD. Of course. What else would they talk about?

"But worth it," she said.

He sipped his coffee. "I suppose."

That was better. With a subtle challenge like that, she was on much safer ground. Recognizing their old argument about CAD versus hand drafting, she issued a challenge of her own.

"You don't think that the ability to draw any three-dimensional object with shaded surfacing and a minimum of sixteen colors is worth it?" she asked silkily.

He shrugged. "I just meant that very little of my professional training focused on three-dimensional geometry."

She was about to make a sharp remark to that when she reconsidered. It suddenly occurred to her that maybe she should try to get along with him—until the field trials were over with, that was. It would make things easier.

So instead of being sarcastic, as she'd intended, she said, "Mine didn't focus on it, either, but I was still fascinated by the process. You've seen it in action, of course."

"Yes, I've seen it," he said with another shrug. But she saw the shadow that had flitted across his face, and suddenly she wasn't so sure he felt as casual about the computer as he pretended.

"My system is up," she said. "Would you like to try it?"

The instant the words were out of her mouth, she regretted them. She hadn't meant to say them at all; what with all her inner turmoil, she'd intended to cut short the conversation as quickly as possible and show him out. Already, despite her vow to not let herself be affected by him, she could feel herself being drawn to him. She was having trouble keeping her glance away from his eyes, his face... his hands.

"Are you serious?" he asked.

She couldn't back down now; it would not only be rude, but ungracious. *I can handle this,* she told herself, and gestured toward the chair in front of the console. "There it is. Help yourself."

Slowly, he turned and looked at the screen. Then his glance came back to her. She could tell he wanted to try; she knew by the longing in his eyes, and suddenly she didn't feel so superior anymore. They were professionals, colleagues, peers. Couldn't they enjoy at least one facet of this curious and strained relationship? They both loved their work; they'd talked about it previously. Why shouldn't she share the process with him? What would it harm? Did they have to be adversaries *all* the time?

"Here," she said, setting aside her coffee cup. She took the chair herself. "Let me show you." Realizing how that sounded, she looked up at him. "Do you mind?"

He hesitated. But she could see the interest in his eyes, and before he answered, she turned back to the screen, her fingers already flying over the keys. "It won't take a minute to set this up," she murmured, concentrating. "Why don't you pull up another chair?"

He did, surprising her by saying, "Why don't you start at the beginning?"

She looked at him in surprise. "Do you have time?" she asked, then gave an embarrassed laugh. "The reason I ask is that once I get going on this, I'm liable to talk your arm off. As my sister says, I tend to get a little obsessed with the subject of CAD."

"Fire away," he said, smiling. "I've got plenty of time."

He was so close she could see those flecks of black in his blue eyes, so close she caught another whiff of his after-shave. Then that dimple flashed in his cheek, and she turned hastily back to the screen. Her thoughts were all ajumble, and she wished now she hadn't started up. She hadn't expected to be so breathlessly aware of him sitting beside her. To her dismay, her fingers shook slightly when she started to type. Fiercely, she pulled herself together and tried to think how to begin. She didn't want to patronize him by starting too simply, but would a little background hurt? She didn't know, but she had to say something, and so she began.

"I've tried several methods of communicating with the computer," she said, resolutely keeping her eyes fixed on the screen, "and like everyone else, I guess, I've finally come up with a combination of devices that's comfortable for me. In the beginning, I used the digitizer for large drawings—" she pointed to what looked like a large plastic pad she kept to one side of the computer "—but I soon found out that it's no more accurate than manual tracing, and of course, it won't correct dimension errors, so I rarely use it now. I prefer the mouse—" she smiled briefly, remembering Anson McAdam's puzzled reaction to the term during that first interview "—because it's easier to reach for than a stylus, especially when I'm doing a lot of keyboard input."

He looked at her intently. "Was it difficult learning to use the mouse after a good old 3H pencil?"

She laughed. "It was different, at first, I have to admit. As you know, when you draw by hand, you get to know instinctively when to use what pencil to get a desired result. Suddenly, with a mouse, you have this little square box. But—" her eyes twinkled despite herself "—when you see what it can do, I promise you, you'll realize that pencils are about to become obsolete. Here, let me show you."

They both turned toward the screen again as she explained what she was about to do. "When we draw a circle manually, we do it with a compass or a template," she said, "but with CAD, we can draw a circle with the graphics cursor by entering points to define the circle mathematically. Like this...."

Using the mouse, she moved the cursor "cross hairs" to a point on the screen and pressed a point entry key. Then she moved it to another area and pressed that point entry. Moving to the keyboard, she pressed the function key that caused an arc to be drawn from the first point to the end point. Before her eyes, a perfect circle appeared. Cal shook his head.

"What'll they think of next?" he said.

She laughed, appreciating the comment. She was still amazed at the process, and she used it every day. "Of course, some shapes require you to enter more than two points," she said. "The ellipse, for one—a polygon, for another."

"I think I could handle that."

She moved her chair out of the way. "Here, you try."

She'd half expected him to make some excuse, but when he eagerly took over in her place, she was amused—then impressed at his quick grasp of the technique. In seconds, he was creating and dissolving various images. The cursor flew over the screen, guided by the mouse and his own imagination. He was so intent on what he was doing that he seemed to have forgotten her, and as she sat and watched him instead of the images that appeared on the screen, she wondered why, since he was so obviously enthralled with CAD, he hadn't switched over to computers long ago. Then she told herself it was none of her business. Besides, she was almost glad he hadn't; if he'd had CAD, the competition between them would have been that much more difficult. *Difficult,* she repeated with an inward smile, *but not impossible.*

But that thought reminded her of the rivalry between them, and she decided they'd spent enough time on this demonstration.

"Well, what do you think?" she asked.

She was almost sorry she had interrupted him. Blinking, he turned from the screen, as though it were an effort to return to the real world. "That's some system, all right."

"And it's not even 3-D."

"Yeah, right," he said, glancing back at the screen. Then he pushed himself from the desk. "Thanks for the demo. Another few minutes, and you might have had a convert."

She couldn't resist. "I thought I already had one."

"No soap. I've still got boxes of pencils."

"Too bad."

"Hey, someone has to keep the old techniques alive."

"Better you than me."

"We'll see."

"Yes, that's right," she said, knowing she couldn't continue to prolong the conversation or she'd weaken. Already, despite her best resolve, she felt shaky; she knew that the longer he stayed, the worse it would get. She'd managed to get this far without betraying herself, and as she led the way out to the reception area and then, pointedly, to the front door, she told herself to hold on just a little longer. Soon he'd be gone, and then she could collapse. Then she remembered why he'd come in the first place, and she turned to him brightly. "So, what about those field tests?"

He looked blank for a moment, but she was too busy trying to corral her turbulent emotions to notice his hesitation. "I think you should decide," he said finally.

She could hardly think straight, much less make a decision. His presence seemed overpowering, and as he stood there, impossibly tall, too big for her to open the door and shove outside, she could feel herself start to weaken, after all. Hastily, she said, "It doesn't matter to me."

"I don't care, either," he said. "You decide."

Achingly aware of his eyes on her, she tried to counter the sensations bombarding her by wondering why he was looking at her like that. She didn't dare return the glance; she wasn't sure, even after her admirable performance at the computer, that she could trust herself. She'd never felt the presence of any man so keenly, and she stepped back, as though another foot or two of space was going to confer immunity, and said the first thing that came into her head.

"All right, then, I've got the design for my project. All I have to do is get the specs to the fabricator. I'll send them out with my secretary this morning...." Remembering that she'd given Lucille the day off, she nearly groaned. Well, she could always send them out by courier or take them over on her lunch hour. She'd get them out there *somehow.* "I'll ask if they can have them ready by the end of the week. How's that?"

"That soon, eh?" he said, still staring down at her. Why was he looking at her like that? "You must be anxious to get this over with."

Oh, he didn't know, she thought in despair, and said, "Not really. I just thought that the sooner we got this settled, the better."

"All right, if that's the way you feel."

It wasn't the way she felt at all. Part of her wanted the competition to last forever, because that would mean that she could continue to see him. But another part was sounding shrill alarms, telling her to get it over with, to get him out of her life, to get on with her business. That was what she had intended to do, had promised herself she'd do. After struggling so hard to get going, she *couldn't* forget her goals; she'd wasted too much time in the past as it was. Never mind that she was in danger of losing her head completely over this man; somehow she'd just have to control herself.

"Well, I think it would be best, don't you?" she said.

When he hesitated, she nearly flung herself at him, telling him what a liar she was, confessing she didn't think that at all. But she wouldn't let herself do it. Stiffly, she stood there, just wishing he'd go.

"It probably would be," he said after a moment, but as she held her breath, praying he'd leave, he looked down at her again. "Mary Nell . . ."

Even the way he said her name made her feel weak. She didn't want to hear what he had to say, and so she said quickly, "I'm really sorry, Cal, but I've got a lot of work to do. You understand, don't you?"

He stiffened. "Yes, I understand," he said, suddenly cold. "Have your secretary call the office to firm up that date, will you?"

She didn't trust herself to say more than a weak, "Sure. As soon as I know."

He walked away without looking back. She stood there a moment, watching him go, willing herself to stay where she was when she wanted to run to him and throw herself into his arms. She waited a tense few moments, but when he turned the corner without another glance, she let the door swing shut. Stumbling back to her office, she threw herself down behind the desk and put her head in her hands. What was happening to her? She felt exhausted, as though she'd come through a storm.

Unfortunately, she couldn't afford the luxury of feeling sorry for herself. After a few minutes, she forced herself to her feet and went back to the computer. How ironic it was that after so many weeks of wishing for work, she had more at the moment than she knew what to do with. When she wanted to go home and fall into bed and pull the covers over her head, she had two deadlines to meet, Mr. Withers to see this afternoon and those specs to take out to McAdam's on the way back. Trying not to think what the coming weekend might bring, she bleakly got to work.

"NICE TO SEE you," Brad called out when Cal got back to the office. "I'm glad to see you finally decided to come to work."

"Lay off, will you?" Cal growled, not in the mood to joke around. Wishing he'd never given in to impulse and dropped by—*dropped by?* He'd deliberately made a detour—to see Mary Nell, he went down the hall toward the drafting room, hoping Brad wouldn't follow. He felt he'd made a fool of himself yet again, and he wanted to be alone. To think about what a jerk he was? His jaw tightened. To get her out of his mind, once and for all. *Damn* that woman. He didn't know why he'd gone to see her.

Yes, he did. He'd had some juvenile fantasy of asking her if they could just start over. He'd thought about it all weekend—in fact, that was all he'd thought about: Mary Nell. That, and what a mess he'd made of things. He'd decided by the morning that what he wanted was a chance to start anew, to wipe the slate clean and just forget everything that had happened between them already. He wanted to be like two people meeting each other for the first time, deciding they liked each other, agreeing to go out and have a little fun. Something *simple*. None of this heavy stuff, like that out-of-control feeling he had when he was with her. Just...fun. They'd have a few laughs, maybe pay another visit to McNalley's so he could hear her play the piano again. But that was all. He'd planned to say—

He hadn't been sure what he planned to say. Maybe he'd hoped he'd think of something when he got there. He frowned. He'd seen how well *that* had worked out, hadn't he? He'd lost all sense of purpose the instant he'd walked in the door. Damn it all! He didn't know what it was, but he wasn't himself when he was around her. All she had to do was look at him or smile or tilt her head in that way she had, and whatever resolve he'd had flew out the window. He'd never been this way with women, and he couldn't understand it. Where was his sophistication, his urbanity, his savoir faire?

Plopping into a chair, he closed his eyes. What was happening to him? He didn't have time for this; he didn't want it. Even if she was interested—which he was sure she wasn't—he had no intention of getting involved again. He had to straighten out too many other things in his life. This contract with McAdam was one. Long ago—in another lifetime, it seemed—before he'd met Mary Nell and jumped on this merry-go-round, he'd had plans. Big plans. He was going to snag this recreational account, get the business back on its feet again and...take off.

He grimaced. Why did that seem so shallow to him now?

Annoyed, he defended his position to himself. It wasn't shallow; it was good sense. He and Davy weren't interested in the same things anymore, businesswise, that was— maybe even beyond that. It wasn't that they'd grown apart, exactly; it was that their lives seemed to be taking different directions. He wanted to expand into industrial design, while his partner was happy playing around with nuts and bolts. And as for being shallow, he wasn't going to abandon his friend—just dissolve the partnership.

He grimaced again. That didn't sound any better. His head in his hands, he slumped over the desk.

"You look like you've seen better days, buddy. Want to talk about it?"

He looked up. Brad was in the doorway, and when Cal saw his genuinely anxious expression, he couldn't tell him to go away. Instead, he gestured for him to come in. Brad didn't wait for a second invitation. With a strong push of his hands, he rolled the chair up to the desk.

"You're certainly in the best of moods lately," Cal said sourly. "Maybe you should bottle it and sell it to me."

"The way you've been acting, I would if I could. Anything you want to talk about?"

There were a lot of things he wanted to talk about, but he didn't seem able to do so yet. He shook his head. "No, it'll work out."

"Suit yourself," Brad said, and hesitated. Then he said, "As long as you're not talking, do you mind listening to me? I've got something I've been waiting to get off my chest, and now's as good a time as any, I guess."

The prospect of listening to someone else's problems instead of endlessly reviewing his own seemed infinitely appealing at the moment. Leaning back so that his chair was balanced on its two rear legs, Cal said, "Fire away. I'm all ears."

Now that Brad had the stage, he hesitated again. Finally he said, "You know I've been dating Lucy—"

"Lucy, is it now?" Cal said teasingly. "Things must be getting serious."

"Stop kidding around," Brad said. "And for your information, it is. Getting serious, I mean. No, don't say anything yet. Just let me say what I have to say. We've been wanting to tell both of you, but the time hasn't been right."

"Tell . . . both . . . of us?"

Brad flushed. "Yeah, you—and Mary Nell."

"What does Mary Nell have to do with this? I thought we were talking about Lucille . . . Lucy."

"We were. We are," Brad said, and muttered something. "Oh, the hell with it. I'll just say it right out. Lucy is Mary Nell's secretary. We wanted to tell you before, but—"

Cal's chair crashed to the floor. "What?"

"Now, don't go off half-cocked. We meant to tell you, but—"

"What do you mean, you *meant* to tell me? Why didn't you?"

"Don't get mad—"

"Mad! You *knew* Lucille was working for Mary Nell, and you didn't tell me? Why would you keep something like that a secret?" Cal leaned over the desk, breathing hard. "When did you find out?"

Brad looked flustered. "Well, almost from the beginning, but—"

"From the *beginning*!"

"You're making it sound like—"

"Like what? God, I don't believe this! You knew and you didn't tell me? What kind of friend are you?"

"Why are you so upset?" Brad demanded. "You're acting like Lucy is a spy or something!"

Cal had shot to his feet; now he whirled around. "How do you know she's not? Don't you think it was a little too convenient that the secretary of our rival for this big contract just happened to fall into your lap? And that the two of you started seeing each other? *And that you didn't tell me?*"

Now Brad was angry. "I'm a little confused here, buddy," he said tightly. "Are you upset at the fact that Lucy is Mary Nell's secretary, or that I'm going out with her, or that you didn't know we were getting serious? Which one is it—or is it all three? For crying out loud, you're acting like we've been passing state secrets or something!"

"Don't be ridiculous! It's just that this contract is important, and we need every edge we can get! How do we know what things your Lucy has been telling Mary Nell? What have you told her?"

"Nothing! But what difference would it make if I did? For Pete's sake, this is just a stupid recreational gear account we're talking about. It's not a direct line to the Pentagon! What's the matter with you? Where's your perspective?"

The thought flashed through Cal's mind that Brad was right and he was wrong, and that he was making too big a deal out of this because he was really upset about other things. But he was too proud to back down now, and he shot back furiously, "Where's yours? If you'd get your head out of the clouds for a minute, you'd realize that McAdam *is* a big account. We need it, and I want it!"

Brad looked at him a moment longer, his jaw working. "Has it occurred to you," he said finally, "that you might have that backward? Maybe the truth is that *you* want that account more than *we* really need it."

"That's bull—"

For once, Brad overrode him. His eyes hard, he went on, "And while you're wondering, ask yourself why you never consulted me about taking this on. Who's keeping secrets from whom, old buddy, huh?"

"Now, just wait a—"

But with one swift, powerful motion of his hands, Brad spun his wheelchair around and sailed out, slamming the door behind him. Wondering how his friend had managed that little feat, Cal started to follow, then stopped, muttering. Maybe it was better if they both took a while to cool off, he decided, and went back to his desk. Righting the chair he'd flung down during his tantrum, he threw himself into it again. What else could go wrong today?

He found out an hour or so later when a client called to tell him he wasn't pleased with a circuit design that had been sent more than two weeks earlier. That meant that he had to redraw the entire thing in meticulous detail, a chore that never failed to bore him to death. Normally Brad took over the repetitive tasks, but after their blazing argument, he was not going to ask his partner for anything—not today. Brad had stayed in his own office since he'd stormed out, and as Cal resignedly sat down at the drafting board and pulled a fresh sheet of paper toward him, he was irritated all over again at the thought of how easy the job would be with Mary Nell's computer. That reminded him of Mary Nell, which led to thinking of her secretary and then full circle to the argument with Brad. Feeling put-upon and thoroughly out of sorts, he grabbed a pencil and started to draw the first line. The lead broke.

"Damn it all," he muttered, and picked up another. But the line he drew wasn't right, and the next one was off, as well. Exasperated, he threw everything down and got up. He couldn't concentrate with the fight hanging over his head. He'd go down the hall, stick his nose into Brad's office, apologize and get back to work. He jerked open the door.

Brad was on the other side, his hand raised to knock. They stared at each other.

"I was just coming—"

"I wanted to—"

They each spoke at the same time, stopped and gestured for the other to continue. Both fell silent, and Cal decided he'd go first. His attempt at apology was less than graceful, but he got it out.

"I'm sorry, Davy," he growled. "I didn't mean to say all those things. It was stupid."

Looking relieved, Brad said, "And I'm sorry I said all that about the new account. I know it's important. I just got carried away, I guess."

"I did, too. And I don't care if you go out with Lucille... Lucy. In fact, I'm glad you've found someone."

"I'm glad to hear you say that," Brad said calmly. "Because I was just talking to her, and we thought it would be a good idea... sort of clear the air... if we all had dinner together. How about if you and Mary Nell come over to my place Friday night?"

Cal backed up a step. He was sorry they'd had a fight, but he didn't think that was such a good idea. "Oh, I don't know—"

Brad grinned. "I'll cook."

It was a tempting offer; one of Brad's hobbies was cooking. But Cal still didn't want to go. Then he thought of a way to get out of it gracefully. "I don't mind, but I doubt that Mary Nell will—"

"Oh, Lucy's already talked to her," Brad said, and peered keenly up at him. "She says she'll go if you will."

Was this what they meant when they said someone was hoisted on his own petard? Cornered, he seemed to have no choice. But that didn't mean he had to give in graciously. "All right. But I can't promise how the evening will turn out. Mary Nell and I aren't exactly—"

"Just be yourself," Brad said, and then winked. "If you can remember what that's like."

CHAPTER TWELVE

"WHY ARE YOU SO uptight?" Stacy asked as Mary Nell got ready for the dinner party Friday night. Stacy was home for the weekend and was sitting on the bed, watching her sister search through her dresser drawers.

"I'm not uptight," Mary Nell muttered, seizing a belt that looked promising, holding it up, realizing it wasn't what she wanted and then tossing it down impatiently again. She started to riffle through the rest of the drawers. "Where *is* that stupid thing? I know I put it somewhere!"

"What are you looking for?"

Slamming the last dresser drawer shut, she straightened and let out an exasperated sigh. "Never mind. It wasn't important. I'll just wear something else."

Rolling her eyes, Stacy murmured, "And you said you weren't nervous."

"I'm not!" she insisted, although she was. "I just wish I'd never said I'd go to this dinner party, that's all!"

"Why did you agree to go?"

"Because Lucille surprised me, that's why. And because I didn't think Cal would. I didn't know what to say when she invited me. The only answer I could think of was that I'd go if Cal would. I never dreamed he'd take me up on it!" she exclaimed impatiently. "But of course, that's just like him."

"Maybe he was just as startled as you were to find out that his partner was dating your secretary."

"Yes, well, that did come as a bit of a shock," Mary Nell said acidly, remembering how she'd just sat there, her mouth agape, when she'd found out. Lucille had come in to work later that day to confess; she still wasn't sure how she felt about it.

"Well, at least she told you about it," Stacy offered.

"Finally."

"Better late than never."

"Better never at all!"

"I don't understand why you're so upset. What difference does it make if she's dating someone from a rival agency? You trust her, don't you?"

"Of course I trust her! It's just that I...I was surprised, that's all."

"I don't understand how you didn't know. I mean, you and Cal have talked about his partner, haven't you?"

"Yes, but he called him Davy. How was I to know that Brad and this Davy person were one and the same?"

"That would make it a little confusing, I guess. But still, I think it's great that Lucille is finally dating someone. And you did say that it sounds like she and Brad are getting pretty serious."

Mary Nell didn't answer for a moment. Finally, she nodded. "Yes, I am glad about that."

But her expression was suddenly sad when she turned to the mirror and picked up a hairbrush. Behind her, Stacy said softly, "Mary Nell?"

"What?"

"You look so sad. What's wrong?"

With a sigh, Mary Nell put down the hairbrush. "Oh, sometimes I just hate myself."

Surprised, Stacy asked, "But why?"

She made herself say it. "Because I'm jealous, that's why."

"What? Of Lucille?"

"No, not that, exactly," she said unhappily. Now she wasn't sure what she meant. "I'm happy for Lucille, I really am. If you could have seen her face when she was telling me about Brad..." She sighed again. "I knew she was nervous about finally telling me who he really was, and I knew she felt badly about having deceived me, but even so, I could see how happy she was, how much in love."

"And you want that, too."

This was getting too heavy. Mary Nell made herself laugh—or tried to. "Don't we all?" she said lightly.

Stacy looked thoughtful. "Someday, yes. But now?"

She took a breath. "You're right. There's a time for everything, isn't there?" She forced another laugh. "Listen to me. I sound like a real romantic, don't I?"

Stacy smiled. "You are a romantic."

"But I don't want to be!"

She didn't realize how forlorn she sounded until Stacy laughed.

"I know you too well, sis," she said. "Despite all this show about how annoyed you are with Lucille, you aren't really upset that she kept Brad's identity from you until now. Be honest. Don't you think it's just the least little bit romantic?"

She couldn't give in that easily. Stubbornly, she said, "She could have told me before now!"

"With the way you and Cal go at it tooth and nail?" Stacy said. "She was probably afraid to!"

"I don't believe that."

"Think about it."

"I don't have to think about it. There's nothing between me and Cal—"

"Oho, and pigs fly!" Stacy said, genuinely amused. "Come on, Mary Nell, who are you trying to kid?"

"Now you're the one who's being romantic," she said. But she could feel her cheeks warming, and she turned quickly back to the dresser. "Now, do you mind? I've got to finish getting ready."

"You go ahead," Stacy said, still laughing. "I'll wait downstairs for Cal. I want to hear what he thinks about Brad and Lucille."

"Don't you dare ask him!" she cried. But Stacy was already on the way downstairs. Sighing in exasperation, she glanced at the bed, where Stacy had been sitting cross-legged, and saw the belt she'd been looking for. "Oh, for—" she muttered, and snatched it. She was just buckling it when the doorbell rang. Not trusting her sister in the mood she was in, Mary Nell grabbed her sweater and flew downstairs.

Despite her haste, she was too late to intercept. When she heard voices in the living room, she knew Stacy had taken Cal in there, and she headed in that direction. She paused on the threshold just as her sister was saying, "Mary Nell is still getting ready. Can I get you anything while you wait, Cal?"

"That depends on how long the wait is going to be," he said in the deep voice that sent a thrill through Mary Nell despite herself. He sounded amused, and Stacy laughed.

"Knowing Mary Nell, it could be quite a while."

"In that case..."

Listening as they tossed the conversational ball back and forth, Mary Nell wondered wistfully why such easy banter with Cal seemed denied to her. She'd never been able to tease him the way Stacy was doing, and he'd never acted with her the way he was acting with her sister. They were always so tense when they were together. She constantly felt as though she were on some kind of emotional tightrope, afraid to take the next step because she might fall off.

She'd only really felt at ease with him when he had come to the office. She had actually enjoyed those few moments they had worked on the computer. That had been the only time she'd felt that they had been able to set aside the multilayered competition and just...enjoy being together.

Or maybe they'd just enjoyed putting down the swords for a moment, she thought pensively. Acting as professionals, they were on safe ground. There was no danger talking about work. It was only when they strayed from that narrow path that they started playing with fire.

Wishing she'd remembered that earlier—before she'd made the mistake of saying she'd go to the dinner party only if Cal did—she realized she'd stood there long enough. Clearing her throat, she came into the living room.

"Oh, you're here," Stacy said, winking. "We were beginning to think you'd gotten lost."

"Or had decided not to come," Cal said, his eyes following her as she came up to them.

The way he was looking at her made her even more nervous than she already was, and she knew she sounded too brusque when she said, "I couldn't do that. If your partner and my secretary were kind enough to invite us to dinner, it would be rude not to show up."

"Er...I think I've got some studying to do," Stacy said hastily. Moving slightly behind Cal, she frowned fiercely at Mary Nell, signaling her to lighten up. Mary Nell saw the gesture—how could she avoid the mugging pantomime?—but she tossed her head. She knew what she was doing. Or hoped she did. She had to keep the evening on an even keel.

"You look very nice tonight," Cal said when they were on their way. "I like that dress."

She was wearing a knit jersey with a scooped neck and a swirly skirt that skimmed her knees. The belt she'd found earlier hugged her waist, and because he was so tall, she wished she'd worn higher heels. "Thank you," she said, and had to add, "I wasn't really sure what to wear. I've never met Brad." She gave him a cool look. "Or Davy, as the case may be."

He looked a little grim. "Yes. If I'd known the confusion that would cause, I would have abandoned the childhood nickname long ago."

"I suppose it doesn't matter now."

"No," he agreed. "I guess not. Still, you'll like him—by whatever name."

Thinking they were safe as long as they were talking about someone else, she said, "I'm sure I will. Lucille certainly seems to, and she's an excellent judge of character."

His eyes twinkling, he glanced at her. "I guess I won't ask her what she thinks of me."

She hid a smile. "I promise, I won't ask her, either."

"So," he said after a silence, "what did you think when you heard the news?"

The question didn't register for a moment. She'd been preoccupied with wondering why she felt so tense. It wasn't that she was nervous at the thought of meeting Brad or about his being in a wheelchair. It was something else entirely, and when she glanced sideways at Cal, she had to admit that he was the reason she felt so jittery. He always made her feel that way. Only with him was she never sure what to say.

"About Brad and Lucille?" she asked.

"No, about Burns and Allen," he said, and grinned when she flashed him an annoyed look. "Sorry. Feeble joke."

"Yes, it was," she agreed absently. She was debating how to answer. Too embarrassed to tell him what her real reaction had been—how, once she'd gotten over the initial shock, she'd felt so betrayed she'd practically accused Lucille of sabotage before she calmed down and realized how ridiculous she was being—she countered with, "What did you think?"

He seemed uncomfortable, too. "I don't know. Not too much, I guess. After all, we're all adults, and it's not—" he hesitated, as though remembering something he would rather not have remembered "—as though we have anything to hide."

"No," she said, avoiding looking at him. "It isn't."

"After all, we're both working on different projects for McAdam."

"Yes, that's right."

"So, it really doesn't matter if we're all one big happy family."

"I suppose not."

He was silent. After a moment, he said, "It does make things a little awkward though, doesn't it?"

"It does," she said, and glanced out the window. "But I don't know why."

He returned his attention to his driving. "I don't, either. It's not as if it's anything to be upset about."

"No, you're right," she said, feeling more uncomfortable by the minute. Their conversation was so stilted that she was wondering what they were really trying to say, and wouldn't. "In fact, I'm glad Lucille finally found someone she likes."

He kept his eyes straight ahead. "And I have to admit it's done a world of good for Davy—for Brad. I was beginning to think he'd never go out again. After Beth left—"

"Beth?"

His jaw tightened. "Beth was... How do they say it now? Oh, the significant other. He would have married her, but then came the accident, and soon after that, she split."

Mary Nell could tell by his tone how he felt, and she didn't know whether to pursue it or not. But she had to say, softly, "But you stayed."

He shrugged. "He's my friend," he said simply.

She shot him a quick, admiring look. "It sounds like you're the friend. He's lucky to have someone like you."

She had embarrassed him. "Yeah, well, we still get into hassles now and then," he said. "That van of his was one. The doctor and I had a hell of a time convincing him to even try it, but I knew that once he did, he wouldn't give it up."

Intrigued, she asked, "How did you convince him to try it?"

He laughed shortly. "I didn't really convince him. I sort of blackmailed him into it."

"You did? How?"

"I picked him up in it one day. I'd already stowed my bike inside, and I drove us over to one of those picnic areas at Point Defiance Park and told him to drive us home again. When he said he wouldn't, I got my bike out and started back."

"You left him there?" She was horrified.

"Yeah, I did," he said calmly. "I knew he could get back if he wanted to. All he had to do was put the van in gear and drive."

Her eyes were wide. "What happened?"

He grinned at her. "He's here, isn't he?"

She sat back. "I don't think I could have done something like that."

"You could if he was your friend, and you were desperate enough."

Doubtfully, she shook her head. "I suppose so, but—"

"No 'buts' about it," he said. "You could do it if you had to—if you wanted to." He gave her an unreadable look. "I think you could do anything you put your mind to."

Now he had embarrassed her. Quickly, she said, "Lucille told me about the van. She was so excited when Brad let her drive it."

This time his look was one of surprise. "He let her drive it?" he said, and shook his head. "Boy, he must be in love. Once he took command, no one was allowed to touch that van but him!"

"He sounds as possessive as that boy in high school I told you about," she said teasingly.

He grinned at her. "Well, you know how men are. Some of them are as possessive about their cars as some of you women are about your computers."

"That's unfair!" she protested immediately. "I let you do as much as you wanted with mine."

He pointed a finger. "As long as you were there to stand guard."

"I left the room to get coffee," she countered.

"So you did," he conceded. "In fact, you were more than generous with your time. Maybe someday I'll be able to return the favor."

"You're going to invest in a CAD system?" Remembering the quick facility he'd displayed with her computer, she didn't know whether to be surprised or dismayed.

He hesitated, but barely. "No, I meant that maybe someday I'll let you drive this car."

She burst into relieved laughter. "Thanks, but I'll pass."

"You don't know what you're missing."

"I'll take my chances."

"Will you?" he said, suddenly serious. He had stopped the car in front of a house and turned to look at her. His body was half-turned in the seat, and his left arm was casually resting on the steering wheel. But there was nothing casual about the look in his eyes, and she knew that she'd been fooling herself about playing this with a light hand. Even though they'd been successful at keeping the conversation going, she had been aware the entire time of undercurrents, tension, an unidentifiable awkwardness she was sure was there because neither of them were saying what they really felt. The whole drive they'd been using words to fill up the silence—and the fear of committing themselves. Now, as she looked into his eyes, shadowed as they were by the dim interior of the car, she saw that he'd felt it, too, and she knew then that he'd been trying just as hard as her to keep up the pretense. In a flash, she understood also that he hadn't meant to say what he had just now, but since he had, he was glad. Was she? She didn't know. Maybe she didn't want to know.

"I . . . I don't know what you mean," she said, faltering.

"Yes, you do," he said softly, and reached for her.

From the first touch of his hands on her arms, she knew it was no use pretending any longer. She'd wanted this to happen from the moment she'd seen him in her living room tonight; she'd been fighting the desire to touch him during the entire drive, and now, despite everything, she turned eagerly to him, wanting his embrace, seeking his mouth with hers.

He didn't disappoint her. When he took her in his arms, his eagerness matched her own, and even in the awkward confines of the car, his embrace was everything she could have asked for, and more. His kiss was nothing tentative, and as she responded from some inner core to the delicious feeling of his lips on hers, she knew that he'd been just as anxious as she'd been for this, and that he'd been holding himself back too.

"This is a mistake," he murmured after a moment.

Lost in the sensation of being in his arms, she didn't answer right away. He didn't let her go, but held her close to him, his mouth moving against her hair. She looked up at him, her voice a whisper. "How can you be sure?"

"Because this wasn't supposed to happen," he said, tightening his arms around her, pulling her closer.

"I know," she said, and nothing more.

He touched her cheek with a fingertip, as though marveling at the feel of her skin, and she smiled softly and leaned her face against his hand. She wanted this moment to go on forever. The car seat creaked as he shifted his position so that he could sit back and still keep one arm around her, and as she rested her cheek against his chest, she could hear his heartbeat, strong and steady. A tiny breeze brought the ghostly scent of jasmine in through the open car window. She'd never cared for the scent before, but now it seemed the rarest perfume.

"I guess we'd better go in," he said.

"I guess we'd better," she murmured.

Neither of them moved. His arm stayed tight around her, and she snuggled closer to his side. Closing her eyes, she let herself savor the moment. She knew it would end soon enough.

It ended just as he put his hand under her chin, gently lifting her face to his again so that he could kiss her once more. Before he could complete the gesture, they both heard the door of the house open and a voice call down to them, "Hey! Are you going to sit out there all night? We've got a dinner going here, remember?"

She glanced in the direction of the house. "I take it that's Brad?"

He scowled. "That's Brad. He always did have good timing."

She laughed. "Well, you did say we should go in."

"Yes, but I didn't mean this instant."

"If we don't, they're going to wonder what we're doing out here."

"You're right," he said resignedly, and reached for the door handle with a sigh.

She smiled as he got out and started around to open the door for her, but as she was adjusting her belt, she suddenly realized the significance of what she'd said, and she paused. What *had* they been doing? she asked herself, her cheeks burning. More to the point, what had *she* been doing? What had happened to all her staunch assurances to herself that no matter what happened, she was not going to get involved? Mortified at the thought of how easily she had melted inside at his kiss, she drew a shuddering breath. It was time—once more, she thought despairingly—to get things under control.

Then he took her hand as they started up the walk, and she realized that it was too soon to hope for control. Despite her resolve, she was more achingly aware of his towering presence beside her than she'd ever been before, and she wanted to stop right there on the walk and be embraced by him once again.

Fortunately, Brad was waiting for them at the door, and introductions distracted her from all the turbulent emotions roiling around inside her. Lucille was nowhere in sight, but by the time Brad backed up his wheelchair with a flourish so they could get past him and inside, she had recovered her poise. She hoped.

"I'm not sure whether to call you Brad or Davy," she said with a smile after he had taken her hand in his and expressed his delight at meeting her at last.

"Oh, call me anything you like," Brad said with a twinkle in his eye. "Cal just uses Davy because it's easy to remember—Davy Davidson. It was funny when we were in grade school. Sounds a little silly now."

"Well, you look like a Brad to me," she said, deciding she already liked him. With those kind eyes and that wonderful smile, she could easily see why Lucille liked him, too.

"That's fine with me," he said. "Come in, come in."

Brad's house was a complete surprise. Lucille had mentioned that her beau liked to fool around with inventions, but she hadn't said that it was more than a hobby. When Mary Nell was ushered inside, she saw that most of the living space was taken up by a vast work/recreation room. Several big tables were pushed against walls, each one cluttered with a profusion of equipment and projects in various stages of completion, and as she gazed around in awe, she thought that she'd never seen anything like it. She turned to Brad, and he smiled at her stunned expression.

"It's a little unorthodox, I admit," he said.

"This is..." she started to say, and waved her hand dazedly.

"Not what you expected?"

"I didn't know what to expect," she said. "Lucille mentioned that you liked to 'tinker,' but she never said anything about this."

"Oh, it's just a little hobby of mine," he said modestly. "You know how us design engineers are. We like to fiddle with things, or else we'd never be in the business."

She looked around again. "I like to 'fiddle,' as you say, but I don't do it like this."

"From what I hear, you do it in a much bigger way. Cal tells me you've got a computer system to keep you company."

"I wouldn't say that it's exactly 'company,'" she said with a laugh. "But it does make work easier at times."

"Still, some things are more satisfying if done by hand."

"That's true," she agreed, and glanced wryly in Cal's direction. "Your partner and I have had several discussions along those lines ourselves."

"I've heard," Brad said, smiling. Then he looked toward a swinging door that was closed, but which she presumed led to the kitchen. "Excuse me for a minute, will you? Lucy is so nervous about this dinner, she's afraid to leave the stove. I think I'll go drag her out."

Lucy? she thought, and said, "Can I help?"

"No, we won't be long. Make yourself at home. Cal knows what most of this stuff is—or is supposed to be. He can show you around if you'd like."

"I'd like that very much," she said, and watched respectfully as he sent his chair spinning halfway across the room with a single shove. Another shove, and he had disappeared into the kitchen. She realized then that the floors were parquet, with no carpeting or rugs that might drag on wheels, and that the big spaces between the pieces of furniture had been designed to accommodate the chair. The place was immaculate; aside from the jumble of equipment scattered along the walls and the piled-up tables, nothing was out of place. Wondering if that was Lucille's doing, she turned inquiringly to Cal.

"Would you like to give me the grand tour?"

"I would, but I don't know where to start. Davy's always working on so many things at once."

"He appears to be quite the inventor."

"He does like to tinker, all right."

"It seems to be more than that. This looks like it could evolve into a full-time occupation."

"Oh, I don't—"

Before he could finish his sentence, they heard a shriek from the kitchen. They were still staring in surprise when the swinging door banged open and a protesting, red-faced Lucille made a grand entrance—on Brad's lap. Looking as though he was having the time of his life, he grinned at Cal and Mary Nell as he held the squirming Lucille firmly in place. "I had to wrestle her into the chair, folks, but here she is—my darlin' lil Lucy."

"Oh, Brad, you say the silliest things!" Lucille said, but behind her furious blush she was laughing, even as she in-effectually slapped his hand. Glancing up at their guests— at Mary Nell frankly staring and Cal looking just as stunned—she gave Brad one last little push and got off the chair. "Hi, Mary Nell," she said, straightening her slacks.

Slacks? Mary Nell thought, not knowing what to think.

Lucille smiled at Cal. "Hello. We've met before."

"We certainly have," Cal said, and glanced uncertainly at Brad. "But you looked...different then."

Mary Nell realized it then herself. "You're not wearing your glasses!" she exclaimed.

Lucille—Lucy?—looked pleased. Blinking rapidly, she giggled and said, "I got contacts today. Do you like them?"

Mary Nell couldn't believe the difference. She'd always known Lucille had beautiful eyes, but without her glasses, her eyes were even more lovely—a spectacular shade of turquoise that changed her entire appearance. Then Mary Nell realized it wasn't only the contacts; in addition to the new hairstyle and the new lenses, her secretary had acquired a new wardrobe, as well. Mary Nell had never seen her in anything other than skirts before, and the slacks were a refreshing change, especially with her slim figure. In fact, Mary Nell thought, surprising herself with a tiny stab of envy, everything about Lucille seemed new and refreshing. Was that why she suddenly felt so out of tune?

But that was absurd. Surely she wasn't jealous of Lucille! She was truly delighted at the changes—she was!

But when she saw the expression on Brad's face as he looked at Lucille and how lovingly Lucille looked back at him, she felt another twinge. She didn't know about Brad, but it was easy to see how Lucille had blossomed in this relationship. Everything about her was different: not only didn't she look the same, she didn't act the same, either. The change had been so gradual that Mary Nell hadn't really noticed it, but when she thought about it, Lucille had more confidence, much more assurance now. She wasn't so retiring, so shy; she was no longer afraid to speak up.

Brad had done that for her, Mary Nell thought. Now that she'd seen them together, it was obvious that the couple were in love; she had never seen two people look so happy, so content, so...so right for each other. And she *was* pleased for them. Why, then, did she feel so...left out?

Brad announced dinner just then, and as Lucille nervously started bustling around, so anxious to make sure that everything was right, Mary Nell looked at Cal. He was watching Brad and Lucille, too, and just for an instant, she glimpsed the same longing in his face that she felt. Her heart skipped a beat. Was he thinking the same thing she was, how wonderful it would be to surrender to a love like that? Troubled, and trying not to show it, she took her place at the table.

But her eyes went unwillingly to Cal again and again during the meal, even as she laughed and chatted and told jokes. No one knew what she was thinking, she was sure. But she wondered, watching the naked love on Lucille's face whenever she looked at Brad, if she'd ever feel that way about a man. Glancing at Cal one more time, with the candlelight glowing on his handsome face, she felt a pang. Why wonder? she asked herself dismally. It was obvious, wasn't it? She already did.

THEY WERE BOTH silent on the way home. She didn't know about Cal, but she was exhausted from all that dissembling; she'd tired herself out trying to be entertaining enough so that no one would guess how depressed she felt. Not that she hadn't enjoyed the evening, she thought hastily; she had. How could she not? Brad and Lucille had done everything possible to make them comfortable. The entire night had been ideal from start to finish. They'd been the perfect hosts.

Maybe that was the problem, she thought dejectedly: they'd been too perfect. At times during the evening—although she was sure both Lucille and Brad would have been horrified if they'd known—she'd nearly felt like an interloper upon such bliss. Watching them together had been almost painful, and during coffee and a flaming cherries jubilee, she hadn't been able to meet Cal's eyes; she hadn't wanted him to guess what she was thinking.

"Well, that was an evening, wasn't it?" Cal said when they were almost at her house. He hadn't said a word until now, and she looked at him in surprise.

"You sound as though you didn't enjoy it."

"Oh, I did," he grumbled. "But it was sort of like being a conductor in the Tunnel of Love, wasn't it?"

She had to smile. "You felt that way, too?"

"If things had gotten any sweeter, we would have had to dig our way out with a spoon."

"But I thought you said you were glad Brad and Lucille had gotten together."

"Oh, I am. I guess. It's just that so much bliss is a little stultifying, don't you think?"

She glanced out the window. "I wouldn't know."

"Oh, yes, you're too busy for involvements."

She looked sharply at him again. "I'm not alone in that, am I? You said the same thing."

He switched on a signal light. "Yeah, I did. And I don't."

"So why do you sound like that?"

"I didn't realize I sounded any particular way."

"Well, you did," she said, folding her arms. "I don't want to talk about this anymore."

"Fine by me."

They drove in silence again until he turned onto her street. Her house was in the middle of the block, and as they came closer, she knew she couldn't just let it go this way. She wasn't being fair; he wasn't at fault because she was petty enough to be envious of a friend's happiness.

"Cal," she started to say.

"Mary Nell," he said at the same time, and stopped and gestured.

She didn't protest. In a small voice, she said, "I'm sorry, Cal. I don't know why I snapped at you like that. It must be that this evening was more of a strain than I realized it would be. I'm a little tired, I guess."

He parked the car and sat there, staring out the windshield for a moment, not saying anything. Finally, he muttered, "I'm sorry, too."

"I did have a good time," she persisted. "And I enjoyed meeting Brad. He's such a nice man, and perfect for Lucille."

"Yes, she's good for him, too," he said, and smiled a sickly little smile. "That much was obvious, I guess."

"Yes, it was," she said, and lapsed into silence. Finally, she realized she couldn't sit in the car all night, so she reached for the door handle. "Well, good night...."

He roused himself from wherever his thoughts had taken him. "I'll walk you to the door."

"No, that's not necessary," she protested, but he was already out of the car.

They went in silence up the walk, and she opened the front door with her key. Then she made the mistake of turning to him. She hadn't meant to, but she heard herself say, "Would you like to come in? I could make coffee."

He hesitated. "No, that's all right. I'd better not. Your sister is home."

She didn't know what made her say it. She should have just stepped inside, said good-night from the other side of the threshold and closed the door. Instead, she uttered a shaky laugh and said, "If you're worried about disturbing her, don't. Attila could drive his Huns through here after she goes to bed, and she wouldn't wake up."

He laughed. "Are you sure?"

She wasn't sure about anything. "Yes, I'm positive."

"Well..."

She stepped back so he could come in. The entry was dark and quiet; Stacy had left only one small lamp burning in the living room beyond. "Let me just find the light switch," she muttered, her hand feeling along the wall. "It should be..."

Before she could reach it, Cal reached for her. Murmuring her name, he turned her toward him. "Mary Nell," he said hoarsely.

It was the longing in his voice that did it. As she looked up into his face, she knew that she hadn't invited him in for coffee. She knew, too, that the evening had been a strain, but not because of Brad and Lucille. It had been a strain denying her feelings for this man. She wanted him, and she couldn't deny it any longer. Everything else was forgotten in that one searing moment when she looked into his shadowed eyes and saw the same desire she felt burning deeply in him. Staring down, he pulled her closer; she went willingly, raising her lips for his kiss. His mouth came down on hers as if he were dying of thirst. They were both trembling so much she wanted to sink down right there on the floor.

"Oh, Cal...." she murmured. Her voice was a gasp; he'd reached for her breast.

"You don't know what you do to me," he groaned, raising his head. His eyes burned from the crushing, passionate kiss.

"Kiss me again," she said, and wrapped her arms around his neck. Once more he brought his mouth to hers and then, with a single movement, he swept her into his arms and held her tightly.

"Where can we go?" he asked.

"Upstairs," she said, and didn't remember her sister until he'd started toward the staircase. But with Cal's strong arms around her, she couldn't think of Stacy; all she could think of was the warmth spreading through her, the throbbing desire to throw off all their clothes and lie together, limb to limb, skin to skin. She wanted to feel all of him next to her; she wanted these sensations never to end.

Her head dropped back, and he kissed the hollow of her throat as he started up the stairs.

He shifted her in his arms, lifting his head so that his burning eyes stared down into hers. "Where?" he asked.

"First door to the right...."

His eyes held hers. "'And straight on till morning,'" he murmured, quoting Peter Pan.

She smiled and sighed and put her arms around his neck. Nestling closer to him, she murmured back, "'And straight on till morning....'"

They didn't have until morning; they only had this night—or part of it. As though they were both aware of that, Cal set her down as soon as they entered her bedroom and pulled her tightly to him again so that she could feel his entire length. A thrill ran through her; she could feel him trembling, too. Already she felt weak, disembodied, out of control. She wanted him as she'd never wanted any other man.

He wanted her, too. She could see it in his face, illuminated from the light of the street lamp that shone through the open window. In that silver glow, his features seemed carved of some beautiful argentine stone. Wonderingly, she raised a hand to touch his cheek, but he grasped her fingers and turned her palm to his mouth, kissing her there and then using his tongue to trace a line to the pulse beating wildly at her wrist. No one had ever done that to her before, and she gasped.

"Oh, Cal...." she whispered, reaching for him. As she pressed her body against him, she could feel his erection against her thigh, and her own body responded in a rush of moist heat that seemed to erupt throughout her entire being. Moaning, she put her head back, and his mouth came down hard on hers. Together, they fell onto the bed.

As his weight pressed her down, she thought that she had made love before, but never like this, never with such fierce hunger or intensity. It seemed, even when she was fully clothed, that every nerve in her body was exposed. His mouth was on her lips, then her eyelids, then her throat, and then the curve of her shoulder as he pulled back her dress. In a frenzy, she ran her hands over his chest, tugging at his shirt buttons, pulling at his belt. In one motion, he got to his feet, pulling her with him. Together, they tugged and pulled at all the restraining clothes until they came together, skin against skin. She could feel his heart pounding inside his chest as her breasts were crushed against him, and she moaned again.

"Let me look at you," he whispered, and held her away, an expression of awe and humility crossing his features as he gazed at her nakedness. After a moment, he raised his eyes to hers. "I knew—" he started to say, and cleared his throat. "I knew you'd be beautiful...."

That did it. With a stifled cry, she flung herself at him, wanting to bury herself in him, wanting him to be buried in her. They clutched at each other in renewed frenzy, falling onto the bed again, oblivious to anything but the sensations flooding them. Everywhere she touched seemed like a revelation; she couldn't get enough of him. He was big and powerful and lean and strong, and in a wild moment, she bit down on his shoulder, only to hear him laugh softly.

"I knew you'd be like this," he said, and laughed again before he rolled on top of her. He looked down into her eyes, suddenly sober. "You..." But words failed him. With a choked sound, he buried his hands in her hair and spread her legs with one muscled thigh. He reached down with one hand to cup her breast, and with the other, caressed the pulsing area between her legs.

That touch aroused her even more, and she wrapped her legs around him, desperately seeking release from the excruciating desire he had evoked. Her hips began to move of their own volition, and when she drew him inside, he groaned and plunged in deeper.

"I wanted to wait...." he gasped.

"So did I...." she said, and gasped herself as he began to move inside her.

Her body was no longer her own; she was possessed by him, filled with him, swept away on such a flood of sensation that she could no longer hold back. Pleasure began as a pinpoint, expanded swiftly and then exploded inside her.

"Come with me!" she cried, clutching him, holding him tighter and tighter. And he came.

They held on together, their bodies straining as the tide claimed them and swept them into oblivion. The feeling was indescribable, the most exquisite she'd ever experienced. She clung to him, wanting never to let him go. An endless time later, he lifted his head, kissed her tenderly and started to roll away from her.

"Where are you going?" she cried, holding him tightly.

He laughed softly. "I thought I was too heavy for you."

"Never," she said fiercely, and wouldn't let him go.

He laughed again and simply turned her with him. Smiling to herself, she nestled in the curve of his shoulder. "That was wonderful," she said, and drifted off to sleep.

Some time later, she heard him moving around and looked up. In the glow of the streetlight, she could see he was already dressed, and she sat up abruptly. "What are you doing?"

Holding his jacket, he came to give her a tender kiss. "Going home," he said. "Your sister's here, remember?"

She put her arms around his neck. "She's a big girl."

He looked down. The sheet had fallen away, and she was bare to the waist. Groaning, he pulled it up again. "Don't tempt me," he said, kissing her again. "I'll see you tomorrow."

"Tomorrow?"

He laughed. "You've forgotten the field test?"

"No, of course not," she said, although until this moment, she had.

He laughed again at her expression, and held her gently back when she started to get up. "Don't. I know the way out. Just go back to sleep...."

More content than she'd been in a long while, she obeyed. And as she snuggled down into tumbled blankets and pillows still warm from his body, she smiled sleepily to herself.

CHAPTER THIRTEEN

MARY NELL WOKE the next morning feeling totally disoriented. When she saw what time it was, she grabbed the alarm clock and shook it. Why hadn't the thing gone off? she wondered, and then she realized she'd been too preoccupied the previous night to set it. Settling back again for just an instant, she allowed herself the luxury of remembering what a wonderful night it had been. Then, still smiling like an idiot, she threw back the covers. If she didn't hurry, she'd be late.

She rushed through a shower, gave her hair a quick brush, tossed on a pair of jeans and a fresh cotton blouse and raced downstairs. When she heard voices coming from the kitchen, she thought Cal had already arrived, until she realized both voices were feminine. It was Lucille, with Stacy. When she came in, they were sitting at the table, having coffee. "Well, hi," she said to her secretary. "I didn't expect to see you this morning."

"I thought I'd come by and wish you luck," Lucille said. "I didn't want to mention the field trial last night. I thought it might be...awkward."

Awkward? Given her state of mind the previous night, she thought, it probably wouldn't have mattered. But she was grateful for such tact, and as she reached for a coffee cup, Mary Nell said, "Thanks. I appreciate that. By the way, I had a good time last night. I really like Brad."

Lucille smiled shyly. "I hoped you would."

Stacy spoke up. "Lucille's been telling me about Brad's house. It sounds like Santa's workshop."

Relieved that no afterglow from her romantic interlude with Cal showed on her face, as she'd thought it would, she brought her coffee to the table. Now that the euphoria had passed, she felt uncomfortable about what had occurred. Where had her resolve gone? What had happened to the woman who wasn't going to get involved?

Deciding that she'd have to think about Cal and all those implications later, she forced her mind onto the conversation. "Santa can't compare," she said. "The whole place is fascinating." She smiled at Lucille. "Almost as fascinating as the change in you."

"Yes, I noticed that right away," Stacy said with a grin. "I think she looks great."

"Oh, stop it," Lucille said. But they could see she was pleased by the pink tint that rose to her cheeks.

Still smiling, Stacy turned to Mary Nell. "So, are you all set up for this test?"

Wondering if she was, she said, "If I'm not now, I'll never be."

"You're not nervous about it, are you?"

Thinking that she was suddenly nervous about a lot of things this morning, but—mercifully—not about the success of her trailer hitch, she shook her head. "No, this time I'm *sure* everything is going to be perfect."

"Of course it is," Lucille said, turning eagerly to Stacy. "Have you seen the new design? It's wonderful. Mary Nell is so clever!"

Stacy winked. "She is, indeed. And no, I haven't seen it. My sister is superstitious about things like that. She never shows me her designs."

"That's not true!" Mary Nell protested. "I would have shown you, except we didn't get the trailer until last night, right before it was time to go home. Cal is supposed to pick it up on the way here. You can see it then."

"Maybe this afternoon, okay?" Stacy said, gulping down the last of her coffee as she left the table. "I've got an early tennis date. I'll talk to you later. It was nice seeing you again, Lucille."

"Thanks. You, too."

"Luck, Mary Nell," Stacy said, giving her a quick hug before she went to the door. "Not that you need it, of course. Say hi to Cal for me."

Lucille smiled as the door slammed behind her. "She hasn't changed at all, has she?"

Looking wry, Mary Nell shook her head. "Not much, I grant you. Do you want some more coffee?"

"No, thanks, I've really got to be going." She grimaced. "It's Saturday—cleaning house day."

"Thanks for coming by, then. And I really did enjoy the dinner party last night, Lucille."

"I'm so glad. I hoped you would. Brad and I felt so awful about keeping our relationship from you and Cal. We never intended to, but then, when things started getting...serious—" She broke off, flushing becomingly. "Well, anyway, I'm glad it's out in the open now."

"So am I."

Lucille looked anxious. "You do like him, don't you?"

"Brad? Of course I like him. I can't imagine anyone who wouldn't."

"Neither can I," Lucille said with a breathless sigh. "Can I tell you a secret?"

"Absolutely."

"I'm thinking about getting my own place."

She nearly spilled her coffee. "What?"

Lucille giggled. "I knew you'd be surprised."

"Surprised! I'm flabbergasted! Does your mother know?"

"I've mentioned it. Just to test the water."

"Was it boiling?"

Lucille giggled again. "That's not the word for it. But she'll get used to the idea."

Mary Nell didn't know what to say. Was this the Lucille who less than a year ago had believed the height of daring was taking an extra five minutes on her lunch break? Marveling anew at this further evidence of change—and the love Lucille's man had wrought—Mary Nell sat back, shaking her head. "Well, this is a surprise. But I think it's great."

"I'm glad, because I owe it all to you."

"Oh, now—"

"No, no, it's true," Lucille insisted. "If I hadn't come to work for you—if you hadn't given me a chance to prove what I could do—I never would have met Brad. And if I hadn't met him, I never would have thought about moving out or... or anything else. So you see, all the credit is due to you."

"I think you're overestimating my part in all this."

"I don't. Can I tell you another secret?"

"You've got another one?"

Giggling, Lucille said, "I seem to be full of them today, don't I?"

"You certainly do," she said, and added only half in jest, "Just don't tell me you're going to quit work. I don't know what I'd do without you."

Lucille looked shocked. "Oh, I'd never quit my job!"

"Well, I'm glad to hear that. So, what's the big secret?"

"Promise you won't say anything?"

"You know I won't."

"Because Brad doesn't want me to say anything—but I'm sure he didn't mean to you," Lucille said earnestly. "I mean, he knows what good friends we are, so I'm sure it'll be okay. Just don't say anything to Cal, will you?"

"Cal? Does this have something to do with Cal?"

"In a way," Lucille said, and looked flustered. "Oh, dear, I might as well just tell you. You know how interested Brad is in his inventions. Well, he's never told Cal, but what he'd really like to do is leave the office and just concentrate on them."

That was a surprise. "Why doesn't he?" she asked curiously.

"Because they're partners, and because Brad feels guilty about all Cal has done for him. After what they've been through, he can't just quit. He knows how much Cal loves the business." She looked anxious. "You understand, don't you? And you won't say anything?"

Slowly, she shook her head. "No, I won't say anything. But it seems a shame. From what I saw last night, Brad is really clever."

"I agree." Lucille sighed. "And maybe someday..." She brightened. "I've already told him that I'll back him. I've got all sorts of savings, you know." She laughed. "Until I met you and Brad, the only thing I ever did with my money was bank it. A penny saved, and all that."

Hearing echoes of Eunice Hendershot, Mary Nell laughed, too. "Speaking of your mother, what does she think of Brad? I gathered last week that she didn't quite approve of your young man."

"Oh, it wasn't that. She just doesn't like all these changes in me, I think. She likes Brad, I know. And she'll come around to the idea of me moving out eventually." Lucille winked. "You won't believe it, but Brad already has her wrapped around his little finger!"

Mary Nell gave her a look. "You're right. I don't believe it."

They laughed, but then Lucille sobered and leaned forward. "You won't say anything to Cal, will you?"

The doorbell rang just then. "Speak of the devil," Mary Nell said, suddenly tense. She got up, stopping to give Lucille a reassuring pat. "Don't worry. My lips are sealed. I won't say a thing, not until Brad does. He does plan to tell him sometime, doesn't he?"

"Soon, I hope." Lucille sighed again and went out with her to answer the door.

Fifteen minutes later, after Lucille had duly admired the pop-top Cal had hitched to the back of his car and blushingly accepted his thanks for the dinner party the night before, Mary Nell and Cal were on their way. Because she felt awkward, she tried to delay facing him by turning around in her seat and waving until they were out of sight, but when they rounded the corner, she had no excuse. Slowly turning around again, she gave him a sideways glance. She couldn't read his expression, but because he seemed a little tense himself, she said, "Thanks for picking up the trailer."

"No problem," he said. "I had a hitch on my car, you didn't. It was easier this way."

She glanced behind them again, as though to make sure the trailer was still following them, but actually she was trying to think of a safe subject to discuss. She still wasn't sure how she felt about the events of the previous night, and because he hadn't mentioned it, either, she felt even more uncertain. She'd started thinking about the possibility of a business collaboration after what had happened, but in the cold light of day, she was beginning to wonder if that was such a good idea. Maybe she'd just been swept away by the emotion of the moment, she thought, and rowned. Realizing the silence had stretched on too long, he decided to break it.

"Where are we going?" she asked. Because he knew camping areas so much better than she did, she'd left the choice of the field test location up to him. "The lake?"

"The site of our former triumphs?" he said, and shook his head. "No, I thought we'd start with a clean slate for this round. We're going to a little campground I know. It's just up the road."

"Oh," she said. She couldn't think of anything else to say. He glanced at her.

"You sure you're ready for this one?"

Because she was feeling more uncomfortable by the minute, she came off sounding more curt than she'd intended. "I was ready for the last one."

"Right."

She shot him a quick look. Was he laughing at her? Lifting her chin, she said, "This time nothing's going to go wrong."

"You're sure of that."

"I'm positive," she said. She did have confidence in her design—but she'd also been confident about those tent poles. Trying not to think about that, she glanced out the window again.

"Mary Nell," he said.

"What?"

"I had a good time last night."

She could feel herself getting red. "So did I."

"You don't sound so sure."

It was out; she had to discuss it. But she still felt uncomfortable, and she said, "I am—about last night, I mean. I did have a good time. It's just . . ."

"Just what?" he prodded when she didn't go on.

She wasn't ready to talk about it, after all. And because she felt so awkward herself, she resented him for pushing her. Impatient with him, with herself, with the entire situation, she gestured with her hand. "Just—oh, I don't know. Things seem so complicated now."

Hearing the irritation in her voice, he remained silent for a few moments, glancing at her once or twice. Finally, he said, "We're back to that now, are we? You're remembering that you didn't want to get involved."

"I thought you felt that way, too," she said resentfully. Why was he making it sound as though this were all her fault? "After all, you said you weren't interested in a relationship right now—"

"No, you said that, not me."

"You said it, too!"

"Well, that was before I met you."

And my computer, she thought, and was surprised and ashamed of herself. Where had *that* come from? Why was she so suspicious? Because she wasn't sure of her own motives—or his?

"And now?" she said.

"And now..." He stopped and shook his head in frustration. "I don't know what now. You've got me all confused."

Oh, this was too much. Erupting, she said, "*I've* got *you* confused? In one instant you're telling me you don't want to get involved, and in the next... What are you telling me, anyway?"

"I'm not telling you I want to get involved," he said. "All I said was that I've changed my mind about...about seeing you."

"Oh, well, thank you, sir," she said sarcastically. "Does that mean I'm supposed to clear my calendar?"

"Why are you getting angry?"

"I'm not angry! I'm just trying to understand what we're talking about here."

"I don't know what we're talking about, okay? So, why don't we just forget it?"

"Fine with me!"

They subsided, both glaring out the windshield. But after a few seconds, she started again. "I don't know why we're arguing about this—"

"We're not arguing. The subject is closed."

"May I finish one sentence, please? Would that be too much to ask?"

He gestured. "Go ahead."

Now that she had the floor, she realized she didn't know what she wanted to say. "Never mind," she said. Beside her, he muttered to himself. She ignored him.

They drove in silence for a while. As she stared fixedly out the car window, she knew she was being deliberately difficult. She was sorry now she'd let her feelings run away with her after the dinner party; she never should have allowed their lovemaking to happen. Now that it had, things were going to be even more difficult. Resentful that she couldn't seem to go forward or backward, she sat there, fuming. Why had she ever thought collaboration of *any* kind with this man would be a good idea? Why was everything falling apart?

Because she hadn't remembered her resolve, that was why, she thought, despising herself. She hadn't remembered any of her promises to herself about keeping on track, getting her business going and sacrificing her personal life for the time being to establish her professional reputation. She'd gotten involved with a rival, something no professional ever did. It was as simple as that.

All right, she'd made a mistake. That's all it was, a mistake. It wasn't the end of the world, and all she had to do now was get through this. She could do it; she knew she could. But when they drove—finally!—through the entrance to the campground, she didn't even notice the name of the park; she was too focused on doing her job and getting home again before she made a fool of herself.

Nothing is going to happen this time, she told herself firmly. *Are you sure about that?* a little voice whispered from the back of her mind.

They had to stop for a permit at a little ranger's hut stuck in the center of the road, and she scowled when the cheerful ranger struck up a conversation with Cal. The longer she waited, the more impatient she became. She was just about to honk the horn to get Cal's attention when she realized how petulant she was being. What was wrong with her? She wasn't usually like this. No wonder Cal was delaying getting back into the car. If their positions had been reversed, she would have walked right out of the park. Immediately deciding to put aside her resentment and act more naturally, she forced herself to relax. She was uptight because she feared something might happen despite all her resolve, but when she thought about it logically, she knew nothing could happen. This was a public campground; other people were here. Okay, so she'd made one mistake. She'd already told herself it wouldn't happen again. And they weren't alone. What could go wrong?

With that thought, she forced a stiff smile. Cal had finally waved to the ranger and was climbing into the car again. He handed her a little ticket with a number marked in grease pencil and said, "This is the campsite we've been assigned. If you see it, let me know—okay?"

"Okay," she said in a small voice. Now she felt very badly about the way she had acted. Just because she was confused and afraid of her own emotions where he was concerned was no reason to take it out on him. As they

started off again, she said, "I'm sorry, Cal. I didn't mean
to be so difficult. I just want everything to go well this
time."

He glanced at her. "I understand," he said finally, and
added, although both of them knew it wasn't the reason
for the tension between them, "This field-testing business
has been a strain—for both of us."

"Then you accept my apology?"

He gave her a smile that made her heart turn over.
"Accepted. Let's forget it, okay?"

"Okay," she said, and quickly glanced away. By some
miracle, she spotted their campsite number up ahead, and
she quickly pointed. "There. That's it, isn't it? Number
thirty-two?"

The section of the campground they'd been assigned to
had been designed for trailers. The spot where they were
to park was long and narrow, enabling Cal to drive in
nosefirst. A branch scraped the side of the car as he did,
and she glanced quickly to the rear. Even though he'd
pulled all the way in, they still seemed awfully close to the
road, and she looked at him doubtfully.

"Do you think this will be all right?"

He seemed confident. "If we were going to camp for a
day or so, I'd reverse the vehicles, but since we're only
going to be here awhile, it's good enough."

"But we're so close to the road."

"There's not much traffic. We'll be okay."

She was still skeptical. "You're sure."

"Trust me," he said with a grin.

"Not on your best day," she told him haughtily, and got
out.

He met her at the rear of the car. "Since this is your milk
run, what do you want me to do?"

"Stay out of the way," she said promptly.

He smiled. "How about if I set this trailer up? We came all this way—the least we can do is have lunch. That is what you had me put in the trunk, isn't it?"

Remembering their ruined picnic from the last time, she'd put something simple—very simple—together for today. "Don't get excited," she warned. "It's nothing fancy."

"I'm sure it will be just fine."

Was that his way of apologizing? She told herself to accept it that way and tried another smile. When he smiled back, she began to hope that the day wasn't going to be nearly as bad as she thought.

"Why don't we eat after we do this test?" she said.

"I'm not sure I can wait," he answered with a grin. "This clean air makes me so hungry, I could eat a bear."

Not realizing he was teasing, she glanced quickly around. "Do you think there are any?"

He laughed. "If there are, they're more afraid of you than you are of them."

"How can you be sure?"

He looked at her curiously. "You're not really scared, are you?"

"No," she lied, telling herself there couldn't be any bears within miles. "I just don't like the idea of some huge forest creature sneaking up on me, that's all."

"Then I promise I'll give a yell if I see one."

"Thanks," she said sarcastically. "Now, if you're through cracking your clever little jokes, would you mind putting the camper up? Then I'll demonstrate this easy-lift design."

"As you wish," he said solemnly with twinkling eyes. Grabbing the cooler from the trunk, he carried it back to the trailer and set it on the ground so he could open the pop-top. Once extended, the shell that rose from the rectangular box looked almost like a tent out of the *Arabian Nights*, with two ells projecting out on either end, and everything else—ministove, refrigerator, table and seats that turned into beds—tucked cleverly inside.

"I'll just put the drinks in the refrigerator," he said, taking down a two-step ladder and leaning inside.

Waving her hand absently in agreement, she turned her attention toward her hitch. She had already tested the thing in the parking lot behind the office, so she knew it worked perfectly; he knew it worked, too, having brought the trailer over for her. But she still had to prove it under field conditions, and after unfastening the safety chain, she looked back with her hand on the hitch to see where Cal was. Without realizing it, she put her hand over the handle, and—just as she'd designed it—the gas lift worked fine. The wheel descended, lifting the trailer effortlessly from the ball that connected it to the car. It all went exactly as she had planned. With one exception. When she'd tested it before, Cal hadn't been inside the trailer, and the whole thing had been parked in a level parking lot. Now they were on a slight incline, and neither of them had thought to block the wheels. She didn't remember that until—to her horror—the trailer started to move.

Her voice rising in alarm, she said, "Cal!"

It was too late. Cal was bending over to put the drinks in the tiny refrigerator, somewhere at knee level. The slight jerk the trailer gave as it started off was enough to throw him off balance, and he went to one knee.

"What the hell..." he exclaimed. His voice was muffled, hollow; already the trailer was moving away.

"Cal!" she cried, reaching ineffectually for the hitch, the trailer, anything she could hold on to. Her fingers slipped off the smooth surfaces. Before her eyes, the little vehicle smartly backed down the small incline and started tooling merrily down the road with Cal inside.

For a frozen instant, she watched it. *This can't be happening,* she thought blankly. *It can't be!* But the trailer trundled along, gathering speed, and as it started to disappear around a bend in the road, she blinked and started after it, screaming, *"Cal!"*

"Mary Nell . . . ?"

She could hear him; she could even see him, sitting inside and glancing around with a puzzled expression. But she couldn't catch up. Terrified that the cart was going to run right into a tree, she started waving her arms and screaming as loud as she could for help. She'd never been a good runner, and she felt all arms and legs and bobbing elbows and knees, like a female Ichabod Crane—but she was running toward the headless horseman instead of away from it.

"Cal! Oh, someone help! Please! Help!"

She ran as fast as she could, her hair flying out behind her, flapping her hands and shrieking like a banshee. And the whole time, Cal just sat at that little table and looked around. She was in a frenzy, and he could have been sitting down to Sunday dinner! Why wasn't he scared? She was petrified. She thought of the picture they made: he trundling along serenely in the camper, sitting at the table; she running behind him like some deranged lunatic, her hair streaming in the breeze.

The image vanished when she saw a fork in the road. Oh, he was going to be killed; she was sure of it!

"Cal!" she shrieked again, and then she saw the most welcome sight of her life. A ranger had come out curiously to the road to see what the screaming was about; he'd obviously been policing one of the campsites, for he had one of those forked sticks in one hand and a bag in the other. *Thank God!* she thought, and screamed again.

"Oh, help! He's going to be killed! You've got to do something! Help! Help! *Help!*"

The ranger was too busy looking at the strange sight coming upon him to look at her; motionless, he watched the cart amble toward him. He didn't move.

"Do something!" she screeched upon seeing him just standing there. She still hadn't caught up to the cart; it was too fast for her. But she couldn't keep up this pace any longer. Already her breath was searing her lungs, and her legs felt on fire. She couldn't keep going, and yet she had to. Oh, why had this happened? She'd been so sure nothing would go wrong!

"Cal!" she screamed again. It sounded more like a gasp for air. She had to stop; her legs wouldn't carry her another step. Panting, she hurled herself along, going more on terrified energy and willpower than strength. She looked up in time to see the ranger step out onto the road just as the cart with Cal in it trucked right on past. Incredibly, she saw Cal lift a languid hand and smile at the man. He waved as he went by.

He *waved*? She was hysterical, dreaming; she was so exhausted from all the running that she hadn't seen what she'd thought she'd seen. Staggering behind, she bobbed past the ranger, who was still looking dazedly at the cart, but she was too out of breath to say anything, much less to scream. Just when she was sure her strength was completely gone, she looked up and stopped in sheer horror. They'd gone deeper into the campground, and the little trailer with Cal in it was heading straight for a tree! Screaming again, she flung her hands over her eyes. She couldn't bear to watch what was going to happen next. Oh, it was all her fault!

But the loud crash she'd anticipated didn't materialize, and after a moment, she spread her fingers slightly and peered through the gaps. She could still hardly breathe; she was gasping so hard that everything kept jumping: the tree, the cart, the entire scene. Expecting to see a limp body at the side of the road, she dropped her hands. Was that...? No, it couldn't be. She'd fainted or was hallucinating. It was all some kind of mad, exercise-induced dream. Was that really Cal leaning outside the net door, beckoning to her from inside, holding aloft a bottle of champagne?

"All this way, and I didn't spill a drop!" he called, and disappeared into the tent again.

She didn't know what to think. Her eyes wide, her breath still coming in fiery gasps, she ran toward the trailer. Incredibly, it seemed to have come to a gentle stop right in front of the tree, one of the wheels firmly blocked by an exposed root. She was still looking at it in disbelief when she realized Cal hadn't come out. Terrified of what she might see, she snatched back the net door and looked right into his laughing eyes.

"Boy, when you design something, you really go all out, don't you?" he said, and held out a champagne flute.

She couldn't move. "You..." She had to clear her throat. "You're not hurt?"

"Of course not. Here, take a sip."

Gasping, she looked from him to the glass, then back to him again. She'd nearly died from fright; she'd run her legs into the ground; she'd made a complete fool of herself in front of this entire camp; and he wanted to celebrate?

"You...you...you..." She was stuttering, incoherent. Still panting from exertion, she gripped the nylon net.

"What?" he said, sounding confused.

"What?" she wheezed. *"What?* How can you ask me that? I thought you were hurt! I thought...I thought..."

She couldn't finish; her breath was a rasping fire in her throat. Tears sprang into her eyes. This had to be the worst day of her life!

Cal saw the tears and looked alarmed. "Hey, don't cry!"

"I'm not crying!" she cried, furiously scrubbing at her face. First she'd made a fool of herself with that damned hitch, and now this! She'd never live it down, she thought, and whirled accusingly around. "It's all your fault!"

He looked surprised. "My fault?"

She knew she was being unfair, but she couldn't help herself. She'd never felt so humiliated; this was absolutely the worst. "If you had blocked the wheels, none of this would have happened!"

"But—" he started to say, and then saw her face. He got out of the trailer and took her arms. "Mary Nell, I think you should calm down. You're getting hysterical."

"I've never been hysterical in my entire life!" she said shrilly.

He tried another tack. Soothingly, he said, "All right, but you're upset. Now come on inside and we'll talk about this."

Her eyes blazed. "Don't you dare patronize me!"

"I'm not patronizing you. I just think you're overreacting a bit, don't you?"

"Overreacting?" she screeched. "Over*reacting*! You're almost killed, and you think I'm making too much of it?"

"I wasn't almost killed," he said reasonably. "That trailer was going four miles an hour, tops. I could have jumped out anytime. The truth was, I thought it was funny."

Her voice rose. *"Funny?"*

He saw the look in her eyes. "Well, not funny," he said quickly.

"What, then?"

They were interrupted before he could answer. The ranger had finally remembered his duty, and as he approached, he called out cheerfully, "Everything all right, folks?"

Cal stepped in front of her. "Everything's fine," he said, holding her behind him with an effort.

The ranger looked at him doubtfully. "You sure you don't need some help?"

She was trying to struggle out from behind him, but Cal held her firmly. "No, I'll just get the car and pull it out. Mind if we have lunch first?"

He wanted *lunch*? Behind his back, Mary Nell gave him a fierce look. She'd see that he got lunch.

"No problem," the ranger answered. "Take your time." He chuckled. "It's not as if you're taking up a camp space, right?"

"Right," Cal said with an answering laugh, and waved as the other man started off. Turning around, he grabbed her by the shoulders and practically propelled her into the trailer.

She gave him a steely glance. "Why did you do that?" she asked, scraping every word.

"Would you rather I told him what really happened?"

She was silent. "You think this is really funny, don't you?"

He tried to hide his smile. "It had its moments, you have to admit," he said. "When I think of you running behind me, screaming your head off..." He saw her expression again and finished lamely, "Well, it seemed funny at the time."

"Yeah, a real laugh riot," she said sourly, but now that she wasn't so scared—or angry—she was beginning to see the humor despite herself. Still, she wasn't ready to give in, and she glared at him again. "Was that why you just sat there and didn't do anything?"

"What did you want me to do? Scream *my* head off? I was never in danger, you know."

"You were going at least fifty miles an hour!"

"Four," he repeated, and then looked at her curiously. "Do you mind telling me what happened?"

"I told you, we didn't block the wheels!"

"I thought you were going to wait until we were ready."

"I did!" she said, and then blurted, "My hand slipped."

He was obviously trying not to laugh. "Well," he said finally, "at least we know the hitch works."

That did it. She'd been seesawing with emotion all morning: highs and lows and everything in between. She'd gone from hysteria to panic to sheer horror and back again, and suddenly it was all too much. "Yes, it does that," she said, and despite herself, she started to smile.

"See?" Cal said, encouraged. "It wasn't so bad, was it?"

"It was terrible," she said. "It was the worst moment of my life."

He was smiling now, too. "I thought the worst moment was when my propeller took wing and dumped you in the lake."

She bit her lip to keep herself from laughing aloud. "That was pretty bad, I admit."

"How do you think *I* felt?"

"At least you didn't have to run like a wild woman down the road, screaming your head off."

"No, but I had to dive into the lake and haul a mangled boat out again. You think that was better?"

"Yes," she said, and laughed.

Sensing that the worst was indeed over, Cal grabbed the champagne he'd poured. Handing her a glass, he said,

"You know, after the way things have been going, maybe we should collaborate."

And suddenly, the air seemed charged. "You think so?" she said.

Silently, he set his glass aside. "What do you think?" he said softly.

She didn't want to think; it was happening again, that longing to be with him. Again, despite all her resolve, she couldn't resist him. One look, and she was lost. She wanted him; she couldn't deny it. He wanted her; he didn't try to hide it.

"Cal, maybe we should—"

His arms were around her; his lips against her hair, her temples, her cheek, her throat. "Are you worried that someone will see us?"

"Well, we are out here in the open...."

Pulling aside her blouse to kiss the curve of her shoulder, he murmured, "We're not in the open—we're in a tent." His mouth moved lower. "Do you really care?"

His lips were on the curve of her breast; already she felt as though she were on fire. "Not in the slightest," she breathed, and let his weight bear her down on the trailer's hard mattress.

He raised his head to look at her in concern. "This isn't too comfortable...."

"Who cares?" she whispered. She wasn't paying attention; she wanted to feel him against her, and she quickly unbuttoned his shirt, slid her hands under the material and slipped it off his back. His chest was broad and muscled, his skin smooth and bare. Running her hands over that wide expanse, she looked up at him and whispered again, "Who cares?"

"Not me," he groaned, and buried his face in her disheveled hair. Of their own accord, her hands had moved lower, to the belt of his jeans. He shifted position so she could undo the buckle, and when her hand slipped under it, he closed his eyes. "This isn't fair," he said, and moved her over.

With sure hands he pulled off her blouse. Her body was aflame; she wanted to rip away her wisp of a bra so she could feel his lips on her skin. Pushing her hand away, he took on the chore himself, raising her up so that he could find the catch that held the lacy thing together. He located it, released the clasp and dropped the bra onto the counter.

"You're so soft," he murmured, touching her with wonder. His fingers drew trails of fire, and she moaned and pulled his head closer. The sensation of his tongue circling her nipple sent a flood of warmth all through her, and she moaned again and drew his head lower.

"So soft," he breathed, and tugged at her jeans at the same time she reached for his. Both pairs dropped to the floor in seconds, and, just as she'd dreamed of, they were suddenly lying naked next to each other. The narrow cot seemed a most luxurious haven; she reached for him, guiding him closer.

"I never thought this would happen again," he said wonderingly, raising himself up on one elbow to look down into her eyes. "After last night ... and then this morning..."

"Don't talk," she said, and reached for him again.

When he slid over her, her legs opened of their own volition, and she took him inside. He filled her as nothing had filled her before. Uttering a groan of pleasure, she wrapped her legs around him and drew him in deeper. He responded by moving with her, touching her, stroking her, calling up every sense and sensation she'd ever felt or forgotten or hadn't known existed. She felt as though he'd tossed her up on a mesa of pure pleasure, so that every kiss, every caress, every fondling grasp, encouraged her higher.

And she touched and caressed and fondled him, too, until he was groaning with pleasure. She couldn't get enough of him. His body was so beautiful, so strong and so sturdy. She could feel the play of muscles under her fingers, a contraction here and there as she ran her fingertips down his spine or cupped him in her hand.

"I...can't...take much...more of this...." he panted.

"Oh, yes you can," she whispered, starting to undulate her hips, making him gasp even more.

But soon passion took over, and their hips moved as one, faster and faster. "Don't stop," she gasped. "Oh, don't stop...."

She could hold back no longer. Their movements were frenzied; they'd passed the point where their bodies were their own. With a cry, she arched upward, clutching at his back, trying to hold him even more tightly to her. With a cry, he grabbed her, too, and rolled over just as the wave of pleasure swooped down on them and carried them away.

"Oh, Cal," she murmured, much later.

CHAPTER FOURTEEN

SATURDAY MIGHT HAVE started out to be the worst day of Mary Nell's life, but the rest of the weekend was sensational. When she and Cal finally came wearily back to the house after the field test at the campground, Stacy took one look at their fatuous expressions and decided to go back to school a day early.

"I've got some studying to do—or something," she said, grinning and waving goodbye. "You two enjoy yourselves."

Her little blue Volkswagen hadn't turned the corner before Mary Nell was in Cal's arms. Together, they went upstairs, stopping every few steps for a lingering kiss. By the time they reached the bedroom, neither wanted to linger. It was as though it were the first time all over again. When he took her in his arms, pulling her toward him and kissing her once more, she answered with the same passion that had burst into fiery life in that little pop-top tent caught under the tree in the campground. With his mouth eagerly seeking hers, she clung to him, inhaling his scent, loving the feel of him against her, luxuriating in the strength of his arms even after he'd released her to look into her eyes.

"Oh, Cal," she whispered, not caring at the moment what might happen, longing only for the feel of his hands on her, the touch of his lips, the union of their bodies. "I never dreamed it could be this way...."

"Neither did I," he said, and held her even closer. They stood like that for an endless time, wrapped in each other's arms, and for her it was a perfect moment. The house was quiet with the hush of late afternoon. The birds were twittering in the trees, and there was the merest whisper of a breeze coming through the open window. The sun's rays were lengthening across the bedspread, filling the room with a golden light, and she even felt that their two hearts were beating as one.

Unconsciously, she sighed and put her cheek against his chest. The faintest fragrance of pine filled her nostrils, and she closed her eyes, breathing it in. She knew that the scent would always remind her of this time. She could smell it now, in his hair and on his skin when she unbuttoned his shirt and pushed the fabric aside to put her lips against his chest. She had never felt so alive. Raising her head, she gave him a smile.

He smiled softly in return, lifting one hand to trace her jaw, to touch her cheek, to feel her skin. "You're so soft," he murmured, his expression marveling. "Why are women so soft?"

She had no answer for that; she wanted to ask him why men felt so strong and powerful. But she didn't have time; an instant later, he was kissing her again, and when he bore her down on the bed with his weight, she couldn't think of anything but how wonderful he felt and how she wanted the moment to go on, and on . . . and on.

The rest of the weekend passed in a daze of delight. Sometime that Saturday night she went downstairs and fixed them an omelet to eat; the next morning she lounged lazily in bed while he got up to fix breakfast. She hadn't expected him to go out and bring back strawberries and croissants and champagne, and she was touched—and thrilled—that he'd gone to so much trouble for her. They

pent a crumbly, silly morning popping berries into each
ther's mouths and laughingly downing them with sips of
hampagne. He'd thought to bring the Sunday paper, too,
nd later, after making love again, she cuddled next to
im, her head on his chest, while he read the book review
ection out loud. She confessed a fondness for spy stories,
nd he told her he preferred nonfiction. They both laughed
t the pretentious "glitz" novels. That afternoon, she
layed the piano for him, and later, they had dinner on the
atio. As though Stacy had sensed something like this
night happen, she'd thoughtfully left two steaks in the re-
rigerator, flanked by baking potatoes on either side and
crisper full of salad greens. Silently blessing her sister,
Mary Nell made a mental note to give her a call later, and
hen proceeded to make a feast fit for a king.

Because it was a beautiful evening, they barbecued the
teaks and then sat for a long time after dinner on the pa-
io in the dark, with only a guttering candle for company
nd the living room stereo turned down low for back-
round. Eyes closed, she put her head back against her
hair and breathed in the soft night air. She'd had such a
vonderful time, she didn't want it to end. Even more, she
lidn't want Cal to go. Wondering what he'd say if she
sked him to stay, she opened her eyes and looked his way.
They'd been sitting silently for quite a while; she'd thought
e was as content as she was, but when she saw his expres-
ion, she got her first indication that all was not well.

"Is something the matter?" she asked cautiously.

He blinked, returning from where his thoughts had
aken him. "No. Why?" he said, but he wouldn't meet her
yes.

"You look so—I don't know...sad."

"Sad?" he repeated, and shook his head. "Well, maybe in a way I am. I was just thinking that I didn't want the weekend to end."

She was so relieved that she spoke without thinking. "It doesn't have to."

"What do you mean?"

She wasn't sure what she'd meant; she hadn't intended to say that, and she hesitated, wondering if she really wanted to go on. Then she knew she didn't have any choice. Cal was like an elixir; one taste and she was lost. She'd already broken so many promises and vows and fervent resolutions to herself, what was one more? It had been hopeless anyway, right from the start. She could no more deny her feelings for this man than perform surgery on a broken heart.

"Remember what you said about collaboration?" she asked.

Before her eyes, he tensed. After a long moment during which her heart began to beat a little faster, but with apprehension and not excitement, he said cautiously, "Collaboration. Do you mean personal . . . or professional?"

She felt as though he'd slapped her across the face. Suddenly, she knew she'd made a terrible mistake, and through a swift, sharp stab of pain, she tried to think of some clever answer that would hide the hurt she felt. Her mind went completely blank. The only thing she could think of was a wondering, *how could he say that to me after all we've been to each other this weekend?* Shocked into speechlessness, she just looked at him.

He tried to make it better—or at least, to make it hurt a little less. "I didn't mean to say it like that, Mary Nell," he said quietly.

Her lips felt stiff. "How did you mean to say it, then?"

This time it was he who flinched. As though ashamed to look at her, he glanced away. "I didn't mean to say it at all," he muttered. "It's just..."

His voice trailed away. She thought that he was waiting for her to tell him it was all right, that he didn't have to explain. She knew he wanted her just to nod politely, shake his hand and let him go away. But she couldn't do that. He'd hurt her, and she wanted to know why. She wasn't going to let him off the hook that easily.

"Just what?" she said. Some of the chill she was feeling had made its way to her voice, and she was glad. She needed a little pride right now, she thought, and wondered where it had been when she needed it the most. Refusing to think of that, she stood. He stood with her, looking even more unhappy than she felt. She wondered how that was possible, or if he really felt that way at all. Had everything been an act? Had this entire weekend only been a ploy, a diversion, a whim—a mistake? Maybe his goal had been to become partners—but in business only. Maybe, like her, he'd gotten carried away by the moment and regretted it. That was the only explanation, the only reason he would have asked that question. Her cheeks began to burn. How could she have been such a fool?

"Which did you think I meant, Cal?" she said. Pain had given way to anger, and that had become fury. She wanted him to answer her; she wanted to know if he had the courage to say it.

"Look, Mary Nell," he said awkwardly. "I...I really enjoyed this weekend. I'm sorry if I upset you just now—"

Her voice was steely. "You didn't upset me, Cal. Just answer the question. Which did you think I meant? No, wait. Maybe I should put it another way. Which would you have preferred?"

He looked so unhappy that she knew. "Never mind," she said contemptuously. "I think we both know the answer to that."

He tried again. "Mary Nell, you've got this all wrong. Let's just sit down and try to discuss this calmly, all right? I'm sure we can work it out."

Just for a second, her resolve nearly failed. Oh, if only they could! she thought. But then, without warning, her mind flashed back to that day he'd "stopped by" the office. He'd been fascinated by the computer, by all her equipment. Then had come that first night with him. Remembering, she hardened her heart. It was obvious what he'd been after, and she'd just been too blinded—as she always was—by her emotions and her treacherous heart to see things clearly.

"No," she said, "we can't work it out. I think you should go now, Cal. I'd like to be alone."

Looking even more unhappy than before, he tried again. "I wish it hadn't gone like this."

She gave him an icy stare. "So do I. Please close the door on your way out."

Left with no choice, he started to leave. At the door, he turned back. "What about the last field test?"

She'd forgotten about that. Briefly, she shut her eyes. Would this never end? She was too upset to give him a choice. Just wanting to get it over with, she said, "We'll do it first thing next Saturday morning. I'll meet you at the lake."

"That's what you want?"

What she wanted was never to see him again. Her chin lifted. "You have an objection to that?"

He hesitated. Finally, he shook his head. "No, no objection."

"Fine, I'll see you then."

She didn't see him to the door. But as soon as she heard it close behind him, she put her hands over her eyes, trying to squeeze back hot tears. What was the matter with her? Would she never learn? She'd always made mistakes where men were concerned; she always wanted more from them than they were prepared to give. But she'd thought Cal was different. She'd been so sure of it! They had so much in common: music, the business...

Bleakness crashed down upon her. The only thing they had in common was the competition for McAdam's damned recreational gear contract. She was certain now that that was why he had suggested collaboration. *That* was what this weekend had been all about! Lucy had told her how much business had fallen off at Stewart-Davidson because of Brad's accident; it was obvious that an account like McAdam's would help put them back in the black. But Cal hadn't emerged any more victorious on his first test than she had on hers, and when they'd gotten involved the second time around, he must have been a little nervous—especially when he'd seen what her computer could do that day he came to the office. And when her trailer hitch had worked so well, he must have really squirmed. They both knew it was good, they both knew it would work—and they both knew Anson McAdam would bite. Since Cal still had his oven to test, he must have decided to give himself an edge. He'd tested the waters with the collaboration idea, and then, for added insurance, he'd tossed in the weekend as a dividend. That way, even if his second field test went wrong, he wouldn't completely lose out. They'd be partners, sharing the same contract. He just hadn't expected her to go overboard; when she'd given signs that she wanted a more permanent romantic relationship, he'd backed away. It had all been a ploy. Why hadn't she seen it before she'd gotten hurt?

Drained, she sat out on the patio until very late. She didn't want to go inside, where memories of Cal resided now. She definitely couldn't go up to her room. When the chill night air finally drove her into the house, she glanced once at the stairs, shook her head, grabbed a quilt and slept on the couch. And, for the first time since she'd started the business, the next morning she called in sick. After the fool she'd made of herself, she just couldn't face anyone, especially the radiant Lucille.

"OH, BRAD," Lucille said worriedly. "I'm so concerned about Mary Nell. She hasn't been herself this week. I've never seen her like this."

They were sitting in Brad's van, having dinner at the local drive-in. It was one of the last places in town—in the world, Brad had told her jokingly—that still served food from trays hooked over car doorjambs. He'd been horrified when he'd found out that his lady had never pigged out on junk food; he'd immediately proceeded to initiate her into the delights of greasy French fries and hamburgers dripping with mayonnaise and cheese. Gamely, Lucille was trying. But the most she'd been able to get down so far was half a burger and a handful of fries; the synthetic milk shake she couldn't touch at all.

"How can people eat like this?" she exclaimed.

"I know, isn't it wonderful?" Brad said with a wolfish grin, and drained the last of his shake. "Now, what's this about Mary Nell?"

Lucille played with a straw. "I don't know. She says the field test with the trailer hitch went just great, but she's been so depressed ever since she got back. I don't know if she's sick or what."

"She's sick, all right," Brad said, finishing her fries. "Just like Cal."

"Do you think they both caught something?"

Brad shook his head fondly. "Oh, my darling," he said. What am I going to do with you? They've caught something, all right. What's wrong with them is that they're both lovesick. That and silly pride. All one of them needs to do is pick up the phone to put things right, but do you think either of them will? Noooo. That would be too easy, wouldn't it?"

Lucille looked at him for a moment, then she smiled. "I'm so dense at times, aren't I?" she said.

"No, just innocent," Brad said, and took her hand. "And I wouldn't have it any other way."

Twining her fingers with his, she sighed. "Oh, this is wonderful," she said. "About Cal and Mary Nell, I mean. Except—" Raising her head, she looked at him. "Except, what are we going to do?"

"Nothing," Brad said, pulling her close. "They have to work it out." He smiled fondly at her and raised her fingers to his lips. "Just like we have."

"Oh, Brad." Lucille sighed again, and leaned her head against his shoulder. "I hope one day they'll be as happy as we are."

"They will be," Brad said. "Those two were made for each other." Then, with Lucille looking hopefully at him, he added glumly, "They just don't know it yet."

THE TWO in question still didn't know it at the end of the week. Cal had spent the time alternating between fits of temper and bouts of depression. He felt awful, and he knew he looked it. He couldn't even stand to look at himself in the mirror when he was shaving; he'd never felt so low in his entire life. A dozen times he went to the phone, intending to call Mary Nell and tell her exactly what he thought. The only problem was that he wasn't quite sure

what that was. Every time he tried to sort out his feeling
for her, he felt more confused and disordered than ever
and he ended up even angrier than before. Then he'd de
cide to hell with it—only to be staring longingly at th
phone again five minutes later, wondering if he should call
after all.

It didn't help his state of mind to be around an exasper
atingly cheerful Brad, who wheeled through the office
whistling to himself. Toward the end of the week, the noise
got on Cal's nerves to the point where he wrenched open
his office door and yelled down the hall.

"For Pete's sake, do you have to make such an infernal
racket all the time?"

Brad calmly wheeled out into the hall. "What racket?"

"That whistling! It's driving me up the wall!"

Brad folded his arms. "There's no reason to take you
bad mood out on me."

"I'm not in a bad mood!"

"What do you call it, then?" Brad asked, starting to
sound a little exasperated himself. "Look, why don't you
make it easier on both of us and just call her, okay? Say
you made a fool of yourself—you did do that, didn'
you?—and beg her forgiveness. Then maybe we can ge
some work done around here."

Cal was enraged. "For your information, I *am* work
ing!" he shouted. "Or at least, I would be, if I had a little
peace and quiet so I could concentrate!"

With that, he stormed back into his office and slammed
the door.

Across town, Mary Nell wasn't faring much better. By
the end of the week she was in such a funk that she would
have forgotten an important appointment if Lucille hadn't
reminded her—twice. With supreme effort, she managed
to put her problems out of her mind long enough to meet

ith a new client and win another account, but she was
xhausted afterward and wondered what was wrong with
er.

No, she knew what was wrong with her. She kept eye-
ng the phone, wondering if she should call Cal and apol-
gize. She would tell herself haughtily that *he* should call
er, but she knew the chances of that happening were slim.
he wished *something* would happen to break the nerve-
acking silence.

"Why don't you call him?" Lucille suggested quietly
ne evening as she was getting ready to go home. She'd
een tiptoeing around the office all week; she'd wanted to
elp, but she hadn't known how. Things were so *compli-
ated* with Cal and Mary Nell, not at all like they were with
er and Brad.

Mary Nell gave her a sour look. "And what do you
hink I should say?"

"You can say that you're calling to make sure the field
est is still on," Lucille offered.

"Oh, it's on, all right," Mary Nell said bitterly. "He
vouldn't miss that for anything!" Her mouth tightened.
'And I can't wait for him to fail!"

"Mary Nell!"

"Well, it's true. It would serve him right."

"But I thought you and Cal . . . I mean, don't you—"
Lucille stopped and bit her lip. "Oh, dear, I knew I
houldn't have said anything! Brad said I should stay out
f it, and he was right."

Now Mary Nell felt bad. She knew Lucille was trying to
elp, and she gave her a quick hug. "You tell Brad there's
othing to stay out *of*," she said. "Now, stop worrying.
t's going to be all right. All I have to do is get through this
hing tomorrow, and I'll be home free."

Lucille didn't remind her that she still had another hurdle to cross after the field test: she and Cal had to meet with Anson McAdam a final time. The secretary only said, "And Cal?"

Mary Nell grabbed her purse. It was time to go home. Switching off the office light, she said, "Cal and I are history, a closed chapter—a book that never should have been opened."

"Oh, but you could work things out."

"Never. We look at things completely differently. I'm glad I found that out now." Her expression indicated the subject was closed. "Now, would you like a ride home, or is Brad swinging by to pick you up?"

"Brad's picking me up," Lucille said in a small voice. She looked uncertain. "Should I wish you good luck tomorrow?"

Mary Nell's mouth tightened again. "Not me. Cal's the one who's going to need it."

Shaking her head at such stubbornness, Lucille said, "I'll call you in the afternoon to see how things went, all right?"

With that, they went their separate ways: Lucille out the front door, locking it behind her; Mary Nell out the back, to the parking lot. But once inside the car, she just sat there with her keys in hand, feeling exhausted. It had been such a long week; she'd thought it would never end. And it wasn't over yet. She still had tomorrow morning to get through, and with that thought she put her head back and sighed. She rarely drank anything stronger than soda, but tonight she was going to have a glass of wine with dinner. Hoping that would help dissolve the knot in her stomach, she started the car and went home.

SATURDAY DAWNED WARM and clear, without a hint of clouds or storm. Mary Nell was awake long before the alarm rang, staring glumly out the kitchen window while she drank her coffee. She'd hoped there would be a hurricane or even a tornado warning today, just so she'd have an excuse not to go, but no; the morning was so beautiful it almost made her head ache. Wishing she'd never agreed to the crazy scheme McAdam had proposed, she threw on a pair of jeans and a blouse. She felt so low that she didn't care what her hair looked like, and she bundled it into a ponytail, from which tendrils promptly escaped. Staring at her reflection, she thought sourly that she looked about fourteen years old. Well, so what? It didn't matter what she looked like; the only thing that mattered was getting the field test over with. Throwing a jacket in the back of the car, she drove out to the lake.

Cal was already there, ostentatiously glancing at his watch every two seconds as she drove up. She checked her car clock. She was right on time; there was no need for such behavior. Annoyed already, she slammed the car door when she got out.

"I'm here," she said curtly. "Are you ready?"

"As ready as you are," he said, and shrugging into a backpack, he promptly turned and started off.

Her eyes narrowed. All right, she thought, if that was the way he was going to be, she'd go along. He was doing it deliberately, she knew, trying to see how much she could take. Thinking that in her present mood, she could take all he dished out, she glanced in satisfaction at the tennis shoes she was wearing. Today she'd come prepared, and right now, she didn't care if they walked all the way around the lake.

They walked for miles in tense silence. She hadn't realized the lake was so big or the sandy shore around it so

wet. Her canvas shoes were soaked in no time, further ig-
niting her smoldering temper; when he finally did stop, she
couldn't help making a sarcastic remark.

"Are you *sure* this is the right place?" she asked with-
eringly. "I mean, shouldn't we be looking for a special tree
or a certain rock—something really distinctive to mark this
occasion? Or have I missed something?"

His eyes were like flint. "I thought you might be getting tired, that's all."

"Don't worry about me," she flashed back. "I don't
care if we trudge around this entire lake. I don't want you
to charge me with unfair judging."

His jaw tightened. She knew she was really pushing him,
but she didn't care. She wanted to make him angry, because then she could stay angry with him. She'd keep her
distance then, something that was becoming increasingly
important the longer they stood here. As infuriating as it
was, she still felt that devil attraction to him, and it didn't
matter how much he had hurt her or what he had said.
Some treacherous part of her wanted to believe it had all
been a mistake, a misunderstanding, that if they tried, they
could sort it all out.

And then?

She wouldn't allow herself even to consider it. If she
started wondering about what might have been, she'd be
lost. But every time she looked at him, she wanted to cry,
"Oh, Cal, what happened? It was going so well! What
went wrong?"

Horrified at her weakness, she pretended she had a rock
in her shoe and sat down. For an awful instant, she
thought he was going to offer to help her, and she nearly
broke the shoelace trying to get it undone. "Well?" she
said coldly, ostentatiously shaking out the nonexistent
rock. "What are you waiting for?"

For an instant she thought she'd gone too far. There was a flash of blue fire in his eyes, but he was more adept at disguising his feelings than she was, for all he said was, "I was waiting for you. I figured since I was the victim of your trailer launch, you should test the oven."

Outraged at his choice of words, she flung back, "That wasn't my fault! If you remember, the hitch worked perfectly. The only problem was that you forgot to block the wheels so the cart wouldn't roll!"

He gave her a cold look. "Yes, so you mentioned. It does seem as if all these things are my fault, doesn't it?"

"I can't think of everything!" she snapped. "The hitch was my responsibility. I figured you could at least watch the wheels!"

He reddened. "Fine," he said. "Since this is my test, I'll set up the stove, and you can watch the beans. Fair enough?"

"What beans?"

He spoke with infuriating patience. "The test wouldn't be any good if I hadn't brought something to cook, would it? I thought the easiest thing would be beans."

She hated him. How dare he sound so reasonable and calm when she felt as though she were going to fall apart any second? She glared at him, but the effect was lost, for he wasn't looking at her. Obviously just as anxious as she was to get the test over with, he'd knelt and was taking several things out of the knapsack he'd pulled off his back. The first was a flattened aluminum square, which, when opened and spread apart, would act as a stove top. Since this test was for the oven only, he put it aside. Despite her annoyance, Mary Nell was impressed.

But she wasn't going to let him know it, and she watched in chilly silence as he proceeded to build a small fire. As though aware of her eyes on him, he glanced up. "You could help, you know."

She gave him an icy look. "What would you like me to do?"

Reaching into his knapsack, he took a can and an opener out. "Here. The beans. I didn't bring a pan. I figured we could use the can."

"Fine," she said, and turned away so that he wouldn't see her struggle. She'd never been able to manage the kind of opener that clamped onto the side of a can and had to be manually turned; the stupid thing always fell off. Trying not to think of her electric opener at home and how much easier it made her life, she vowed she'd get the can of beans open if she had to do it with her teeth. Finally, through sheer willpower, she managed to mangle the top of the can enough to prize it apart. She held it out to Cal, daring him to say a word. Just one word.

He looked at it without comment, but she was sure he was hiding a smirk. Then he stood. "I thought *you* were going to conduct this test."

Sure that despite his innocent expression, he was laughing at her somehow, she tightened her lips. Reaching down, she jerked open the little oven door with the pot holder he'd silently handed her, and practically threw the can inside before slamming the door again.

"All right. The beans are in the oven. How long are we supposed to wait?"

"That's up to you. You're supervising this field test."

Eyes narrowed, she glanced at her watch. "Fine. We'll give it five minutes."

"Do you think you can stand to be out here alone with me that long?"

"I don't know. I'll try."

They stood in silence for another moment or two before he tried again. "Mary Nell, I'm sorry. I told you—"

She tightened her lips again. "I don't want to discuss it."

He fell silent, but not for long. "Can't we at least talk about it?"

"No."

"You're not being fair."

That did it. Whirling around, she cried, "Fair! You talk to me about being fair! How dare you!"

"Now, wait a minute—"

She was too angry to care what she said. All the resentment and hurt she'd tried to bury during the week suddenly boiled over, and without warning, she was furious. She wanted to have it out with him; she never should have kept it in.

"No, you wait a minute! It might have taken me a while, but I've got it figured out now. The pity is that I didn't catch on to you sooner! I might have saved us both a lot of trouble!"

"What are you talking about?"

"You don't know?" she said acidly. "Well, let me fill you in on a few details, then! What was the problem, Cal? Did you get in a little deeper than you intended? Did you really think your charm was so blinding that I wouldn't see what you were up to?"

He looked genuinely confused. "I don't know what you mean. If you're talking about last weekend—"

"Oh, yes, let's talk about last weekend," she said withringly. "That was when things got a little heavy, remember? That was when the price suddenly got a little higher than you wanted to pay."

"What price? What are you talking about?"

Infuriated, she cried, "Don't play the innocent with me! You know damned well what I'm talking about! You backed out because you hadn't anticipated more than one-night stand—or a series of them! *That's* what I'r talking about!''

His face red, more from growing anger than embar rassment, he said, ''You've got it all wrong, Mary Nell. didn't back out—''

''What do you call it, then?'' she cried. ''Wasn't it al about collaboration? That was why you came on to me Cal, to make sure you'd get—''

''Came on to you? Came *on*?'' He was really red now his eyes flashed. ''Is that what you thought I did?''

''What else could I think?'' she snapped back. ''Every thing was fine until you thought you were trapped! Wasn' that what last weekend was all about? Weren't you jus trying to wriggle your way into my life—into my com puter system?''

''That's the most ridiculous thing I've ever heard!''

''Enlighten me, then!''

Facing each other over the fire at their feet, neither o them noticed the little oven starting to jiggle on the rocks Engrossed in their argument, they didn't hear the omi nous rattlings, either.

''I'm telling you, Mary Nell, you've got it all wrong,' he said. ''There's nothing to explain, I swear. It was jus one of those things that ... happened. That's all.''

She knew he was lying; she could see it in his face, in the quick shift of his eyes away from her. Furious that he wa still trying to play her for such a fool, she said, ''It didn' just happen. You planned it. Are you going to deny thi contract is important to you?''

''Of course it's important. But it's important to you too.''

''Yes, but *I* wasn't the one who suggested collabora tion!''

"Will you *forget* about that stupid collaboration idea?" he shouted, suddenly enraged. "It was only a joke!"

The little oven gave another series of rattles, these slightly more pronounced than the first. If they'd been listening, they would have heard the slight hissing sound of steam trying to escape. But they weren't listening.

"A joke!" she repeated, outraged. "Just like last weekend was?"

"I told you, last weekend was a...a mistake!"

"A mistake? A mis*take*! Is that what you thought it was?"

"I didn't mean it that way."

"Then tell me how you did mean it!"

He never got the chance. The oven had held out as long as it could. This time neither of them could ignore the ominous hissing from inside the aluminum box; they both looked down just as the oven did a last little jig on the hot coals.

"Oh, no!" Cal said. "I think—"

She thought so, too. Snatching up the pot holder she'd flung in a rage to the ground, she dropped to her knees and made a grab for the door. She was too late. With a muted roar of relief, the top door of the oven flew open with a bang, and before either of them could take shelter, a fountain of beans spewed high into the air along with an escaping hiss of steam.

"Look out!" Cal cried, trying to protect her. It was a futile gesture; the explosion had flung some of the sauce onto the fire, and because she was kneeling, the resulting black smoke rolled over her like a blanket. The beans hit the apex of their journey seconds later and started to come down. Suddenly she was caught in a hailstorm of little brown pellets and sticky sweet gook. By the time the smoke cleared, she was covered in beans and cooling brown sauce, her face black from the smoke. In silence, she listened to the last little hiss of the fire. When the noise died out, she looked expressionlessly at Cal.

"What happened this time?"

Silently, he held out his handkerchief. "Are you hurt?"

She looked down at herself. She was a mess. If her clothes looked this awful, she could just imagine what her face and hair were like. Tentatively she raised a hand and touched her hair. When it came away covered with sauce, she sighed.

"No, I'm not hurt. You wouldn't happen to have a shower handy, would you?"

He was obviously waiting for her to explode as the oven had. Nervously, he said, "There's always the lake."

With as much dignity as she could muster, she stood. Beans fell off her with little plops to the ground. By this time Cal was so tense waiting for the eruption he was sure was going to happen that he started to laugh. She gave him a sharp look.

"This . . . isn't . . . funny, Cal," she said, carefully spacing her words. He only laughed harder. "I mean it. This isn't funny!"

He tried to control himself. "I know. I'm sorry. It's just—" He started laughing again.

That was the last straw. Her nerves were strung as tightly as his after their argument, and when he started laughing at her, she lost her temper again. "You did that on purpose!" she said accusingly.

That wiped the smile off his face. "No! It was—"

"An accident?" she cried. "Maybe it was a *mistake*!"

"No, I designed it to be airtight, and it was. We should have watched the beans—"

"*You* should have watched them! You designed that oven to explode on purpose!"

Two spots of color appeared in his lean cheeks. "That's ridiculous! Why would I do a stupid thing like that?"

"How do I know?" she cried. She was trying to get the sticky stuff out of her hair. Bean sauce clung to everything, and she was furious. She looked and felt a mess; something was dripping down her back.

"Mary Nell, please calm down—"

"Calm down? Calm *down*?" she shrieked. "This whole thing was a farce from day one, and we both know it! How dare you take it out on me!"

"I don't know what you're talking about. We just forgot to watch the stupid beans, that's all—"

"No! You planned it! I know you did!"

"Yeah, and maybe you sabotaged the oven so that you'd get the contract. What about that?"

"I don't need to sabotage anything! My work stands for itself!"

"So does mine!"

"You're not going to get this contract, Cal. I mean it!"

"We'll see about that!"

"We certainly will! It's more important to me than it is to you! We've seen that."

He stiffened, taunted finally into losing his temper. "You don't know what you're talking about! That contract is my ticket out. It'll set Davy up in the business for good and leave me free to do what I want!"

She was just as enraged. "If that's what you think, you'd better ask your partner how he feels!" she cried, flinging another handful of smashed beans to the ground. She'd finger-combed them out of her hair, and she shook her hand in rage. How could this have happened? Why was he just standing there? She felt as though someone had dipped her in a vat of taffy.

"I don't have to ask him, I know!"

She put her hand up to her hair again, but her sticky fingers stuck to the strands, and she had to jerk them free. Tears came to her eyes, and her temper boiled to the surface once more. "You don't know anything! If it were up to Brad, he'd dissolve the partnership and stay home with his inventions! But no, he has to keep on because you won't let him go! He can't—"

The look on his face stopped her in midsentence. Choking into silence at his expression, she took a step back. The beans forgotten, she put her hand over her mouth. Dear God, what had she done?

It was a moment before he could speak. Finally, his voice strangled, he said, "How do you know all this?"

She didn't want to tell him. Impaled by the look in his eyes, she said unwillingly, "Lucille told me. I wasn't supposed to say anything. I'm sorry, Cal. I was . . . upset."

Without a word, he turned on his heel and started off. Frozen, she watched for a second or two, then cried, "Wait! Where are you going? What about the test? We can't just leave all this stuff here!"

"Leave it, toss it. I don't care. It's not important now."

"Cal—wait!"

He didn't even turn around.

CHAPTER FIFTEEN

ON MONDAY, wondering if she'd ever felt so awful in her entire life, Mary Nell dressed for her last meeting with Anson McAdam. She was so depressed that she didn't care what she wore; grabbing the first thing that came to hand from her closet—the detested gray suit—she put it on with barely a glance and finished her makeup. Gazing at herself in the mirror, she thought that the only good thing about her appearance was that she'd finally washed the beans out of her hair. Suddenly reminded of Cal and that horrible scene at the lake, she quickly switched out the bathroom light and went downstairs to finish her coffee. Despite her dawdling, she was still early and couldn't leave yet. But after she'd come to a decision during the tense weekend, she was anxious to get out to McAdam Recreation and get it over with.

"Don't think about him!" she told herself fiercely over another cup of coffee. "Just don't think about him!"

But Cal was all she'd been able to think about all weekend—and Brad, and Lucille, both of whom she'd felt she had let down. Lucille had entrusted her with a confidence, and she'd destroyed that trust. What effect that would have on Brad and Cal's relationship, she didn't know. But she had felt so awful about it that she'd called Lucille at Brad's as soon as she'd cleaned up on Saturday.

She wanted to know if she could come over and talk to them for a minute.

"Of course, come right over," Lucille said. "But Brad isn't here. Cal came by a while ago looking like thunder, and he and Brad went off somewhere. Does it have anything to do with the field test?"

That was worse than she'd thought. Since it was obvious Cal was already having it out with Brad, she had to confess what she had done. "I'm afraid so," she'd said unhappily, and told Lucille the whole awful story.

"Oh, Mary Nell." Lucille sighed when she'd finished. "I think you'd better come over. We'll wait for Brad together."

Lucille hadn't offered a word of reproach, and that made her feel even guiltier. The drive to Brad's house seemed endless, and she felt as though she were on the way to the Bastille. How could she have done such a thing? She felt terrible. She felt even worse when she saw Brad's van in the driveway when she got there; she couldn't even postpone the inevitable. She got out of the car and trudged up the walk, not knowing what she was going to say. But what did it matter? She couldn't offer excuses—she had none to give.

Lucille answered the door, Brad right behind her. Before either of them could say anything, she burst into an abject apology. "I can't tell you how sorry I am for all this. I know I shouldn't have said anything, and I feel just terrible. I didn't mean to tell him, but we were arguing, and it . . . it just slipped out. Is there anything I can do to make it right?"

"Sit down, Mary Nell," Brad said kindly, ushering her in. "There's no cause to be so upset."

"But there is! I know you have no reason to believe me, but I've never done anything like this before. I'd give—"

"Mary Nell," Lucille broke in. "It's all right."

She was too miserable to accept that; they were just being kind, and she didn't deserve it. "No, it's not all right. I broke a confidence, and I shouldn't have. I'm so sorry."

"Apology accepted," Brad said. "And now, believe *me* when I tell you that I'm glad it happened."

She'd been so sure Brad would despise her that she could hardly believe what he'd said. "You're . . . glad?"

"Yes. I've been wanting to let Cal know we've been heading in different directions for a long time now, but I haven't had the nerve. You did it for me, and I'm grateful. It's made things so much easier."

Bewildered, she looked from one to the other. Lucille nodded encouragingly and Mary Nell looked back at Brad. "Are you sure you're not just saying that?"

"Not a bit. Cal and I had a long talk, and we've decided to dissolve the partnership after we settle a few things at work." Smiling, he reached for Lucille's hand and held it tightly. "Lucy's going to back me financially if I need it, but in any case, we'll do just fine."

Mary Nell couldn't believe this was happening; she felt a heavy weight sliding off her shoulders and sat back. "I think you will, too," she said, and then for the first time she noticed the ring Lucy was wearing. Her eyes widened as she looked from one to the other again. "Is that what I think it is?"

"It is." Lucy giggled, and like every other engaged female the world over, she blushed and held out her hand so that the little diamond could better catch the light. "Brad asked me to marry him this morning."

Grinning from ear to ear, Brad interjected, "And she accepted. Do you believe that? I'm going to marry her this afternoon before she changes her mind!"

Blushing again, Lucille protested, "Oh, Brad, you know that's not possible. What would Mama say?"

"You've told your mother?" Mary Nell asked. "What did she say?"

"She's already planning how many people to invite," Lucille said with a happy laugh.

At that, Mary Nell sprang up from the couch and gave them both a hug and a kiss. "Congratulations," she said. She was delighted for them; she really was. But their obvious happiness only served to underscore what a mess she'd made of things in her own personal life, and she left soon after that.

Brad went with her to the car, and on impulse, she leaned down and gave him a hug. "I'm glad that things worked out so well—between you and Lucille, anyway," she said. "I know you're going to be very happy together."

"I know it, too," Brad said. "Lucille's a wonderful woman. I couldn't ask for better."

She smiled. "Neither could she."

"Thanks," Brad said, and hesitated. "Are you all right?"

She'd made it this far; she couldn't crumple now. "Yes, I'm fine," she lied.

He looked up at her. "It's going to be okay, Mary Nell," he said.

It was no use pretending—not with Brad, who saw too much. Leaning against the car, she shook her head hopelessly. "No, it's not. I've ruined everything. I'm grateful that you've forgiven me, but I know Cal never will."

"Trust me. He will."

She shook her head again. "No, it just wasn't meant to be, I guess. I thought—" She couldn't go on; her throat was closing, and in another moment she would cry. She nearly did when Brad reached out and took her hand.

"There are a few things about Cal I think you should know, Mary Nell," he said quietly.

She wanted to tell him there was nothing she wanted to know, but she couldn't lie. She was parched to hear anything and everything she could about Cal. Even so, she said, "I know what you're trying to do, Brad, but it's not going to do any good."

"Don't be too sure," he said. "For instance, did you know he was married before?"

"Yes, he mentioned it. But that was all. I gathered the subject was too painful to discuss."

"Well, it was a bad time. But it was also a youthful mistake—something that never should have happened." Brad smiled slightly. "You'd never know it now, but the two of us—Cal and I—were once pretty wild. It's amazing that we ever got Stewart-Davidson off the ground. In those early days, we were always too interested in having a good time to really settle down. Cal was so good at everything he did. He always attracted a lot of women—you know, the ski-bunny type, the groupie. He married one of them."

She couldn't stifle her curiosity. "What happened?"

"The inevitable. She moved on. After a while, so did he."

She leaned against the car again. "So what you're telling me is that he's afraid of relationships because his marriage ended in divorce?"

"Not exactly," Brad said. "He was just starting to come out of it when he met Anna Maria."

She hadn't heard about her. "Anna Maria? Who was she?"

"A violinist with the Seattle Symphony."

She asked because she knew she had to. "And he married her?"

"No, I think he wanted to, but she got an offer to join the Philadelphia Orchestra."

"A musician." She groaned, suddenly remembering that night at McNalley's when Mort had embarrassed her into playing the piano. If only she'd known! But Cal had said he liked music, and he'd asked her to play the weekend they'd stayed at her house. Was that only last weekend? Already it seemed a lifetime away. She looked miserably at Brad.

"It sounds like Cal's had about as much luck with women as I've had with men," she said.

Brad squeezed her hand. "He'll come around. Give him time."

She gave him a bleak smile as he bent to kiss his cheek again. "I'm not sure I have that much to give," she said. "But thanks, anyway."

She drove home in a haze of tears, thinking about what Brad had told her. There were times the rest of the weekend when she tried to convince herself that it would have made a difference if she'd known, but she knew that wasn't true. What would she have changed? Would it really have helped if she hadn't played the piano?

She'd come out of her reverie this Monday morning. With the weekend finally behind her and only one chore left to be done, she shook her head. None of it would have made a difference, she thought now; she and Cal just weren't meant to be together. She knew that. She'd tried to steel herself against it. But was it her fault that despite everything, she'd fallen in love?

Abruptly, she threw out the coffee that had cooled while she'd been standing deep in thought. She glanced at the clock. It was time to go. After thinking about it all weekend, she had decided to withdraw her name from the competition; she didn't care what McAdam had decided. Win or lose, she wouldn't wait to hear about it; she was going out to his office this morning well before her appointment to tell him to give Cal the contract. She couldn't accept the account now, even if she got it. She'd always associate it with Cal, and it would be an endless source of pain. She didn't need that; things were already too painful as it was.

Her sister's face flashed into her mind just then, and she bit her lip. She hadn't told Stacy about her decision; they both knew how much she'd counted on this to see them through until the end of the school year. But if Stacy knew, she'd resign from the graduate program, and Mary Nell wasn't going to allow that. She'd had her chance; Stacy deserved hers. She'd come up with other sources, that's all. She'd managed without Anson McAdam before; she'd do it again. She was just picking up her purse when the phone rang.

"Hello?"

"You're up early," Stacy said.

"I was just on my way out the door."

"Another early appointment?"

"Yes," she said. She didn't want to elaborate.

"In that case, I'll make it quick. What do you think about a grant for my graduate program?"

She thought it would be the answer to her prayers. "I think it would be great, if you can get it."

"Say no more, then," Stacy said with a giggle. "You're talking to the recipient of the Charlotte Grayson Chalmers Grant for graduate study in nursing. What do you think about that?"

It was too much to hope for. "Who is Charlotte Grayson Chalmers?"

"She's a woman who graduated with honors about a hundred years ago, married a rich man, established a couple of hospital wings and then took pity on all the struggling nursing students who came after her. Aren't you pleased?"

She was starting to dare to believe it. "I'm overwhelmed," she said. "But how—"

"How did it happen? Ah, I knew you would ask."

"Are you going to tell me?" Relief was making her giddy; she had to sit down while she clutched the phone.

Having obtained Mary Nell's full attention, Stacy was only too happy to oblige. "Well, I know how pressured you've been feeling about money lately, so I—"

"Did I say that?"

"Give the girl a little credit, will you? Of *course* you didn't say it. You didn't have to. But I knew you were."

"I told you we'd work something out."

"Do you want to hear this or not?"

She subsided. "I do. Go ahead. I won't interrupt you again."

"Okay. Well, I thought that since it was my idea to go to school for another year, I should help pay for it, so I started looking around. I heard about these grants, and after studying the qualifications, I applied for the Chalmers, and voilà! Here I am, the proud possessor of a scholarship that pays all my expenses for graduate school! Come on, tell me how proud you are of me.''

"I'm so proud of you I don't know what to say.''

"That's a first—you speechless. But before we break out the Dom Perignon, remember I still have to come up with living expenses and a few extras. I'll have to hit you for a loan or two, but at least the big stuff is taken care of, so we won't have to worry about that. Pretty nifty, huh?''

"Pretty nifty," Mary Nell agreed fervently, and took a relieved breath.

"So, how're things with you?''

She didn't want to talk about it, especially after Stacy's wonderful news. "I'll tell you later. I've got to leave for my appointment right now.''

"Okay, but call. I'm dying to know how the thing with Cal turns out.''

Thinking bleakly that it wouldn't turn out at all, Mary Nell left the house. She knew she should be happy that Stacy had removed such a heavy financial burden from her shoulders, and she was. Now it didn't matter whether she got that contract or not; she could even refuse it with a clear conscience. So she should feel pleased. Instead, she was so depressed that she was nearly in tears. Thankful that she'd decided to meet early with Anson McAdam, she started the car. The last thing she needed at this point was to see Cal again.

MUTTERING A CURSE, Cal looked at the blood welling on his jaw where he'd cut himself shaving. Grabbing a piece of tissue, he stuck it on the spot and glared at his reflection. Damn it all! Nothing had gone right since Saturday; he'd spent the entire weekend in a rage, wondering how everything had gone so wrong. The only ray of light in the

entire mess had been his talk with Brad. But when he re-
called the circumstances that had led to that discussion, he
ripped off the bit of tissue and went to get dressed. After
endlessly going over it, he'd decided last night to withdraw from the competition for the McAdam contract. It
seemed the least he could do for Mary Nell.

Mary Nell. With a fierce frown, he reminded himself
that he wasn't going to think about her anymore. That was
done, over with, dead in the water, finished before it began. If he had any doubts, all he had to do was remember
what a fool he'd been.

Wincing again, he decided he didn't want to remember
that, either. He'd think about that meeting with Brad, instead. He'd been so furious at what Mary Nell had told
him that he couldn't wait to talk to his partner and friend.
He wanted to hear from Davy himself that he wanted out
of the business; he wouldn't believe anything until he'd
heard it from Davy's own mouth.

He'd heard, all right. After listening to his partner rant
and rave for a while, Brad had calmly interrupted and said,
"I'd rather you hadn't found out this way, but yes, it's
true."

Even then, Cal didn't trust his own ears. "Let me get
this straight. You *want* out of our partnership?"

"I thought we were going to discuss this calmly."

"I *am* calm! I just want to know what the hell is going
on! Why didn't you tell me this before?"

"Because I . . . I didn't want to be disloyal—"

"*Disloyal!* Is it more honorable to lie?"

"I didn't lie," Brad said. "We didn't discuss it."

"I . . . you . . . we . . ." Realizing he was stammering, he
tried to get himself under control. He didn't know why he
was so upset; after all, dissolving the partnership had been

his idea, too. He'd been thinking about it for a long time now. He had no reason to feel so betrayed. But even so, he felt ready to explode, and he gripped the edge of the desk. Fittingly, he thought, he and Brad had gone to the office for this little discussion.

"I wanted to tell you, Cal," Brad said unhappily, "but I knew how hard you worked when I was going through rehab, and I knew it was going to take both of us to get things going again. And then when this McAdam thing came up, I thought it was the perfect solution. With all your sports experience, I knew you were a shoo-in. I didn't know Mary Nell would—" He saw Cal's face and hastily went on, "Anyway, I was sure you'd get the contract, and then we'd at least be in the black enough so that I could...I could tell you I wanted out."

The thought flashed through Cal's mind that that had been his reasoning, too. Why did it sound so traitorous coming from Brad? Gripping the edge of the desk even harder, he said, "To work on your inventions."

"Yes," Brad said. "To work on my inventions."

"And that's really what you want to do? Tell me the truth, Davy. We've been tiptoeing around this long enough. Is that really what you want?"

Brad took a deep breath. "Yes."

It was like a weight lifting off his shoulders. Where he'd felt furious and outraged and betrayed only seconds before, the instant Brad told him that, he felt relief. They'd both wanted the same thing; he couldn't believe it. Shaking his head, he said, "I wish we'd talked about this before."

Brad reached out and gripped his knee. "So do I, buddy," he said. "So do I."

So now he was free to take the business in any direction he wanted. Or he would have been, if he hadn't decided to tell Anson McAdam this morning that he wasn't going to take the contract. Win or lose, he'd already decided to bow out and let Mary Nell have it. She deserved it; he didn't. He'd just have to figure out something else. His mouth twisted. It was about time, wasn't it?

And Mary Nell?

Well, it was too late for that. He'd really made a mess of things there. If only she hadn't hit him so quickly with that commitment business; he just hadn't expected it.

No, that wasn't the reason he'd insisted that glorious weekend was a mistake; the plain truth was that he'd scared himself. Against all reason, he'd fallen so hard for Mary Nell that he knew it would destroy him if he made a commitment and then sometime in the future she wanted out. After all, Donna had, and so had Anna Maria. One had divorced him, and the other had run off to play the fiddle. What guarantee did he have that Mary Nell wouldn't leave him, too?

There are no guarantees, buddy, he remembered Brad telling him once. *Only a fool asks for that.*

All right, so he was a fool. He'd certainly proved that. Quickly, he finished dressing. It was over, and that was that. It was no good thinking about Mary Nell, wondering what might have been. Grabbing his sport coat, he shoved his wallet in his pocket and went out to the car.

MARY NELL WAS nervously flipping through a magazine in Anson McAdam's outer office, waiting for his always-absent secretary to return so she could tell the girl she was here, when she heard someone else come in. She looked up. Her heart stopped. *This isn't happening,* she thought and squeezed her eyes briefly shut. But when she opened them warily again, he was still there. She couldn't ignore him; she was more sophisticated than that. Still, the best she could manage was, "Hello, Cal."

He seemed as surprised to see her as she was dismayed to see him. "Hi," he said, and sat down in the chair farthest from her. "You're here early, aren't you?"

She wanted to lift the magazine again, but her fingers seemed paralyzed. "So are you," she said.

He looked uncomfortable. "Yes, well, I wanted to make sure I was on time. How about you?"

"Oh, I ... er ... wanted to see Mr. McAdam about ... something else."

"Oh," he said, and looked away.

She dropped her gaze to her magazine again, but her mind was churning furiously and she wasn't even seeing the printed page. *What is he doing here now?* Oh, this was going to make things a thousand times worse! Why hadn't she just called in her decision to withdraw? Why had she ever come?

Unable to help herself, she glanced covertly at him when he reached for a section of newspaper from the cluttered table beside him. He looked so handsome sitting there, so sure of himself, so calm and cool and composed. Didn't he feel *anything*? She wanted to dash across the room, fling herself against him and beg for his forgiveness, asking if they—by some miracle—could start all over again.

With an effort, she got hold of herself. Where was her pride? She was being ridiculous. It was obvious that he felt none of those things. He'd made that perfectly clear Saturday morning. By a supreme act of will, she looked down at the magazine again. Praying that the secretary would return or that McAdam himself would miraculously appear, she turned some pages in a pretense of reading. But she was so aware of Cal sitting opposite her that she wanted to scream.

On the other side of the room, Cal pretended to read his paper, but every time Mary Nell finished turning a page, his eyes went quickly to her and then away again, before she could see him. How could she look so calm, so composed? He felt as if he were about to explode. *What is she really doing here so early?* he wondered, and then told himself it was of no consequence to him. But why did he want to throw himself across the room, fall to his knees and beg her forgiveness for being such a buffoon? Without knowing it, his hand clenched. The urge to reach out and touch her was so fierce that it was almost a physical ache. He made himself return to his paper, but the lines blurred, and he thought agitatedly that if someone didn't come to rescue him, he was going to go berserk and tear the office apart—that, or run out and never look back. *Damn it, Mary Nell,* he thought bleakly. *Why did things go so wrong? We're meant to be together. We should be together. Why aren't we?*

They both jumped when the door to Anson McAdam's office opened. McAdam stepped out, laughing and saying something to a mountain of a man who dwarfed him...who dwarfed the *doorway*, Mary Nell thought, her eyes wide. She'd never seen anyone so...big. Who was he? *What* was he? A new species? Unconsciously, she leaned back in her chair.

Cal got to his feet. Her neck stiff, Mary Nell turned to look at him, and her eyes widened again. As tall as Cal was, this...this tree of a man towered over him. She was looking from one to the other in shock when she realized that McAdam had stopped and was staring at them in surprise.

"Oh..." he said uncertainly. It was clear that he hadn't expected them so early, and he looked up at the towering man beside him.

Cal obviously didn't need to be introduced. Holding out his hand, he said, "Dwight Kennebaker, right? My name's Cal Stewart. I'm a fan."

Slowly, Mary Nell stood, too. Obviously, this man was a sports figure. She racked her brain. He had to be a football player—or a wrestler. Who else would be so huge?

"Pleased to meet you, Mr. Stewart," the man said in a surprisingly high voice. He turned his bulk in Mary Nell's direction. She had to fight not to shrink back.

"And I'm Mary Nell Barrigan," she said, holding out her hand. It was immediately engulfed in his big one, and she braced herself. But for such a huge specimen, he was surprisingly gentle. After giving her fingers a quick shake, he dropped her hand and smiled. He was missing his two front teeth.

McAdam seemed to feel he should say something. "I see my secretary didn't call you."

She obviously hadn't given him her message about coming in early, either, Mary Nell thought, and decided she didn't like the sound of this. "No," she said. "She didn't."

"Oh," McAdam said again. Then he seemed to decide to get whatever it was he had to say over with. "Now that you've met Dwight here, I guess my secret's out," he said with a nervous laugh. "I might as well tell you that Dwight's agent and I have been negotiating for some time, and after a lot of fancy footwork, old Dwight's finally going to join the fold."

"Join the fold?" Cal said.

McAdam turned to Dwight. "How about waiting for me in my office, my man? I've got a few things to straighten out here. I won't be long."

Dwight seemed agreeable to that; from the almost childish look of anticipation on his face, Mary Nell thought they'd probably find him playing with that airplane hanging over the desk when they went inside. With a wave of a hamlike hand, Dwight disappeared.

Rubbing his own hands together, McAdam gestured toward the couch.

"Why don't we sit down?"

"No, thanks," Cal said with a glance at Mary Nell. "I've got a feeling this isn't going to take very long."

She had the same feeling. "Why don't you just tell us what's going on?"

Nervously, McAdam rubbed his hands together again. "Well, as I said, I've been negotiating over Dwight for a long time now, and when his agent called me last night and said they were willing to discuss a product endorsement deal, well, I...I couldn't pass it up." He gave an embarrassed laugh. "In this state, who'd say no to a Redskin, anyway?"

"Especially one who weighed three hundred pounds," Cal said neutrally.

"Yes, well...er..." McAdam said, and went on. "Well, the point is that with Dwight on the team now, I won't have to redesign my lines. We can use him to endorse the old ones. It'll make it easier on everyone, don't you see?"

Mary Nell saw it very clearly. After all their work! she thought, and glanced quickly at Cal.

As though he'd read her mind, McAdam hastily continued, "Of course, I know how much time and effor you've put into those designs I asked you to do, and I'm grateful. Yes, indeed, grateful. And I don't intend to let such hard work go unrewarded—"

"You've already paid us for that," Cal interrupted. He didn't like this, either.

"Yes, yes, I know, but it's not your fault that Dwight came along right when I needed him, so I intend to compensate you for your time. Yes, indeed, compensate."

Mary Nell didn't want his charity. "I don't know about Cal, but that's not necessary where I'm concerned."

"Oh, I don't know that you should be so quick to refuse my little conciliatory gesture," McAdam said. "As I said, I remember how hard it is to start up, and I've had a little talk with some of my people. I was fascinated, most fascinated, by that explanation of your CAD process, and when I learned about that new 3-D system, well, I saw how we could all come out ahead. Something like that should be sufficient compensation for losing out on my account. What do you think?"

Mary Nell couldn't believe her ears. A 3-D system such as the one he was talking about was worth . . . well, it was worth more than she had expected to be paid during the next five years. Dazedly, she looked at Cal. He seemed as stunned as she was.

"Yes, yes, I thought so," McAdam said happily. "Well, I do like to please people who have tried so hard to please me." He raised a warning finger. "Of course, at those prices, I do intend to buy only one. What you do with it is your affair. How's that sound?"

She didn't know what to say. "It sounds fine," she said faintly.

"Cal?"

But before Cal could answer, there was a crash from inside McAdam's office. They all looked in the direction of the door, and then McAdam said resignedly, "They warned me this might be a little difficult. You'll excuse me, won't you? My office will get back to you with the details later this week, if that's all right with you."

After quickly shaking their hands, he saw them out into the hall, and then he ran back to his office. Feeling dazed, Mary Nell walked toward the elevator. Looking similarly stunned, Cal followed. She let him punch the button; at the moment she couldn't remember which floor they were on.

"I don't believe that just happened," she said.

"I don't, either. Maybe we'll wake up and find out it's all been a dream."

She looked at him. "A nightmare, you mean."

"Was it that bad?"

"It was awful."

"But look what came of it."

"Yes, and what are we going to do about that? There's two of us and one computer."

Cal looked down at her with that intense blue gaze. "There's always share time," he suggested. His voice sounded strange.

"I don't think that would work," she said. She was having a hard time breathing herself, and it wasn't because of being summarily dropped from the McAdam account.

"We could give it a try," Cal said.

Despite herself, her treacherous heart leaped. The desire to share more than computer time was clear in that deep blue gaze; she was sure of it. But she no longer trusted her instincts. After all that had happened—the highs and

lows, the joys and the sorrows, not to mention the pain—
she had to be absolutely sure.

"Well, I have been thinking about moving to a bigger
office," she managed finally. She couldn't look away from
him; they seemed to be the only two people in the world.

"And now that Brad's leaving, I'm going to have some
space," Cal murmured. His hand trembled; he wanted so
to reach out and touch her, but he didn't dare. Her lip
trembled, and it was all he could do not to take her in his
arms. His chest felt tight; he could hardly breathe. Would
she refuse? He didn't know what he'd do if she did.

She looked up at him with that clear green gaze. "Well,
I suppose we could try it for a while," she said. She seemed
to be holding her breath. Was he reading her right? He
hoped so; what if he was wrong? There was only one way
to find out.

"And if it doesn't work?" he asked.

She wouldn't conceive of that happening. Not now, not
when they were finally so close. Her heart taking flight at
the expression of love and worry—and fear that he'd lose
her—so naked in his eyes, she could no longer dissemble.
She was sure of him now, as sure as she was of herself.

"How could it not?" she said, looking up into his eyes.
"Weren't you the one who suggested we collaborate?"

He held back with an effort, searching her face. "I
thought you didn't want that."

This was the last test. "And I thought you didn't want
a commitment."

He held her eyes. "I was a fool. And afraid."

"Of what?"

"Of losing you."

She couldn't believe this was happening; she thought she might faint with joy. "And if I could assure you that won't happen?"

The barest hint of a smile touched his mouth. "Someone once said there are no guarantees."

She searched his face. "That someone was wrong."

His voice shook. "You mean it?"

She'd never meant anything more in her life. Her heart singing, she looked up at him, at this man she loved so fiercely with all her heart. "There's just one thing...."

Instantly, he looked concerned, almost afraid to ask. "What?"

"Who *was* that man?" she asked bewilderedly.

Cal laughed, a release of tension, a sound of love. "You don't know who that was?"

She shook her head. "Only that he was the biggest thing I've ever seen!"

"That was Dwight Kennebaker, nose tackle for the Redskins."

"Nose tackle?" She drew back. "What in heaven's name is that?"

Laughing again, Cal reached for her and held her tightly. "Can we talk about this later?" he asked.

The instant his arms closed around her, she forgot all about nose tackles and mountainous men and computers and competitions and everything else. Gazing up at him with love, she said, "We don't have to talk about it at all...."

The elevator finally arrived, and the doors opened with a whoosh. But none of the passengers, primed and ready to rush outside, moved; the scene that greeted them was too good to miss. Cal and Mary Nell were oblivious to anyone else. Wrapped in a tight embrace, they were busy redesigning their future with an old-fashioned kiss.

Harlequin Superromance

COMING NEXT MONTH

#362 WORD OF HONOR • Evelyn A. Crowe
As a child, Honor Marshall had witnessed her
mother's death in an air disaster. Years later, when
she found out it was murder, she vowed to seek
revenge. Special agent Travis Gentry agreed to help.
But his price was high.

#363 OUT OF THE BLUE • Elise Title
When a wounded Jonathan Madden showed up in
Courtney Blue's bookstore, it was like a scene from a
thriller—and Courtney had read plenty of those!
Jonathan was no mere professor, as he claimed to be.
But he was definitely hero material....

#364 WHEN I SEE YOUR FACE • Connie Bennett
Mystery writer Ryanne Kirkland couldn't allow
herself to think of a future with Hugh MacKenna,
the charismatic private investigator from Los
Angeles. Firstly she was blind, and secondly there
was a possibility she'd have to live her life
on the run. Hugh only wished he could make her
understand that his life was worthless
without her....

#365 SPRING THAW • Sally Bradford
When Adam Campbell returned to her after a
twenty-year absence, Cecilia Mahoney learned the
meaning of heaven and hell. Heaven was the bliss of
love regained, hell the torment of being unable to
find the only child Adam would ever have—the one
she'd given away.

Your favorite stories
with a brand-new look!!